AMETHYST WITCH

A STACY JUSTICE MYSTERY

BARBRA ANNINO

Dane House

INTRODUCTION

Stacy Justice is a young reporter who lives in Chicago, far away from the kooky, small town of Amethyst, Illinois, where she was raised by a family of witches. She's perfectly content with her career, her cat, and her lack of a love life ... until her cousin informs her that their grandfather is deathly ill. Stacy road trips home, only to discover that her grandfather was poisoned, her grandmother has confessed to the crime, and there's a new chief in town who is easy on the eyes, but tough on witches.

Now, the reluctant witch must prove her grandmother's innocence, save her grandfather from meeting an untimely end, and fight the killer that's bent on destroying them all.

This is the first novel in the Stacy Justice mystery series— where secrets only lead to more secrets, and being the member of a family means that you make sacrifices which can lead to murder.

*I*t all started with a penny.

Earlier that day, in a mad rush to grab a bite before the copy was due on my editor's desk, I rushed through the revolving doors of the *Chicago Chronicle*. As my luck would have it, I didn't exactly ... well, revolve all the way.

The moron behind me chose the moment my shoulder strap slipped to test his bicep strength. As I bent to retrieve my bag, the glass slapped my forehead roughly. For a moment, I bounced around like a human pinball without an escape hatch. Then I landed on all fours, ass in the air, not entirely pleased with myself for choosing this day to wear my new $1.99 cotton Wonder Woman panties.

"Hey, sweetheart, when you're done flirting, can we move it along?" asked the charmer behind me.

I flipped him the bird and returned to a bipedal position. Then I gave the door a shove.

It didn't budge.

Again, I pushed the glass, but it was stubbornly holding its ground.

Kick, smack, shove, pound, slap, scream.

"What the hell?" I muttered.

"It looks like it's stuck on the bottom," an amused bystander pointed out.

I knelt down, checked out the rubber sweeper thing that all revolving doors are born with, and saw she was right. Wedged inside, standing completely upright, was a penny.

Extracting it, I checked the date, as I always did.

It was the year I was born.

"Uh-oh," I whispered. Then the door swung into action and I was tossed onto the street where four people applauded and exchanged bills.

My cell phone sang out a tune as I wondered what the spirits were trying to tell me with that date. I shoved the penny in my pocket, an uneasy feeling sweeping through me.

You see, long ago I learned from my grandmother, Birdie, that some pennies, when found under bizarre or unique circumstances, acted as messages from our spirit guides. Those were the ones you hung onto, at least until you decoded the message.

Not that I still bought into her nonsense, but old habits died hard.

I answered the call with, "Stacy Justice."

"Hey there." It was Cinnamon. My younger cousin and closest friend.

"Hey, what's going on, Cin?" I could hear the clinking of glasses over the airwaves, telling me she was at the bar. Her bar, actually. Cinnamon owned the Black Opal in my home-town of Amethyst, Illinois, about three hours from Chicago.

"I need to talk to you. You busy right now?"

My stomach fluttered, anticipating the worst. No one ever said, "I need to talk to you," before delivering good news. It's never, "Hey, can I talk to you? You just won the lottery!" Nope. Does not happen.

"What's up? Is something wrong?"

Cinnamon took a deep breath. "Well," she started, then paused and shouted to someone else. "Scully! You touch that tap and so help me the next beer you drink will be through a barbed wire straw!"

Yikes. Cin was about as tall as a Bratz doll, but what she lacked in stature she compensated with in tone and creative threats.

"Sorry about that. Listen, Stacy, Gramps is sick. Birdie asked me to call you. She thought you might want to come home."

I sunk onto a nearby bench.

"What's wrong with him?" Our grandfather was seventy or so, but he was in good health last I heard, so I wasn't expecting this.

"Actually, I don't know." Cinnamon sighed. "No one knows. It's very strange what happened."

"What happened?" I glanced at the huge clock on the building. It was early afternoon on Thursday.

"Late last night, Pearl noticed he seemed disoriented, almost like he was drunk."

Pearl was my grandfather's girlfriend. She owned a restaurant in town called Pearl's Palace. Ironically, she bought it from another woman named Pearl. "That doesn't make sense. Gramps hasn't had a drink since he divorced Birdie."

"I know. Thirty years. They ran some tests. Thought he might have had a stroke, but the tests showed no signs of that. He's been vomiting a lot, too."

Oh boy. Not Gramps. If my family were a circus act, he'd be the guy standing near the ropes making sure a lion didn't eat one of the kids. He was the only stability I knew. In fact, if something happened to him, then it would be up to Birdie to …

A thought occurred to me then. "Cin, where was Gramps last night?"

She blew out a long sigh. "He was there."

Good grief. "Please tell me you don't think—"

"What, that she finally followed through with it? Hell, I hope not."

"I'm on my way."

2

'*S*he' was our grandmother. My mother's mother, Brighid Geraghty, who insisted everyone call her Birdie. She was named after the Celtic goddess of fire and hearth. It means 'one who exalts herself' and, well, let's just say that it suited her.

Every third Wednesday since I could remember, Birdie and her two sisters hosted a family dinner at their guest house. Divorce or not, Gramps was still family, so the invitation extended to him.

Just so everyone knew where she stood on the idea, however, every so often Birdie would pass Gramps the pot roast and say things like, "Oscar, are you wearing your good teeth? Wouldn't want you to choke on a piece of meat." Or, "Does anyone smell something funny? Lolly, you didn't mix up the rat poison with the flour again, did you? No matter. Oscar will taste it first." Always with a wink and a smile.

Of course, everyone laughed and Gramps shook his head, but he did have a habit of smelling his food before tasting it.

But she didn't really want him dead.

I was almost seventy-five percent sure of that.

This was why I wasted no time clearing the absence with my editor. Currently, the cat was in the carrier, a bag of clothes on the backseat, the Jeep was pointed west, and I was on my way home.

The area where I grew up was beautiful, almost magical, although I would never say that in Birdie's presence. Carved into the cliffs and valleys of the Mississippi River region in Illinois, Amethyst stood out like a jewel in the crown of the Midwest. Where the rest of the landscape was flat, the town looked like it was hijacked from New England and dropped there by a spaceship.

Which was fitting, since Amethyst was like the *Twilight Zone* on acid.

It was after six when I crawled up the hill to my grandmother's inn. The sun had just begun to slip into the valley as the wind scattered leaves across the yard. The Queen Anne house looked the same as when I had last seen it a few years ago. A porch hugged the circumference, garnished with chippy-painted wicker rockers and ferns. The spindles and gingerbread contrasted the creamy base color with pops of plum, teal, and red. Like a mature woman who loved to show off her jewels.

Parking at the edge of the driveway, I got out and stretched. The rosemary still clung to its greenness near the garden gate, unusual for late October. Rosemary for remembrance. That's what I had painted on the marker when I was fourteen, the day after my father died. The same day Birdie spoke of spirit guides, and my mother faded into the shadows.

The smoky scent of burning leaves tugged at me. Gladys Sharp was busy raking her yard across the street, but she took the time to wave. I waved back, wondering if she was still a groupie.

You see, the Geraghty Girls, as my grandmother and her two sisters were called, were a bit of a legend in this town.

A few houses down, Bea Plough stuck her head out, scowled, and slammed the door.

And like all legends, they were not without enemies.

Taking a deep breath, I circled around the Jeep, and swung open the passenger door. "Well, Moonlight, you ready to meet the family?"

Moonlight yawned and meowed.

I hoisted him from the car, shutting the door behind me.

The brick path trailing to the front entrance was peppered with pumpkins and gourds. Nylon spiderwebs hugged the porch railing, and a mannequin wearing a purple cape and pointy witch's hat filled the corner. I couldn't help thinking that was redundant as I cranked the bell.

With three witches inside, why would they need any out here?

Ella Fitzgerald belted out a tune from somewhere in the house as I waited to be greeted. "Let's call the whole thing off ..." After a moment, Aunt Lolly appeared. The oldest Geraghty Girl.

"Oh, hello." Her hair was a mop of copper, springing from her head in all directions like loose wires. Her checks were adorned with orange circles of rouge, and her aqua eyes glowed beneath glittered shadow. "Do you have a reservation?" she asked.

Her appearance, coupled with the blank expression on her face, told me the boat was in the harbor, but the captain was below deck, sipping a cocktail.

This had to be handled delicately, so I began cautiously. "No, Aunt Lolly. It's me, Stac—"

"I'm terribly sorry," she smoothed the sequins on her chiffon gown. Lolly always dressed like she was hosting Oscar's night. "We're all booked up."

I saw the door shift a second too late. "Wait!" I tried to stick my foot inside, but she was faster than she looked. Closed and locked.

Damn.

I sighed and rang the bell again.

From farther away, Fiona called, "Lolly, honey, get the door."

No, no, no. Didn't Fiona sense me? What good was all that hocus-pocus if you didn't know when your own grand-niece was standing on your front step?

I put the cat down and searched the plants and the welcome mat for a key. Nothing. Then I pulled up a rocker, climbed on, and steadied myself while I felt above the threshold.

"Excuse me?" someone said.

I screamed, tipped back on the rocker, wobbled for one fleeting moment, then dove toward the hedges. My sneaker got snagged in the stupid nylon spiderweb and it clung to me, dipping me up and down like a teabag. Head in the bushes, head out of the bushes. Head in the bushes, head out of the bushes.

"Ahhh!" I yelled.

They weren't those soft evergreens that you could touch without needing stitches either. Nope, these were the real prickly deal.

Then a flashlight blinded me, and a man's voice asked, "What the hell are you doing?"

What kind of question was that? Did he actually think I planned this impromptu plunge over the railing for the amusement of the neighbors? Did he not see me fall? "I'm redecorating, Einstein. I thought the hedges needed a living, bloody display to better scare the kiddies. What does it look like?"

"It looks like you were trying to break into this house." He was stern as a high school principal. When did they get a neighborhood watchdog group?

"I wasn't breaking in. Who looks for a key before they break in? This is my family's home."

I still couldn't see the guy ... or anything for that matter since the flashlight was pumping out some high wattage directly into my retinas. It also didn't appear help was on the way, so I performed the hardest sit-up of my life and pulled over the banister. The flashlight darkened, and I turned to see who was behind it.

Through the faint dusting of the remaining sun, I could make out his features. His incredibly sexy, angular features, highlighted by a five o'clock shadow. He didn't carry himself like a man who grew up in a small town, and I certainly did not recognize him.

For a brief moment, I fantasized about shaving him in the shower. Then I remembered it was his fault I just had an evergreen facial.

"I've never seen you before," he said. "Are you related to the Geraghtys?"

"What are you, a cop?"

He cocked his head. "Yes, I am as a matter of fact. Now it's my turn. Why are you sneaking around the Geraghty porch?"

Foot in mouth disease ran chronically in the family. "You really are a cop? You aren't wearing a uniform." In a small town like this, police officers didn't roam around in leather jackets.

He flashed a badge. "I'm going to ask one more time. Who are you?"

I was tired of this guy's attitude, cute or not. "You got me." I picked up Moonlight. "I'm a cat burglar. Get it?"

He mumbled something about 'gotta be related' and 'nuts', but I didn't catch it all because he was rounding the porch and heading up the stairs.

Then, miracle of miracles, my Aunt Fiona opened the door. "What's all the activity?" she asked in that throaty voice that said she should be working the receiving end of a 900 number.

"Hi, Auntie."

"Mrs. Geraghty," nodded Cop Guy.

"Oh, Stacy, it is so good to see you!" She pulled me in for a hug and whispered in my ear, "You're so pretty, why must you always look frightful? And in front of this handsome man."

She stepped back and cocked her head. Then, in a louder voice, "Leo, have you met my gorgeous niece, Stacy?"

Subtlety was not a Geraghty trait.

Smiling, Leo held his hand out. "A pleasure."

I leaned in to flash a sexy pose and clasp his hand, but there was some lingering sap on my eyelids and I forgot the web was wrapped around my foot. Luckily, a ripe pumpkin broke my fall.

"Jeez, are you okay? Let me help you." Leo bent down, reaching for me.

I lowered my head and put my hand up. This was so embarrassing. The first hot guy I'd met in months, and not only did he think I was a criminal, but he was probably certain I had vertigo. "I'm good, thanks." I turned my attention to the orange goop splattered on my sweatshirt and the knots around my feet.

Fiona said, "Leo, my darling niece has had some trying news of late, not to mention a very long trip. I'm afraid she's quite taxed and isn't herself this evening. Now then, how may I be of assistance to the law on this fine day, you sweet boy?"

Man, she was good. She was one of those women that you just knew was a pinup girl at one time and probably still could be.

Leo replied, "Ms. Geraghty, I was hoping to talk to your sister, Birdie."

I perked my ears and managed to rip the web off my feet.

"I'm afraid she isn't here at the moment. Something I might help you with?" Fiona asked.

Leo was about to speak, but then he stopped. He shot me a look as if I had just escaped a mental hospital. Then he answered Fiona, "No, that's all right. It can wait. I'll come by another time."

I couldn't help noticing how well his jeans molded to his backside as he stepped off the front porch.

"Stacy, I have the cottage all fixed up for you. Why don't I take you back there so you can freshen up while Lolly finishes dinner? By that time, your grandmother should be home from her errands." Fiona handed me a key.

"Thanks." I picked up the cat carrier and started back down the porch steps, following Fiona. The guest cottage was to the left of the main house, set back on the property. It was painted a creamy white with a sharply slanted roof and a porch swing.

"Here we go." Fiona stepped into the cottage. "Don't you love it? I decorated it myself."

For a brief moment, I wondered if Fiona had been the

first choice for *I Dream of Jeannie*, but Barbara Eden beat her out of the part. Because this place could have passed for the inside of Jeannie's bottle.

A fuchsia velvet sofa played center stage, adorned with coordinating silk pillows. A silver champagne bucket sat at the heel of a chair shaped like a stiletto. The two windows were draped with miles of pink, purple, and red brocade fabric tied with beaded tassels, and the floor was covered with a leopard print rug.

Fiona grabbed a remote control.

"Okay, honey, now here's the switch for the fireplace."

Poof! The fireplace turned on.

"And this is for the stereo."

"Ohhhhhh, my love, my darrrrlin', I hunger for your touch ..." sang a Righteous Brother.

"And this works the Jacuzzi."

If Barry White had bobbed his head up from the water, I would not have been a bit surprised.

"Can't you just see a young couple falling in love here?" Fiona clapped her hands together, her fingers flittering with tiny sparks.

Actually, I could see a young couple plowing through a box of condoms here, but who was I to judge?

My phone rang then, and I scrambled around in my pocket for it.

It was Cinnamon.

"Hey, Cuz. Are you in town yet?" Pool balls cracked in the background.

"I am."

Fiona motioned that she was going to leave. I waved to her.

"Oh good. Well, I'm not sure how long I'm going to be

stuck at the bar. You want me to call you when I'm done? I doubt I'll be able to visit Gramps with you tonight."

It was nearly seven. I was tired, hungry, and in desperate need of a shower.

"I'm not sure I'll make it to the hospital tonight myself. I'm just getting settled in. I need to change and clean up. Plus, if I leave before Birdie gets home, I'll never hear the end of it."

Fiona had the door open, but stopped and turned back. "Dear, I'm sure Oscar will understand if you can't see him until tomorrow. What with all that's happening, you should rest before the spell." Then she shut the door behind her.

"So, Cin, why don't I call you when I know more? But—"

Wait a minute. Did Fiona just say the word 'spell'?

"Cin, I gotta call you back."

3

*B*y the time I chased after Aunt Fiona, she was already back in the main house, which, unfortunately, I still had no key to open.

Deciding to pretend I never heard the word spell, I fetched my bag and cat supplies from the car.

There were bigger things to worry about than Birdie trying to mold me into a witch, although it was hard to believe she was still at it. Ever since I was a kid, she made it her personal mission to teach me all about the Old Ways. Birdie's roots traced back to a pagan tribe from County Kildare in Ireland, and she, Lolly, and Fiona have lived their entire lives by the theology passed down from generation to generation. They even have their own personal bible called the "Blessed Book" although I had never seen it, nor did I care to. It's unnerving enough living with the things I have seen.

I peeled off my clothes and climbed into the shower, washing away the pulp of the jack-o-lantern. The steam seeped into my pores, relaxing my muscles, and I decided to take a nap after I fed Moonlight.

. . .

THE DREAM CONSUMED ME IMMEDIATELY. My father sliding on ice. His head split wide. Blood mixing with the paint of the fire hydrant. And then, a scream. Mine, as I was wrenched from the nightmare.

"Anastasia." Someone was shaking my shoulder, jostling me from sleep. "Wake up."

Birdie. She had an energy I could sense, smell even, without opening my eyes.

"Five more minutes," I muttered, and rolled over.

She poked my shoulder a little harder than necessary, and I turned to face her. She was propped on the edge of the bed, a black wool cape dripping down her legs. The hood engulfed her auburn hair, a frame for her face.

"Birdie, what the hell? I just laid my head down." I squeezed my eyes tight.

"You know I don't believe in Hell." Birdie plucked a stray hair from her cape. "Was it the dream again? What about the prehnite stone I gave you for beneath your pillow?"

Magic was her answer for everything. Got a stomachache? Mint tea should clear that right up. Big exam? Dab some basil oil on your forehead to increase concentration. Killed your father? Put a crystal under your pillow to make the nightmares go away.

She stood, stiffening her spine. "You have to face your demons sometime." She pointed her chin at me and tossed the coverlet off the bed. "Dinner is ready."

I watched the back of her cape head for the door. Her tone was all business, so I rolled off the bed, threw on a pair of jeans and a sweater, and darted after her. "Wait a minute, Birdie. Let me get my boots."

She had the front door open as I yanked one boot on

and then the other. I stopped when I felt something inside of the left one. I tugged it off as Birdie kept going and shook out a penny.

The date was earlier than the one from the revolving door. I didn't recall ever finding two in the same day, at least not under such unusual circumstances. The knot in my belly tightened as I tucked the coin in my pocket and rushed after my grandmother.

Clouds were rolling in, and the temperature had dropped a bit. Birdie was almost at the back door of the house, the entrance that entered into the kitchen. I caught up to her, leaves crunching with every step, as she pulled the door open and stepped inside.

Rosemary and garlic seeped from the wall oven, perfuming the air. I had always loved the rustic kitchen of the Geraghty House. It was a roomy, box shape marked with open shelving and dark wooden beams from which seasoned cast-iron pots dangled like earrings. The meals made in those pots were too numerous to count. The chips in the pottery, all well-earned. There were herbs and spices and dried fruits everywhere like they had been tossed on a shelf and forgotten, but I knew better. I knew those old jelly jars filled with juniper berries or lavender buds were used often, if not in a meal, then in a shampoo or spell.

Aunt Lolly was near the stove, stirring something in an old copper pot. Fiona pulled her head away from the fridge at the creak of the door.

"Lolly," Fiona called over her shoulder, "Stacy's here."

"Stacy?" Lolly asked. "He's in the Summerland." Then she returned to cooking.

Some pagans believe that the Summerland was where a soul rested for twenty years after the death and where it prepared for re-birth. Lolly could read past life records. It was this one that tripped her up.

"No, honey. His *daughter,* Stacy," Fiona nudged gently.

I was named after my father, although Birdie refused to call me by my given name.

Lolly glanced up from her pot. "Birdie's daughter?" she asked, brows arched. Literally. They were drawn in that way.

"I'm Birdie's granddaughter, Aunt Lolly," I offered.

I could almost see the spark ignite in her eyes as the elevator made it to the top floor. "Oh my goodness. Stacy! Come, give us a hug." She motioned me toward her.

"Great to see you, Aunt Lolly." I rushed over, and she wrapped her arms around me and squeezed.

"Dinner's almost ready," said Fiona. "Why don't you go into the dining room and open some wine?"

The house was built with thirteen rooms. At the entrance, a winding oak staircase carried guests of the inn to the second-floor suites, but the kitchen and dining room were on the first floor near the rear of the home.

"What's for dinner?" I asked.

"Roast pork with maple cider sauce, rosemary new potatoes, and baked apples." Fiona set salt and pepper shakers on the table as Birdie disappeared into the pantry.

"Can I help?" I asked.

"No, no. Everything's under control." Fiona winked at me.

I grabbed a bottle of wine from the rack and went into the dining room to uncork it. There were crystal goblets in the china cabinet, along with gold-rimmed dishes and antique flatware. After the table was set, I poured myself a generous glass of wine and sat down.

Fiona delivered the pork to the table, Lolly trailed with

the potatoes, and Birdie brought up the rear with the baked apples.

We all sat down, Birdie at the helm, and gave thanks to the goddess of the hunt, Diana.

I filled my plate generously. "This looks delicious, Lolly. Thank you."

"No problem, toots." Lolly took a belt of the wine.

For reasons I will never comprehend, alcohol had the exact opposite effect on my Aunt Lolly than it did the rest of the world. It seemed to sharpen her senses.

"So, Birdie, where were you? I thought you would be here when I arrived."

"I was visiting Oscar."

I nearly choked on a potato. Fiona patted my back, and I spit it out into a napkin.

"Anastasia, honestly." Birdie clucked her tongue

"Why? Why would you visit Gramps without me?" If ever two people needed a buffer, it was them. Well, just Gramps. And maybe Pearl. I was sure she wouldn't be thrilled with a visit from Birdie.

"Excuse me, child. I was not aware that I needed your permission to pay my respects to a man I was married to for twenty years."

I didn't like the way she said 'pay my respects'.

"Twenty-two," sang Fiona as she arranged her potatoes around a slice of pork.

So maybe Birdie was softening in her later years. I could buy that. "Do the doctors know what's wrong with him yet?"

"Doctors." Birdie reached for the potatoes and waved her hand dismissively. "What do they know?"

Then again, maybe not.

Lolly glanced up from her wine, and Fiona stopped cutting her pork loin.

Taking a deep breath, I set my fork down. "Did something happen?"

"Of course not." Birdie arranged the food on her plate. "I simply brought in a remedy of burdock root, dandelion leaves, and lemon balm to purge Oscar's system. I tried to give that nurse instructions on the dosage and temperature at which to brew the tea but she wouldn't hear of it. So I got rid of her and fed him the tonic myself."

I didn't like the sound of that. "Birdie, they don't even know what's wrong with him yet. You can't go around administering potions to a patient in a hospital. What if it makes him even more ill?" Or worse. And what if someone had seen her? I couldn't imagine that would go over too well, considering the fact that Pearl wasn't fond of Birdie, and half the town had heard my grandmother threaten my grandfather's life on more than one occasion.

"Oh, please. What will make him ill is that terrible slop they feed people in those hospitals. That and Pearl's cooking." Birdie smirked as she bit into an apple. Then her green eyes caught mine and she practically dared me to contradict her. This was a dangerous sport that had landed me on the injured reserve list so often I quit playing altogether. I held my tongue.

"Besides, why shouldn't I give him healing aid? I am an herb practitioner. For thousands of years, medicine men and women have healed the sick. No Geraghty has needed a doctor in years." She snapped her wrist as if to dismiss the ridiculous discussion.

A smart person would have let it go, but at some point I would have to meet these people, and it would help to know if I needed an alias and a disguise.

"Then what happened?" I asked.

Birdie stabbed a piece of pork. "Nothing."

"Nothing? You just left and that was it?" I studied her carefully, like a jury studies a witness.

"Yes, I left. I'm sitting here, aren't I?" She folded her hands in front of her.

I relaxed in my seat and took a sip of wine.

"After they escorted me to the door."

There it was. "You got thrown out of the hospital?" I would probably need to rent a clown suit just to get past the reception desk.

"Don't be so dramatic. No one laid a hand on me. I was asked to leave, and after I completed the spell, I did."

I could just hear how that went down. *Security, would you please escort this crazy redhead as far away from the building as possible?*

Like a bad episode of *I Love Lucy*.

Fiona was brave enough to change the subject as I downed my wine and poured another glass. "Lolly, this pork roast is lovely."

"Thank you, Fiona. I slow cook it in a roasting pan at two-hundred degrees for the first hour—that's the secret—then I turn the oven up to three-hundred."

Everyone agreed the dinner was excellent, and the conversation shifted to tomorrow's guest check-in as we finished the meal. The inn had three guest rooms. They were expecting a young couple on their honeymoon, two girlfriends, and a married couple celebrating their twenty-fifth wedding anniversary.

I wondered if I should call Cinnamon and warn her about Birdie's hospital antics while we cleared the table. The sink was filling with suds as the water rushed over the plates, so my ears weren't entirely focused when the words *cape*, *ritual*, and *Anastasia* were spoken across the room.

I turned the water off, not certain if I had heard that right.

"Yes, but shouldn't we wait until the Moon is in Virgo?" Lolly asked.

"Or at least until Sunday. Isn't that best for healing?" chimed Fiona.

"No, no. I have just the spell in mind," Birdie said. "Now that my granddaughter is here, all four winds will be represented. And the work will be that much stronger."

Oh no. Spellcasting? Me? That couldn't possibly end well. My days of practicing magic were well behind me and for good reason. "Okay, you three. I'm not sure where you're going with this, but count me out."

"You want to help your grandfather, do you not?" Birdie had changed into her ritual cape—a thick, red velvet number that, on a woman of average height, would sweep the floor. On Birdie, it just grazed her ankles. "I should think you would do everything in your power to aid his recovery."

The remark smacked of manipulation and I resented it. Of course I loved my grandfather. Of course I would do anything to help him. But I was a grown woman and I didn't like being told what to do. Especially if what I was being forced into was dangerous. Birdie knew how I felt about casting. She knew my magic could harm. "The question I have is why do *you* want to help him?" I parked a hand on my hip and steadied my gaze.

Immediately, I regretted the question. Her face flinched as if she had been slapped. I stepped toward her. "Oh, Birdie, I'm sorry, I didn't mean—"

"It's fine." Her voice was tight as she turned her back.

Lolly and Fiona shuffled out of the way, fussing with the center island, clearly avoiding the conflict.

After an awkward silence, Birdie said in a low voice,

"Stacy, just because I could not live out my days with him, and I argue with him periodically does not mean I don't care about your grandfather."

"You forgot about the death threats." It just slipped out.

"Now you know that's my little way of a joke." She sighed. "It's not my place anymore to watch after Oscar. I just assumed that you would want to help in any manner you could. But I wouldn't ask you to do anything you might be uncomfortable with, dear."

Sighing, I placed a hand on her arm. "Sure, Birdie. You win. I'll help with the spell."

She smiled like a cat who caught a mouse. Ever the victor.

"But if I make things worse, it's not my fault. I just want that on record."

*a*s I stood in the heart of the home, huddled around the apothecary table, staring into a big, white box, I wondered for the millionth time if I was adopted. I mean, with my father long buried and my mother out of the picture since high school, there was no concrete proof that I wasn't swiped from a shopping mall at the age of two. Except for the fact that my coloring was similar—red hair, green eyes, fair skin—the family resemblance was nil.

"What's this for?" I asked.

Fiona's voice was excited. "It's your ritual cape, Stacy. Lolly was up early this morning fashioning it for you."

That was an interesting choice of words, because if there was anything this garment was not, it was fashion. I smiled at Lolly who was chugging back the ritual wine. She wiped her mouth with the back of her hand and grinned back.

The cape spilled to the floor as I lifted it from the box. It was a primary blue crushed velvet crime with white satin lining and an air of comfort. It smelled of sea and storms. How appropriate.

I assessed Fiona. Her cape was a rich emerald green

embroidered with lighter green spirals. Lolly's was a sunlit yellow, trimmed with gold ribbon. Birdie's ritual cape was red, accented with a gorgeous black triquetra, the pattern symbolizing the three-fold rule of pagan law which states that everything you put into the universe, you receive back times three.

So why was I cursed with the Smurf robe?

"Go on, dear, put it on." Birdie and her sisters took their place around the table.

I shoved my arms through the sleeve holes, fastened the top button, and sighed. I'm 5'6" and a size six, but this thing could have covered a linebacker. Who was her model?

Lolly frowned. "Well, I suppose I could take it in quickly before we get to work."

"No, Auntie, it's fine. Let's get on with it."

"All right, then, but I will need to do the alterations before Samhain next week."

Samhain falls on October 31st and is a major pagan holiday. It marks the beginning of the dark part of the year and the Celtic New Year. It's also believed to be a magical night when the veil between this world and the Otherworld thins. The departed are honored, and some lucky believers have been known to catch a glimpse of their ancestors. I was not among them. I also had not planned on sticking around that long, but I didn't say so.

After my wardrobe was situated, the three of them fanned around the table to their respective positions to perform the spell.

I looked at Birdie. "Where do you want me?"

She rolled her eyes. "Do you mean to tell me that you don't know where to stand?"

It felt like rush week at a sorority house. Except I was hoping *not* to get in. "No, Birdie. Give me a hint."

"Why don't we begin with a test of your knowledge then?"

"I didn't study for a test."

Birdie ignored me and continued. "Look at your Aunt Fiona. Can you tell me what her cape and position represents?"

The fact that all three of you are wacko? But it was easier to just play along. I stared at Fiona. Her ritual cape was green. Green was the color of money, grass, luck, and fertility. Gramps needed none of those things. Green. A mixture of blue and yellow make green. Half and half.

"Balance." With that one word, the early lessons taught to me in this very kitchen, in the garden, in the woods behind the property, all flooded back to me. "And she's standing at the north end of the kitchen. She represents the north wind."

"Very good." A tiny smile tugged at my grandmother's lips. "Now look at Lolly."

Her cape was yellow. The color of the sun. Sunrise. Sunset. With each day, a new cycle begins. Each month marches toward a new season. Each season toward a new year. A new year brings change. That had to be it.

"Change," I said.

"And?" prompted Fiona. Lolly was on Fiona's left.

"And she represents the east wind."

Fiona clapped.

Good. Now I was cooking with gas, and hopefully, I could get out of here soon and meet my cousin for a drink. A strong one.

Birdie's was easy. I turned to her. "Red is for strength and your wind is south."

"And what about you, Anastasia?" Birdie asked.

Okay, *think.* Blue. Blue is true. Blue is truth. But that

didn't make sense in this spell. The sky is blue. The moon can be blue. Tranquility. The ocean is blue. Waves. Water. Water cleanses. Cleansing leads to healing.

"Healing. Blue is for the healing ritual." Wait a minute. I flicked my eyes to Birdie. "You want me at the center of the healing spell for Gramps? No, Birdie." What if I screwed it up? I could make things worse. Gramps could wake up with a second tongue or something. Or worse. He could not wake up at all. "I don't want that responsibility."

Birdie dismissed my protests. "One link in a chain, my dear. You are the youngest and strongest among us. It is your purpose today. Now we begin."

The apothecary table that rooted the kitchen was covered with a black silk cloth. A pewter chalice filled with liquid sat in the center surrounded by three large fluorite crystals, powerful cellular cleansers. Alternating with the stones were piles of dried herbs—mint, mugwort, and sage. All used for healing. Birdie placed an athame in front of the chalice. A double-edged ritual blade used in spell-casting.

The three of them closed their eyes and took a deep breath in unison.

I did the same, but most likely for a different reason.

Then Birdie's voice boomed. "We call on the Wise Ones to assist in healing the sick. And the spirits to carry our spell to Oscar's door." They all bowed their heads, so I did, too.

"To the Goddess of Green, Airmid, enchant these herbs of health."

Each sister grabbed a pile of herbs and crumbled them into the chalice. Entrails of translucent smoke filtered out, circling the pewter cup.

"And Bran, God of Regeneration, charge these stones with renewed energy."

They each clasped a stone in their hand and the temperature of the room shot up with the intensity of the energy.

"And to Brighid, Triple Goddess of Fire, Water, and Hearth." Birdie pointed to me and nodded to the knife, indicating that I should pick it up.

The tarnished silver handle of the blade called out to me, its vibrations strong, the magic inviting me back into its fold. I hesitated, though my fingers itched to touch it. *This is for Gramps*, I told myself. *It's not like last time. Nothing bad will happen.* I grasped the athame and lifted my eyes for direction on what to do with it.

But rather than Birdie, my gaze locked on a face outside of the back door.

I yelped and dropped the knife.

My grandmother startled. "What is it?"

"I saw someone. There's someone at the back door," I answered.

"Oh for Goddess sake." Birdie swung toward the door, her cape whooshing behind her. Her spine stiffened when she spotted the visitor. She quickly waved her arm and both the smoke and the heat vanished from the kitchen.

I craned my neck to see if I could make out any features, but it was dark.

Birdie opened the door a crack. "Yes, Leo, what can I do for you?"

Leo? Oh great. Officer McHottie Pants was back, and I was wearing a freaking Druid's cape. The room didn't have a trap door or an easy exit, but there was always the option of doing a swan dive on top of the dagger. Or I could just let nature take its course and die of embarrassment.

"Good evening, Mrs. Geraghty, I need to ask you a few questions if this is a convenient time?" Leo tried to peek over her shoulder.

Don't let him in. Don't let him in. Please, Birdie, hear my tele-pathic message and ... Don't. Let. Him. In.

She hesitated for a beat, either ignoring my message or not hearing it at all, because like I said—magically deficient —and let him in. And they wonder why I don't think I'm any good at witchcraft.

"Well, Leo, what is it? You're interrupting our session." Birdie blew out the candles that lit the altar and flipped a light switch, apparently not bothered at all by the fact that Leo was witnessing a ritual.

Jeez, he was even sexier in the light. He had a Mediter-ranean look about him, with waves of hair like thick choco-late, and hazel eyes that could lure any woman down a dangerous path.

Leo scanned the accessories scattered across the table. I watched his gaze trail from the herbs to the fluorite crystals to the chalice. His eyes locked on the athame, and finally, they rested on me.

I pretended to buff my nails.

"Yes, I can see that you're very busy here and I won't take too much of your time. I just have a few questions." I felt his eyes still on me as he said this, and I looked up.

"For my granddaughter?" Birdie's voice had an edge to it. She either didn't like Leo or didn't like the way he was looking at me.

Leo tilted his head toward Birdie. "No, I ... I'm sorry." He turned back to me. "You're Stacy, right?" He bent down slightly as he asked the question, and I realized the hood was covering half my face.

I slipped it off. "You remembered." I flashed my most seductive smile.

Leo gave a crooked grin. "It's not every day I meet a woman upside down."

I put my smile away, and Fiona patted my shoulder.

Birdie cleared her throat, and Leo turned back to her. "I'm sorry, Mrs. Geraghty. I have a few questions to ask you, and I wondered if you might come down to the station with me so I can get them answered."

I stepped forward then. "What? No. No way. What's this about?"

"I'm afraid that's between me and your grandmother." Leo looked at Birdie. "Would you come with me to the station so we can talk about this a little more?"

"Absolutely not!" Now I was pissed. Who did this guy think he was?

"It's fine," Birdie stated.

"Stacy," Fiona interjected gently, "your grandmother knows what's best."

"No. It isn't fine." I angled toward Leo and crossed my arms. That's when I realized I was the only one still wearing a cape. Birdie, Fiona, and Lolly had discarded theirs.

Unbuttoning it, I tried to shimmy free, but I tripped over the fabric and stumbled into Leo. He helped me right myself, and I wrenched away from him, glaring. "What is this about?"

Sighing, Leo scratched his chin, but he didn't answer.

"Are you going to charge her with a crime?" I asked.

He ignored my question. "Mrs. Geraghty, did you visit Oscar Sheridan this afternoon?"

Uh-oh. "Don't answer that, Birdie."

"Why? I have nothing to hide," Birdie said to me. Then to Leo, she answered, "Yes, I did."

I jumped in then, because, frankly, I wasn't certain what happened at the hospital and because Birdie had a tendency to run off at the mouth like a rain gutter. "Birdie, wait. Don't say anything else. Look, Detective, I'm sure you realize that my family has suffered quite a shock from the disturbing news of my grandfather's illness, and my grandmother is quite tired."

"No, I'm not," Birdie argued.

Leo shifted his stance and directed his words at me. "Look, I just need to ask your grandmother a few questions, that's all. She isn't the only one I've questioned, but I need her version of the events of both yesterday evening at dinner and now this evening at the hospital. Your grandfather's illness is suspicious to the doctors. They're running several tests to determine if it's natural or ... otherwise."

"Oh, dear," Fiona gasped.

"What are you saying?" A lump crawled up my throat. She wouldn't really try to hurt Gramps. *Would she? No, no, no.* Birdie was a lot of things. But she was not a murderer.

I hadn't realized Leo was still talking. "And his girlfriend isn't too pleased about your grandmother injecting him with her herbs while he was asleep."

At that moment, the world fell from under me. Birdie had failed to mention that little tidbit. That knowledge might have been very helpful before we let the policeman in the kitchen. My words came slowly. "You didn't."

All she did was shrug.

"I think it would be better for everyone if your grandmother came down to the station to give a statement."

I racked my brain, searching for the name of an attorney while Leo waited for a response.

Birdie rose from her chair. "We go."

"Wait. No, Birdie, wait a second. We need to call someone. Who's your attorney?"

"Don't be absurd. I've done nothing wrong, and besides, I abide by Celtic law." She was already gathering her things.

"What the hell does that mean?" I shouted. Leo held the

door open as Birdie stepped out. I grabbed my jacket. "I'm going with you, then."

"This isn't a taxi ride," Leo said.

"Then arrest me," I shot back.

"You can meet us there." The screen door slapped behind them.

I turned to Fiona. "What just happened?"

The booze was wearing off Aunt Lolly, and she shrieked at the slam of the door and tossed a towel over her head.

I wanted to crawl under there with her.

5

The wind wrestled with my coat as I punched my arms through the sleeves, jogging along the path to the driveway. I lost the grip on my keys, and when I stooped to pick them up, I noticed something odd. Seemed all the neighbors decided to step out for a breath of fresh air. At the same time. Coach Malloy was leaning against his front porch, a cup of coffee in hand, watching the night sky. Gladys Sharp was sweeping her walkway. Bea and Stan Plough were watering their dead flowers.

Dammit. Did they see Birdie get hauled away? Or did they hear the news on their scanners?

I waved as I hopped into the Jeep and squealed out of the driveway down Lunar Lane. I made a sharp right onto Crescent and a left on White Hope Road. The station was across from the county courthouse, a block from Main Street. I couldn't find a spot in the parking lot, so I slid next to a meter and hopped out of the car. I checked my pockets. No money. Reached in the Jeep for my wallet. No wallet. *Perfect.* I just broke six laws getting there. I threw my keys on the seat and slammed the door.

The moon hung low in the sky like a silver pendant as I debated whether to call my cousin. It was just after nine. Cinnamon would most likely be knee-deep in customers. Better to stop by there when they were done with Birdie.

I pushed through the station door and spotted Gus Dorsey. He was wearing an Amethyst police uniform that his belt was trying desperately to hold onto. I had heard that he joined the force a few years back, which surprised me since he was voted most likely to join the circus in high school. He had a stun gun in his holster where a firearm should have been, and a basset-hound look on his face.

"Hi, Stacy. How's your cousin?" Gus was a year younger than my cousin and had been in love with her all his life. Cinnamon refused to date any man with biceps smaller than hers, so poor Gus never had a chance.

"Fine, Gus. Where is my grandmother?"

"She's in the interrogation room. Come on." Gus opened the wooden half-door for me to pass through.

Leo came around the corner then. Smiling at me, he said, "I'll take you."

This guy had nerve. He hauled away my grandmother, and then thought he could flash a smile at me? A very sexy smile. He opened a door to a tiny room with a huge window. Birdie was on the other side of the glass.

"Wait a second, I want to go in there with her," I said.

"Sorry. Can't do it."

"Well, she needs an attorney, at least."

"For what?" He shrugged. "She didn't do anything criminal. I know she's into all that new age, natural healing. She was just trying to help."

"You haven't lived here that long, have you?"

He chuckled. "We just need to fill out a report to make the hospital administrator happy."

"But she needs someone in there to, to ..." *To keep her big, fat mouth shut*, was what I was going to say, but I thought better of it.

"Stacy, you're worrying for nothing. She'll be out of here in ten minutes," Leo said. "She can't see you and the speaker is broken, but you can observe what's going on. I'll be right back."

I walked up to the glass and watched my grandmother's face. No expression. Then she cocked her head and stared right at me. She smiled and winked.

Gus entered the room and sat down across from her, a pen and notepad in his arms. I could see his lips moving, and he laughed periodically as he scribbled on the paper. Birdie smiled politely, completely uninterested in whatever he was babbling about.

The door opened and Leo walked back into the room. "What's your pleasure?"

He had two cups of coffee. "No thank you."

"Come on." He brushed his elbow against mine. "I have Columbian roast and hazelnut. You look like a hazelnut."

"I have no idea what that means," I snapped.

Leo crinkled his brow. "I just thought—"

"You just thought what? That you could stand there and flash a sexy smile while that dipstick interrogates my grandmother?"

"You think I have a sexy smile?" He grinned wide and posed in profile view. "Wait, wait ... how about from this angle?" He turned to the other side and curtsied.

I couldn't help but laugh. My shoulders relaxed a bit. Maybe I was worried for nothing. Gus had known Birdie all his life. She was in good hands, even if she did let her mouth run. I accepted the hazelnut coffee, sat down on a cold metal chair, and sighed. "I'm sorry. This has been quite a day."

"I bet." He sipped his coffee.

"It's not every day you have to pick up your grandmother from the police station."

I didn't tell him about the time six years ago when Birdie decided to bring the Summer Solstice celebration, which involves dancing naked under the full moon, to Main Street. Or about my high school graduation when Birdie wanted to get me a car, but she couldn't afford one, so she 'borrowed' a Corvette from the dealership. Still don't know how she got it started.

"So how long are you in town?" Leo asked.

"I'm not sure. A few days, I guess."

Leo sipped his coffee. "Maybe I could take you to dinner?"

Before I could answer, Gus knocked on the window and pointed to the door.

"Think about it. I'll even let you turn on the siren."

He walked out to meet Gus, and I sat there feeling the corners of my mouth lift into a smile. Dinner sounded fantastic. I wondered if I had something to wear. Sure, I had to spend some time with Gramps, but I also needed to eat. And sitting across from those movie star lips for ninety or so minutes sounded like a vacation in paradise. Yep. This day was definitely closing on a high note. Yay me.

I tried to catch Birdie's eye, but she wasn't looking at me. She was writing on the notepad Gus left in the room.

Finishing my coffee, I decided to wait in the room for Leo to come back so I could take Birdie home and we could make plans for dinner.

After twenty minutes, I was wondering what was keeping him. I stood and stretched my legs just as Gus re-entered the room where Birdie was. He handed her a piece of paper. She glanced at it, nodded, then picked up the pen and signed it. *Finally*.

I stepped out just as the door to the interrogation room opened and Gus exited, babbling about the Avengers, Birdie close behind him.

"Gus," Leo interrupted, "take Mrs. Geraghty downstairs. Make sure she's comfortable."

"Wait, what?" I pivoted to Birdie. "What's going on?"

"We'll talk later, dear." She grinned and pinched me on the cheek.

"Birdie!" I started after her.

She waved over her head and followed Gus down the stairwell, a soft breeze trailing her.

I swung back to Leo. "Where is he taking her?"

"To the booking room."

"Why?"

He had that same look I'd given to family members when I was writing the obituary column. "Because she confessed to the attempted murder of your grandfather."

That was the last thing I heard before the darkness.

6

"*S*tacy, Stacy, can you hear me?" A voice was calling my name. It sounded far away. Where was I? I remembered ... Birdie ... and ... and now I was lying down. Thank God. It was a stupid dream.

"Give me that." The voice again. A man.

I was trying to pry my eyes open.

Another voice, female. "Should I call somebody?"

A soothing hand on my forehead. "Hang on. I think she's coming around."

I opened my eyes.

Definitely not a dream.

Gus stood next to Leo, as he hunched over me, his face lined with worry. "You had us all scared there." He was holding a cool cloth to my forehead.

"I'm fine. Did I pass out?" My head was fuzzy. Unfortunately, my memory was intact. Aside from the fact that I wanted to kill my grandmother, everything else seemed fine.

"You fainted after, um ..." I was glad he didn't repeat it.

"How long was I out?" I slowly sat up and planted my feet on the floor.

"Not long." Leo handed me a cup of water.

I sat there for a minute, not sure what to do next.

Leo sat next to me. "Do you want me to call someone to pick you up? Or Gus can drive you home."

"No, I'm good. I just want to see my grandmother. Where is she?"

Leo glanced at Gus. "Actually, she asked not to be disturbed."

The blood was flowing to my brain again, and I could feel a slight twitch in my eye. I hoped I wasn't having a stroke. Did women in their twenties have strokes? I wasn't sure.

I balked at Leo. "Are you freaking kidding me? What do you mean she asked not to be disturbed? Is this the damn Holiday Inn?"

Leo shrugged. "Hey, she's your grandmother."

"There's no proof of that." She didn't even have her own birth certificate, let alone mine. Some kind of mishap at the courthouse in the late seventies. A fire? I couldn't recall, but the fact remained that no one knew the true age of any Geraghty woman. Jeez, what if *I* was older? What if I was losing all my childbearing eggs just sitting here and I didn't even know it?

A voice interrupted my thoughts. "Stacy?"

"What?"

"Um, your phone. It's ringing," Leo pointed to my pocket.

I sighed, stood up, and fished out my cell phone.

"Yes, hello? May I speak with Stacy, please?" Aunt Lolly.

"Hi, Lolly, it's me."

"Hello? Hello? Fiona, come here," she screamed in my ear. I held the phone away. "I don't know how to talk on a cell phone!"

"Aunt Lolly, you aren't on a cell phone, I am."

Leo bit his lower lip and walked away. Bet he wouldn't be laughing after a few hours with Birdie. He'd be banging his head against the wall, begging me to take her home.

"I can't hear her. No. Yes. Yes, I think so. No. You talk."

"Lolly? Lolly!" I yelled.

In the background, Fiona called to her sister, "Turn the phone around, honey."

Shuffle, shuffle, shuffle.

"Hello? Stacy? Is Stacy there?"

Oh, for the love of ...

"Yes, Lolly, I'm here. What do you need?"

"Oh, hello, dear. When will Birdie be home?"

"Why? Is something wrong?"

"Well, see, I do the cooking and the cleaning, Fiona does the laundry and the decorating, and Birdie does the customer service. But Birdie isn't home and we have reservations tomorrow and guests are coming and we don't know what to do. This credit card thingamajiggy is a pistol, I tell you..." Her voice trailed off. Then absently she said, "Hello? Who is this?"

"Lolly, is Fiona around? May I please speak with Fiona?"

"Do you have a reservation?"

"Aunt Lolly," I carefully enunciated, "please let me speak with your sister."

"Birdie isn't here. You'll have to call back." Click.

"Dammit." I shoved the phone in my pocket, threw the empty water cup on the ground, and jumped up and down on it like a two year old. It was cardboard, so it didn't have the satisfaction of a crunching sound. Like when you hang up on someone with a cell phone instead of a landline. Ruined the climax.

Leo sauntered over, sipping a soda. "Trouble in paradise?"

If he wasn't carrying a weapon I might have decked him. "Paradise? Paradise is an island I've never been to, Leo. My home is the Twilight Zone and Rod Serling is the mayor."

"Anything I can do?"

Release my grandmother? Make my grandfather all better? Give me a police escort back to Chicago so I can return to my job and the simple life where all I have to worry about is riots and drive-by shootings?

But I didn't say any of that. "You can tell my grandmother that I will be back later and that she will talk to me if I have to borrow a bullhorn."

Smiling, Leo nodded.

I picked up the smashed cup and tossed it in the trash near where Gus was standing. Then I kicked the can. Gus let out a small yelp.

I stormed out the door just as Leo called, "What about dinner?"

There was only one place to go to help me sort through this mess.

"TAKE THESE," I said to Cinnamon, handing her my car keys, "and give me one of those." I pointed to a bottle of Pinot Grigio, shrugging out of my coat.

Cinnamon grabbed a glass, and I shook my head. "No. The whole freaking bottle."

Laughing, she reached for the wine.

The Black Opal was a Main Street staple. It wasn't too chic, too loud, too dirty, too clubby, too anything. It was one of those places you'd feel comfortable bringing a client or your best friend. You could order a martini, a shot, or a beer, but nothing pink. Cin hated the color pink.

Classic rock-and-roll hummed from the jukebox, but it was slow for a Thursday and I was thankful for that. The only customer was Scully, perched on a center stool. I think Scully was listed as a fixture in the contract Cinnamon signed when she bought the bar. He was as old as the building itself, and I had never seen him anywhere else around town. I waved hello to him.

Cinnamon leaned across from me, brown hair curling around her bare shoulders. She was wearing a black tank top that showed off her tattoo of a phoenix rising from the ashes and her curves.

"That bad?" She handed me the glass.

"Worse," I croaked.

Cinnamon popped open a beer for herself. "Bay," she called toward the storage room, "you're on."

Bay was a local kid who played in a classic rock band. He had a round baby face that made him look twelve instead of twenty-one. He emerged from the storeroom wearing a tee shirt with a picture of Tweety Bird flicking off Sylvester. "I keep tips," he said.

"Fine." Cinnamon walked around to the front of the bar, holding her beer. "Let's get a table in the back and you can tell me what's going on."

I followed her into the back room when WHAM! I was knocked down by a mountain lion. My wine glass flew out of my hand as the booze soaked my sweater. The four-legged mammoth straddled me and licked the wine off my face as I tried not to piss myself.

"Dammit, Thor!" Cinnamon yelled. "Get off." She dragged the beast off my chest and scolded him.

I sat very still on the worn wood floor, afraid to look.

"Stacy, are you okay? I'm so sorry. I don't know why he did that." Cinnamon was blotting me with her hands. She shouted over her shoulder, "Bay, bring Stacy another glass of pinot and a towel."

"What the hell was that?" I struggled to sit up.

"That's Thor. Don't you remember? The dog Tony got me for our anniversary right before I kicked his ass out."

Tony Panzano was Cinnamon's ex-husband who accidentally slept with her arch nemesis. They had had a huge fight, and Cinnamon walked out for three days. Tony was in a drunken depression and Monique Fontaine, who was a one-woman comforting committee, tried to pull him out of it. Unfortunately, she pulled a few things she shouldn't have.

"What are you feeding it? Miracle Grow?" I attempted to wipe off my sweatshirt. I had never seen such a giant dog. The thing was almost as tall as me and his head looked like the front end of a Chevy.

"He's a Great Dane. You know, like Marmaduke. He isn't usually so rambunctious." She glared at Thor who bowed his head dutifully. "He's actually kind of handy around the bar. He's a good guard dog. I don't need a bouncer." Cin helped me to my feet.

"No, but I bet you need a Bobcat to pooper scoop."

Thor sat in front of me, remorse on his face. He grumbled what could have been an apology.

"Thor. God of Thunder, right?" I couldn't pull my gaze from the dog. There was something majestic about him. He had soulful brown eyes, a shiny tan coat and a black mask that covered his face like a secret.

"Mmm Hmm." Cinnamon nodded.

We both stared at Thor. He chuffed and offered a paw the size of a Frisbee. I shook it to let him know there were no hard feelings. His eyes locked with mine and for just a moment, I felt a tether between us. Like we had met before. Strange.

"Come on. Let's sit. Tell me what's happening." Cinnamon guided me to a table where Bay dropped off a fresh drink. Thor marched over and sat sentry next to me, his huge head trained on the door like a soldier ready for battle.

I began with the news that the doctors found our grandfather's illness suspect.

"Does that mean he was poisoned? Or could it have been an accident like mistaking a bottle of Drano for Maalox or something? He is getting up there, you know."

If my grandfather was rounding the corner to senility street, that might be a plausible scenario, but our phone conversations were always lucid. Naturally, I didn't see him as often as my cousin did.

"You would know better than I would. How has he been lately?" I asked.

"Fine. He's been fine. Nothing unusual except—" Cin smacked her forehead. "Crap, I almost forgot. Guess who came into town this week?"

"Who?"

"Wildcat."

"Really?"

Cinnamon nodded. "He and Gramps swapped war stories all night. Birdie hated it, but Fiona ate it up."

That didn't surprise me. Birdie was not Bill 'Wildcat' Panther's biggest fan. He was Gramps' oldest friend, and I wasn't sure what she had against the man, save for the fact that he had a generous helping of the obnoxious gene. He liked his booze hard and his women soft, which didn't appeal to Birdie in the least.

Before Cinnamon launched into the latest gossip, I

decided I better let her know what had happened with Birdie. I took a healthy sip of my wine for some courage. I was interrupted when Thor unloaded the contents of his stomach all over my boots.

I looked down, not really surprised. Wasn't the worst thing that happened today.

Cinnamon jumped up, knocking her beer over and the trifecta was complete as it trailed onto my jeans. "Dammit, Thor. I'm so sorry, Stacy, I'll buy you new shoes." She ran to get another towel.

I eyed Thor, wondering if he thought his first name was Dammit. He looked confused. Like he had never called in sick a day in his life and was mortified by the prospect.

"Here." Cinnamon returned with a towel. "I don't know what the hell is wrong with this dog. He eats everything. One time he lapped up some antifreeze Tony spilled at the shop." Tony was a mechanic. "He was hobbling around like the town drunk, completely out of it. The vet had to pump his stomach."

I spotted the penny just as she said that. From the looks of it, it had been swimming in the dog's stomach. I used the towel to wipe my boots, then picked up the coin with it and cleaned it off. Cin went to get a mop and bucket from the closet behind me.

"Jeez, couldn't that kill him?"

"Yeah. It's poison," she called.

I stopped wiping and looked at Cin. She caught my eye, and I was sure we were thinking the same thing.

"Acting like he was drunk," she said.

"They pumped his stomach," I said.

Gramps.

7

*C*innamon told Bay to close up, and we left out the back door with a bottle of wine and headed to the cottage with Thor in tow.

"So do we call the hospital, tell them maybe he ingested antifreeze?" Cinnamon asked.

"I would think they would recognize the symptoms. Besides, we aren't certain. I mean, that's a stab in the dark." I decided to wait until we got there to tell her that our grandmother was in the slammer.

The streets were quiet as we meandered through the town up the steps to the inn. There was no traffic, no one else walking in the night, and I couldn't help but notice everything looked the same as when I had left it. Old-fashioned lampposts dotted the crossroads, wrought iron fences framed the yards, and painted ladies were still painted. Of course, in a town this small, the people didn't change much either. Everyone knew everyone and each other's business. Even if something exciting were to happen, people heard about it on their home scanners long before it was printed in the newspaper. Not much fun for a reporter.

Cinnamon broke the silence. "So now what?"

"Still think it was an accident?"

Cinnamon blew out a sigh. "I don't know. If he did swallow antifreeze, at least we can rule out Birdie. I'm sure she would choose something much more dramatic to poison someone. Like oleander."

"You're probably right."

Cin gave me a funny look as I swung through the gate.

"What was that?"

"What?" I twisted the knob and let us into the cottage. No one ever locked doors in this town. Well, except for the Geraghty Girls, but that was mostly to keep Lolly inside of the house.

Thor jogged inside like he owned the place and jumped on the couch. I kicked my shoes off as my cousin went in search of glassware and a corkscrew.

"That pitch. Whenever you're hiding something from me your voice jumps up an octave like Mickey Mouse." Cin eyed me closely.

While I disagreed with that analogy, I couldn't ignore the fact that Cinnamon knew me better than anyone. We may look completely opposite, but we had a lot in common. She also lost her father too young and that bonded us together for life. Uncle Deck was my mother's brother and the former chief of police. Which prompted the question, "What's the story with Leo?"

"You met him?" she asked with more enthusiasm than I thought necessary. "Wait. Let me open the wine first."

"I'm going to wash up."

"You're not off the hook, by the way. You still owe me an explanation," Cinnamon called to me from the kitchenette.

Boy did I.

I scrubbed my face and hands, tossed my clothes into

the hamper, and climbed into a pair of pajamas. When I returned, Cin had two glasses of wine poured and she was sitting at the breakfast bar.

"So, how did you meet Leo?" she asked.

"That's not important." I sipped the vino.

"Oh lord, you didn't crash into him with your car or anything did you?" Cin knew I was not the most graceful person on the planet.

"No." I sighed. "Actually, he thought I was breaking into the Geraghty house because I didn't have a key and I was looking around the porch for the spare."

Cin burst out laughing. "No freaking way."

"I'm glad my embarrassment amuses you." I reached for my wine glass.

She waved her hand. "Okay, forget about that. What did you think?" She leaned in closer, her eyes wide.

It was clear she thought I was a good match for this guy, and since he was obviously not her type she seemed eager for me to jump in. I should explain that anyone with a badge was not her type. Between her anger management issues, and her father's profession, I suppose it was inevitable that Cinnamon would have trouble with the law, which she did as a teenager. Except for taking a blowtorch to Tony's fully restored '68 Mustang a year ago, she'd been on the straight and narrow ever since.

I shrugged. "He's cute."

Cin sat back on her stool. "Cute? Your cat is cute."

Moonlight yawned from the top of the stiletto chair.

"You're right. He's gorgeous," I agreed. Not that it mattered at this point.

"You want me to set you up?"

Oh boy. How to tell her that I already had an invitation

to dinner, but breaking bread with the guy who tossed your granny in the big house might not be good karma?

Cinnamon was eyeing me, probably trying to figure out what stupid, clumsy thing I did when I met Leo. "Stacy, what's the deal? It can't be that bad."

If only.

I poured another glass of wine. "I have seen him again, actually. He asked me to dinner."

She scooted her stool closer. "Really? That's great. When are you going out?"

"I don't think we *are* going out."

Cin threw her hands up, exasperated. "Here we go. Every time a great guy comes into your life you push him away."

I rolled my eyes. She could be so dramatic. "That's not true."

"What about Chance?"

"What about Chance?"

"You were both so good for each other and he adored you."

She had a point there, but I wouldn't admit it. The truth was, Chance was a *great* guy. A great friend, a great boyfriend. But that didn't change the fact that we wanted different things.

"Cinnamon, who stays with their high school boyfriend forever?"

"Me."

I narrowed my eyes at her.

She shrugged. "Well, you know, until the divorce."

"I still think there's something screwy about Monique's story." It was true. Tony worshiped Cinnamon, and Monique lived to torture her. I wouldn't be a bit surprised if she had slipped something into Tony's drink that night.

Cinnamon tapped the counter. "Don't change the subject. Why won't you go out with Leo?"

"Well, Gramps is sick for one thing and we still don't know what's wrong." And also, there was the small matter of Birdie's confession.

"Fair enough, but you can't keep watch over him 24/7."

"I may also have to help out at the inn." I took a big gulp of my drink.

"Why is that?" Cin asked.

I sucked in some air. "Cin, I need you to tell me everything that happened at the dinner. Who was there, what you talked about, what was served. All of it."

Cinnamon stood up and parked a hand on her hip. "You're creeping me out. Tell me what is going on, Stacy, right now."

So I did.

When I was finished with the highlight reel, Cinnamon's mouth was skimming the floor. "It has to be another stunt, right?" she asked. "Birdie is forever reaching for the shock value, and she's been trying to get you to move back to town ever since you left. This is her way of keeping you here." Cinnamon sounded like she was trying to convince herself. "She wouldn't really hurt Gramps."

All I could do was nod. I was about seventy percent sure she was right.

Let's face it, neither one of us wanted to believe that our own grandmother would harm our grandfather for real. People toss around threats all the time, but they don't actually follow through. Most people anyway. But we were talking about a woman who once reduced a 6'4" two hundred-eighty-pound plumber to a blubbering pile of tears because he padded the bill. Revenge is an art form to Birdie, deeply embedded in her beliefs.

Over the next hour, I told Cinnamon everything I knew, and she filled me in on that night's dinner. Everyone seemed in good spirits. No arguments, just the usual banter between our grandparents. The menu included pot roast, baby carrots with an orange glaze, twice baked potatoes, and peach pie that Pearl had brought.

"Do you know if Gramps and Pearl went right home or did they have other plans?"

"I'm not sure. You'll have to ask them. Pearl usually pops into the restaurant to close up."

Pearl owned the Pearl Palace. It was a quaint diner on Main Street stuck in the 1950s, complete with skirted waitresses and a revolving dessert case.

"But they still live above it, right?"

Cin nodded.

"So it was just you, your mom, Pearl, the Geraghty Girls, and Wildcat?" I was thinking out loud.

"Actually, there was someone else."

"Who?"

"Chance was there. too."

"Why in the world was he there?" I had no ill will toward Chance. In fact, I had fond memories of our time together. But I wasn't one to keep stray boyfriends just laying around where anyone could trip over them.

Cinnamon shrugged. "I don't know. I think they needed something fixed around the house. It's no big deal."

I sighed and considered this. In a way, Cin was right. So Chance had dinner at the house. So what? He had been a big part of my life once. It was only natural that he would stay friendly with my family. I wondered how his parents were doing. His house was my refuge when things went haywire here. We could watch re-runs of old sitcoms, make macaroni and cheese from a box, play Monopoly, and know that we would never smell the stench of burning sage or accidentally walk in on a soul retrieval session. Which, believe me, was never advised.

It was getting late and I was exhausted. Cinnamon and I made plans to meet the next morning at Muddy Waters Coffee House. Then I would visit Gramps and hopefully straighten out this mess. I scratched Thor behind the ears and said good-bye. He barked in protest.

Cinnamon turned to leave, then stopped and said, "Why would she confess to something so serious if she didn't do it?"

"I don't know, Cin, but I'll find out."

The wind howled through the trees, and a chill passed through her to me.

"Stace."

I looked at her.

"Birdie doesn't lie."

"I know."

8

Sleep was dreamless. Which could only mean one thing in my world—too much wine. I lay in bed for a moment, feeling Moonlight lick my hair. Probably sucking up the pinot that sloshed on me after Thor's greeting last night.

The clock read 6:30. I could get away with another hour of sleep. I curled up on my side and was just about to drift off when the banging started.

I bolted upright, not sure where it was coming from. BANG! BANG! BANG!

From above. *Who the hell's tap dancing on my roof?*

Peeling the covers back, I crawled from my cozy bed, still not clearly focused.

BANG! BANG!

This was so not helping my headache. I couldn't find my slippers, but the boots were close. Didn't bother zipping them as I stumbled into the living room, heading toward the door. The shoe chair helped move things along after I tripped over it and sailed into the tile, which, again, did not help my headache. Finally, I managed to get onto the porch.

"It's 6:30 in the morning," I yelled. My mouth felt like a lint trap. "The birds aren't up yet." The sun was blinding me, so I had to shield my eyes. I stood there squinting at a man on top of the cottage roof. *What the hell?* He had a hammer in his hand, but the sun was behind him so his face was a silhouette.

"Sorry, ma'am, I didn't realize someone was staying here. I can come back later."

Ma'am? I was not old enough to be ma'am. Well, at least the banging stopped.

I turned to go, but then I heard, "Stacy?"

All I could see were work boots, jeans, and a baseball cap. I squinted, fighting to focus my eyes. "Yes?"

"Don't you recognize me?"

"Sun's in my eyes. Who is it?"

He moved with assurance toward a ladder and the light shifted. Recognition slapped me hard. *Oh please, not now. Why does this keep happening to me?*

There wasn't much I could do, so I decided to just enjoy the view as he scaled down the ladder. He still looked like a walking ad for Levi's. Tanned face, wisps of golden hair across his forehead, and there they were ... those blue eyes I used to get lost in.

"Hi, Chance."

Is there anything worse than running into your first love with bedhead, baggy pjs, and a hangover?

"How are you?" His sexy mouth curved into a lazy smile.

"I'm good." *Why did I come out here? Please, goddess, don't let me stink of dog barf.*

He reached in to hug me, and I backed away. "Don't think you want to do that. I haven't showered yet."

"Come here." He pulled me into his strong arms. He smelled of sawdust, autumn leaves, and juniper berries.

Comfort food for the nose. I relaxed into the embrace and it felt good.

After a moment, he asked, "Pinot grigio?"

Jeez, where's a rock when you need one to crawl under? I broke away and tried to smooth out my hair, but I only succeeded in getting a finger stuck. Chance was gracious enough to pretend not to notice.

"Compliments of Thor." After struggling to free my hand, I decided to just sacrifice a few strands and yanked.

We stood there smiling at each other for a beat.

"You look great," Chance said finally.

I burst out laughing. "You're such a liar."

He laughed, too, but then his voice got low. "No, I mean it. You always look great to me."

And with that, it felt familiar standing there with him. Like the first place you ever lived, your favorite spot on the sofa, a classic you read again and again. Chance felt like home to me. But as they say, you can't go home again. "So, I guess you're fixing the roof?" I pointed to the roof as if neither of us knew it was on top of the house.

"Yep. Fiona called me last week. Said she needed a repair job, so I thought I could squeeze it in. Then she changed her mind and decided on a total replacement. I had another job lined up, but the guy canceled at the last minute." He eyed the loose shingles.

Canceled at the last minute, eh? It stank of Fiona's handiwork. Always playing Cupid. Well, that was fine for tourists and townsfolk, but my love life was off limits and I intended to tell her so.

"That was very nice of you."

Chance shrugged. "You know I'd do anything for your family." Then he added, "And you."

I smiled.

"I didn't know anyone would be here, though. She said they weren't going to rent the cottage until I was done. Sorry for waking you."

"No problem, really. So you went into the contracting business with your dad?"

Chance nodded. "It's a good thing there's ordinances that keep people from tearing down these old houses." Chance surveyed the cottage. "A contractor comes in handy in this town. Business is great."

"I'm happy for you, Chance." I meant it. Chance deserved every bit of happiness he could find.

"Well," he clapped his hands together, "I should get back to work." He took a step back toward the ladder.

"And I should get cleaned up." I moved to go inside.

"Stacy?"

I turned back. "Yes?"

"It's really good to see you."

I studied him closely. He had a few more lines than I remembered. A few more pounds that filled him out just fine. The boy I had loved was now a man.

"It's good to see you, too."

Back inside, I leaned against the front door as I gathered my thoughts. Had Chance heard about my grandfather's illness? Birdie? Surely he would have said something if he had. And why did he not mention the dinner?

Catching my reflection in the hall mirror, I smacked my forehead. I looked like the troll doll I used to keep on top of my pencil in fourth grade. Just once, I would like to run into a gorgeous man with hair, make-up, and wardrobe intact.

Moonlight was crying to be fed, snaking my ankles. Scooping him up, I carted him off to the kitchen in search of coffee and food.

The fridge and cupboards were a ghost town, so I was

out of luck, but I did have kitten food in my suitcase. I shuffled off to the bedroom and clicked the locks open, pulling out a can of Happy Kitty chicken and livers. Moonlight recognized it instantly and jumped on my shoulder, purring like a jet engine.

We went back to the kitchen and I dug out a saucer, popped the lid off the can, and emptied the contents into it. Moonlight scarfed his breakfast down, did a figure eight around my legs, and sauntered into the living room, curling up behind the heel of the shoe chair.

I rummaged through the suitcase and pulled out a new pair of low-rise jeans and a knit top with a built-in bra, plus socks and non-cotton panties. No Tinker Bell or Hello Kitty today.

The shower was hot enough to massage my muscles, and the scent of the shampoo I found in the little basket woke up all my senses. I was revived as I stepped out and reached for a towel. Then I saw the mirror and screamed.

It was fogged over except for three words.

I WANT YOU

9

*I*t took twenty minutes to dress and dry my hair, and I was out the door, heading toward the inn, still unnerved by that message. Was it possible a previous guest had left it? A couple scrawling little notes to each other? But certainly, that mirror would have been buffed to a shine by one of the aunts and any impression lost in the process.

Without coffee, this was not going to get sorted out properly. It was still early. Cinnamon and I had plans to meet in an hour, but I needed a jolt now, not to mention a talk with Fiona. How could she not tell me Chance would be around every damn day? I knocked on the back screen door and called out. No answer. The door wasn't locked, so I let myself in.

The kitchen had been cleaned up, all traces of spell work stashed away. In the basement, I suspected, where they stored their tools. It was a sacred place, untainted by outside energy, Birdie once explained.

No one had started the coffee, and I didn't see any muffins in the oven so I had to fend for myself. My hands were deep in the back of a cabinet, reaching for the Columbian roast, when directly behind me someone yelled, "Hey."

I jumped three feet in the air and nearly wet myself.

"Ha, ha, ha, ha, ha, ha." It was a cartoon laugh. Nasal and annoying as hell. I turned around, clutching the can.

He wore a crisp white shirt and black pants. His hair was bottle-blond and spiked with goop, and he used aftershave as an accessory. He reminded me of a skunk sprayed with bleach.

Then I noticed the remains of a faint scar on his forehead where I had once hit him with a fallen tree branch after he tackled me and tried to lick my face when we were kids.

Ed Entwhistle. Suddenly, my stomach ached.

"What the hell do you think you're doing?" I pointed the coffee can at him. Yoga and kickboxing kept my body strong. Pretty sure I could take him again. I could only guess my anger hung like a cloak because he backed off, his face drained of some of its luster.

"Oooo." Ed raised his hands in a defeated gesture. "I give, I give." He laughed. "Drop your weapon."

I just stood there, wondering what the hell he was doing in my grandmother's kitchen.

"You like the new threads?" he asked.

When I knew Ed in high school, he got his clothes at the Farm-N-Fleet. These clothes had the aura of an upscale department store. Personally, I didn't care either way.

Here's the thing. When I first moved to Chicago, I met a woman walking a spider monkey down the street. She was crying because the exotic pet store she bought him from wouldn't take him back and her husband threatened to shoot him if she brought him home. So I took him.

Chester knew lots of great tricks, and for the first few days, we got along fine. I dressed him in little doll clothes, combed his hair, and brushed his teeth. But then Chester began showing his true colors.

He had an uncontrollable habit of picking at his fur and flinging the scabs at me. He also liked to snatch food from my plate and run around the living room with it before mashing it into the carpet. But the last straw was when I had a date over and Chester dropped his shorts and gave us a lesson on sexual healing, solo style. He went to the Lincoln Park Zoo the next morning.

So, you see, the monkey could be primped and groomed, but underneath he was still a monkey. That was how I felt about Ed.

"You look well, Ed. Love the hair."

"Yep." He patted his head. "The store is doing fantastic, and Pop's going to retire soon. I'll be managing things from then on. Then it's all mine." Ed grinned. "Especially when he croaks."

I blanched.

He quickly realized his faux pas. "Not that I want that. I love that old geezer, you know that." He elbowed me. "But think of all that dough, baby. Just you and me riding off into the sunset." He grabbed my waist and pulled me close.

Making a mental note to vomit later, I wriggled free from his grasp. Ed had been trying to get me to go out with him since freshman year, but since I tend to date within my species, it never happened.

Ed's father was Roy Entwhistle, a one-time partner and longtime friend of my grandfather. He and Gramps ran an industrial store together years ago that supplied farm equipment to the entire county. Gramps had the insight to see that factories were replacing farming in the area and he wanted to get out of the business. Roy refused to sell, so he bought Gramps out and lost his shirt. Gramps, on the other hand, made a fortune in real estate investments with money from Roy's buyout. Their store, one of those huge super-stores that have everything from lettuce to lawn chairs, was now sprawled across land my grandfather once owned, but gifted to Roy as a peace offering.

Fiona breezed into the kitchen then. "Oh, there you are, Stacy. How's the kitty?" She sashayed toward the fridge. "Ed, are we all set for the weekend's groceries?" she asked.

Fiona was taxing the laws of gravity with a full-body leotard and a wrap-around mesh skirt. Lolly trailed behind her in a bright floral number with white tights and a tutu.

Friday morning yoga. I nearly forgot. "Moonlight's fine. Aunt Fiona, may I speak with you, please?"

"One minute, dear." She reached into the fridge and pulled out two water bottles and tossed one to her sister. Then she ducked back inside, filtering through the food.

"You're all set, Ms. Geraghty. Everything in its place. I didn't get a chance to wash and put the fruit away, though. That's in the pantry. And I'll need to bring more eggs."

"Thank you." Fiona followed his cue and ducked into the walk-in pantry.

"No problem, ladies, I'll be on my way." Ed swung a jacket over his shoulder as he walked to the screen door. He paused and shot at me, using his hand as a gun. "I'll catch you later, Stacy."

I groaned as the screen slammed behind him.

"Looks like someone is smitten with you." Fiona took the coffee from my hand and prepared a pot.

"I'd rather date an escaped mental patient with a conta-gious skin disease and six fingers."

Lolly gazed at me quizzically, and Fiona raised a perfectly plucked eyebrow.

"Look, forget it. And forget about Chance and I getting back together, too." I directed this at Fiona who was pouring cream into a cup.

She seemed shocked. "Whatever do you mean, dear?"

"Fiona, don't play games with me. He happened to get a cancellation, and you just happened to need your roof repaired, and I just happened to be staying at the cottage at the exact same time?"

"That's right." She exchanged looks with Lolly. Lolly shrugged and went back to twisting her tutu into a knot.

Fiona pulled out the Bailey's and poured a shot into a coffee mug.

"I don't believe in coincidences. If I learned anything in this house, it was that. So what was it, hmm?" Leaning against the counter, I crossed my arms. "Passion flower in his boots? An incantation the full moon before last? Did you tie our yearbook pictures together with a rose vine and bury them in the woods? What?"

"Don't be silly. I would never do any of those things."

The rich aroma of the coffee filled the kitchen, and I helped myself to a cup. Fiona poured some in the mug with the Irish cream liqueur and handed it to Lolly.

Clearly my point had been made, whether she was going to admit to playing puppet master or not.

"If that's the story you're sticking to, you should know that I do not practice magic anymore."

It wasn't that I didn't buy into the principles of my family's nature-centered philosophy; it's that I didn't see the point. Whether you prayed to the Holy Trinity or the Triple Goddess made no difference to me, because when it came down to it, all the magic in the world couldn't save my father. And when I needed my mother most, no matter how many herbs I enchanted, how many spells I cast, she did what I knew in my heart she would.

Disappeared.

Fiona cocked her head and cleared her throat.

"Except for last night, I mean. That was a one-time deal for Gramps."

"Humph." She ran some apples and pears under the faucet. "We'll see what your grandmother has to say about that."

Crap. Between Chance, the mirror, and Ed, I forgot all about Birdie.

"About that, Fiona. There's something I need to tell you."

"What's that, dear?" She was peeling the fruit with a knife, the skins falling in long ribbons into a glazed blue bowl.

Didn't they notice she wasn't home?

"You see, the reason Birdie didn't come home last night is because ... um, because—"

"Because she was at the police station." Lolly belted back the spiked coffee and burped.

"You knew?" It hadn't occurred to me that Birdie would have called.

"Certainly." Fiona quartered the fruit and tossed it with lemon juice.

That was a relief. One less thing to deal with. Lolly seemed to be holding it together, and Fiona was busy putting together a fruit crisp.

"It's all settled." Fiona bent to turn the oven to three hundred and fifty degrees.

She's being released? "Really? She's coming home? When?"

Fiona and Lolly chuckled. "That depends on you," they replied in unison.

Uh-oh. Now, what're they up to?

Lolly kissed my cheek and a whisper ran through my head. "We aren't up to anything."

Did I say that out loud?

"Now, why don't you run along so we can prepare for the afternoon arrivals?" She topped the apples and pears with butter, brown sugar, and oats, then popped it into the oven.

"Fine. I can take a hint." I stood up and put on my wool jacket. "I just have one question. When was the last time someone stayed in the cottage?"

Fiona tapped her chin. "Not since the renovation. Why do you ask?"

"No reason."

I followed the brick walkway that coiled to the front of the house and exited through the iron gate. It was almost time to meet my cousin, but it was a warm morning, so I decided to walk.

I didn't hear the car behind me until it was too late.

10

A black, souped-up muscle car coasted next to me like Jaws stalking his lunch. The windows were tinted just dark enough not to be illegal. All I could see were sunglasses shaped like the ones highway patrolmen wear.

The window oozed down. "Get in," he said.

I stopped walking, sliding my own shades down the bridge of my nose.

"No freaking way."

"Come on. I'll take you for a ride."

He rolled the window all the way down.

"I need the exercise, Tony. Besides, I'm headed to meet Cin and she would kill me if she saw me with you."

"I'll take you down to the corner and drop you off. I need to talk to you, Stacy. Pleeeeeeze."

Jeez, I hated to watch a man beg. I let a cry of frustration and waved my fist to the sky.

Tony took that as a sign of acquiescence. He swung the car door open, and I reluctantly climbed in.

"Where you headed?" he asked.

"Muddy Waters."

Tony sat there for a minute staring at his shoes, the engine idling. I never noticed before, but he could have passed for Cin's brother. Same dark complexion, same thick, wavy hair. Since she was half Sicilian and he was all Italian I guess it made sense. I stared at him, waiting for him to say something. This was not a conversation I wanted to have, but the man was a member of my family at one time and I felt a little sorry for him.

Finally, he spoke. "I miss her, Stacy." His voice was broken, which matched his heart, I supposed, but it was his own damn fault. He was lucky he walked away with only a torched car and a broken heart because Cin could have busted up a lot more. In fact, her restraint surprised me. Very unlike Cin to let someone off so easy who crossed her.

"You screwed up, Tony."

"I know. I know. I'm a bastard." He slammed his hands against the steering wheel. "I know it isn't an excuse, but I was so drunk, I don't even remember that night."

"You're right, that's no excuse," I agreed, but something was knocking on the back of my mind when he said those words. *I don't remember.*

"You gotta help me out here, Stacy." His eyes were all misty, giving me a teddy bear stare.

"Forget it. I value my life." Cin did not take kindly to uninvited advice.

"I'm begging you." His voice was all squeaky.

"What am I going to say?" I threw up my hands. "You cheated on her with the person she despises most in this world. I just don't see how you can mend that fence, Tony."

"Look, she's the one who walked out. I was out of my mind with worry. I thought she left me or ran away or worse. No one knew where she was for days."

He had a very tiny point.

"This is not the time to bring all that up," I said.

Tony gave me an apologetic look. "Aw, hey, I'm sorry. How is Gramps?"

"I honestly don't know."

"I should be there for her," he said as if he were thinking out loud.

Tony loved my cousin. There was no question he would take a bullet for her. In fact, he had already taken his fair share of right hooks for her. Cinnamon's mouth got her in more trouble than a political candidate with Tourette's Syndrome, and Tony had tried to interfere in many a battle.

This was an impossible situation.

I sighed. "I'll do what I can."

"Thank you." He hugged my neck.

I shook my head, feeling as if I just agreed to arm-wrestle an alligator. "Drive."

Cinnamon texted me as Tony crested the hill, and I felt a pang of guilt. She wanted to know if we could just go straight to the hospital and skip the coffee shop. Her distributor had changed the time of his delivery so she had to make the visit quick. I texted back that I'd meet her there.

A few minutes later, after promising Tony I would try to get my cousin to at least speak with him, I was standing in front of the hospital when my cousin rushed toward me, apologizing for the change in plans. I waved it off and we walked through the automatic doors.

Lynn Bernstein, an old classmate, sat behind the reception desk. She was finishing up a call, and hung up the phone before greeting us. Cin explained we were there for Gramps, and Lynn gave us the room number and directions.

Gramps was a few floors up, so we headed toward the elevator just as the door slid open revealing Ed and Roy Entwhistle.

"Dad, calm down," Ed was saying, a hand on his father's back.

Roy hunched slightly, his face pinched tight as if he was constipated. "That jackass," he mumbled.

I cleared my throat, and Ed looked up, his face red. "Hey, Stacy."

"Hello."

Roy marched down the hall, still mumbling something about no-good jackasses.

Ed chuckled, shaking his head. He winked at me like we were in on some private joke together. "Stacy, we have to get together and catch up. How about dinner later?"

I shook my head. "Thanks, Ed, but I don't have the time right now." *Or ever.*

Ed nodded and smiled. "Sure, sure. Maybe another time."

I smiled back and Cin and I slipped into the elevator.

"What was that about?" I asked, punching the floor number.

Cin shrugged as the doors closed. "Who knows? He's a cranky, old coot and his son is three kinds of creepy."

I stared at the worn carpeted floor as the car crept up the shaft.

Was Roy holding a grudge on that old real estate deal? Did he still harbor resentment toward Gramps?

There was a *ding* as the elevator came to a stop, and the steel door slid into the wall. We stepped out into the hall where a doctor was having a tight-lipped conversation with an attractive woman who looked to be in her forties dressed in a red suit and holding a plastic cup. The doctor quickly handed her something and walked away.

Pearl came out of the room then, her eyes wide and happy to see me. "Sugar." She hugged me close, her bangle bracelets clinking in my ear. She was a dozen years younger than Gramps with golden, straight hair, heart-shaped lips, and a behind that proved she made the best cheesecake in town.

Pearl turned to the woman with the cup. "Gretchen, dear, this is Stacy. Oscar's granddaughter."

Gretchen smiled. "A pleasure."

I smiled back and nodded a hello.

Pearl touched Gretchen's arm. "Gretchen is my niece. She's staying with us for a bit. Helping out at the restaurant." She bobbed her head, looking from one to the other of us like she was watching a tennis match. Her eyes fell to the cup. "Is that Oscar's hot chocolate?"

"Yes." Gretchen handed Pearl the cup, and she went into Gramps' room with it.

Cinnamon was hanging back, speaking to someone on her phone.

"I didn't know Pearl had a niece." Funny that she never mentioned it. From what I understood, Pearl didn't have any family. No children, just an ex-husband from many moons ago.

"We lost touch for a while."

Cin walked up then. "Stacy, I gotta go. If I don't meet the distributor right now, he said he won't be back until Monday and I'll be out of Coors Light." She greeted Gretchen with, "Hello again," as if they had met once or twice before.

"Don't worry about it. I can catch a ride. It's no big deal."

She gave me a funny look, and I remembered that she didn't know Tony brought me there. "Fiona dropped me here," I lied.

"Oh. Okay. Well, I'll say a quick hello to Gramps first."

"He isn't in his room right now. They're running tests," Gretchen stated.

"Oh." Cin frowned. "Well, tell him I love him, Stacy. I'll see you later." She rushed down the hall and into an open elevator.

I turned back to Gretchen. "Was the doctor speaking to you about my grandfather?"

She was zipping up her purse, stuffing papers inside. "Oh, no, no. He was just recommending a good chiropractor. I have a terrible ache in my neck and I'm a big believer in holistic medicine."

I nodded, tempted to send her to the Geraghty Girls. Then again, what had she ever done to me?

"Have you heard anything more about his condition?" I asked.

"Not a word. Probably by this afternoon they'll know more. I was just about to take off. See if I can get any work done at the diner."

"Oh?" I asked.

"Paperwork mostly. Help with the schedule, that sort of thing." She checked her watch. "It was nice meeting you." She followed the same path Cinnamon took.

There was a mental knocking on my brain as I watched Gretchen rush off, but before I could figure out what it meant, two arms like rump roasts wound around me and swung me into the air.

I kicked my legs out and screamed.

The deep laugh came like waves in my ear, and the nerves in my body automatically relaxed, recognizing the tone.

Releasing me, he spun me around. "How ya doing there, Kitten?"

Wildcat may have been an older man, but he could probably kick the ass of any guy half his age. He reminded me of Clint Eastwood in that way. Although he was built more like The Rock.

"Hey, Wildcat. It's great to see you again."

"Well, you know I can't stay away from my old buddy too long."

I smiled. "Has it been that long?"

"Give or take a decade." He peered into the room and thumbed a calloused hand that way. "So, is he awake, or what?"

"Actually, he's getting some tests done."

Wildcat shook his long hair. "More tests, huh?" He shifted nervously. "Hope he's okay."

"He will be." I patted his biker jacket.

His eyes flicked to the open doorway, a cloud washing the blue away for a brief moment. Then he clapped his hands. "How about a Bloody Mary?"

"It's ten in the morning."

"Scotch it is."

Jeez, the guy was a grizzly bear. "I think I should wait here for Gramps."

"You can't let an old man drink alone. It ain't safe. I'll bring you back later." He dragged me to the elevator.

Cinnamon was wiping down the bar of the Black Opal when we roared up on Wildcat's Harley. I looked like a cashmere sweater set on spin dry for too long when we walked in. She shot me a raised eyebrow, and I gave her a 'don't ask' look. She wasn't even open yet.

We sat near the curve in the bar that faced the doorway, and Wildcat ordered shots of Jack Daniels.

"To your old Gramps." He lifted his glass.

Thankfully, mine was soda.

Cin went to stock the cooler, and I asked Wildcat what brought him to town this time.

"Me and Oscar used to have big dreams you know, back in the Army. I thought maybe it was time to settle down and live out those dreams."

"Do tell." This had to be burning Birdie up. Wildcat moving to Amethyst? It was bad enough her ex-husband was still floating around. Wonder why she hadn't mentioned it?

Wildcat was shaking his head. "Well, it's like this." He waved a meaty arm in front of me. "War Games."

I raised my eyebrow.

"You know, like laser tag, paintball, only we would have more of a military element. Combat. That plaza would be the perfect setting."

Could that be what Roy was mad about? Did Gramps tell him he couldn't rent the space anymore?

"Course, now, who knows?" Wildcat muttered.

His eyes were on the bar, but his mind was somewhere else.

11

*W*ildcat didn't stick around long, and Cinnamon received her delivery so we decided to head out for sustenance.

I wondered if I should bring up the subject of Tony. Maybe I could write her a note and slip it under her coffee cup.

"This is on me," she said. "Why don't you grab a table?"

After ordering a non-fat latte and a banana bran muffin, I scooted away from the line.

There was a round table near the front window I was just about to claim when Iris Merriweather pounced on me.

"Well, looky here." She wiped the stools with a dry cloth. "When did you blow into town, honey?"

Iris owned the coffee house and she was a close friend of Pearl. She was in her sixties, with frizzy blonde hair better suited for a loofah. She was wearing elastic blue jeans and a white polo shirt with a canvas apron tied around her waist.

"Hey, Iris, thought you would've heard by now." I draped my jacket over the stool.

Iris was the biggest gossip in town, which came in handy

since she was the gossip columnist for the local newspaper. She was also the last one to know anything because nobody trusted her and therefore told her squat.

"Well, I've been trying to phone Pearl all morning and she won't pick up over at the Palace. I'm sure she would've told me," Iris said, trying to convince me that she was well suited for her job. She got no argument from me. And not much else, for that matter.

"I'm sure she would have." Let Pearl tell her that Gramps was sick. I wasn't in the mood to field questions.

"Wait 'til I tell Shea you're back. He'll be thrilled." She tapped my shoulder with the back of her hand. "We knew you'd get tired of that big city life sooner or later." Iris scrunched up her nose and made a face.

"Oh, I'm just here for a visit."

"Well, isn't that a shame." She frowned.

Shea Parker published the *Amethyst Globe*. The paper was founded by my father. Dad handled the news end of things, plus copy and other print work while Parker was the marketing, sales, and distribution arm. It was a small town paper that grew rapidly, eventually taking in several awards, but that changed when Dad died. Parker continued on with the paper, but it lost its spark, because when it came to reporting, he was like a blind man driving a car. He could fire up the engine, but it was only a matter of time before he ran it off the road.

Cin walked up then and handed me my coffee. She and Iris exchanged greetings.

"Well, I'll leave you to it." Iris headed off to check on the young girl behind the counter filling orders.

I thanked my cousin for the breakfast and tore into my muffin. I told her about my encounter with Chance and how I was sure Fiona was up to something as well as missing out on visiting Gramps. I left out the message on the mirror and my ride with Tony.

"So are we going to see Gramps after this? I know he wants to see you, he—" She glanced over her shoulder at the clock and stopped mid-sentence. "Like I haven't had a hard enough week," she grumbled.

I spiraled around to see what Cin was looking at, and there she was in all her tricked-out glory.

Monique Fontaine.

She had been a thorn in Cin's side most of her life, but she crossed the line when she slept with Tony. Now it was war. Monique wasn't French. Her folks hailed from Michigan, but she wore French perfume, smoked thin cigarettes, and called herself Monique even though her real name was Monica.

I was willing to bet the mutual loathing came from the fact that both my cousin and Monique craved unbridled attention.

Monique was teetering on four-inch heels. The motorcycle jacket and leather miniskirt would have looked great on a woman with curves, but she pulled it off like Bad News Barbie with an eating disorder. Her attire usually dictated the kind of man she was after, so her sights seemed set on a biker or a parole officer. Take your pick.

She slid a glance our way, verifying the local Avon lady was still driving the latest model Mercedes.

"So, Monica ..." Cin called.

Here we go.

"What corner you on tonight? Maybe I could shoot you some business."

Cinnamon grinned wide. Monique turned around and put her elbows on the counter, pointing her fake missiles at us.

"Same corner your husband picked me up on, honey," Monique fired back.

Cinnamon jumped off her stool, and Monique sprang to attention.

The bell on the door clanged then, and in walked Tony. He had a smile on his face until he saw who was in the coffee shop. Then he froze. I'm pretty sure he would have bolted, too, if it weren't for what happened next.

I slid off my chair, not sure what the hell I was going to do, but on point just the same.

I was relieved to see Iris circle around the front of the counter ... until she pulled out a notepad and perched on a stool.

My cousin was a foot in front of me. I reached for her arm, hoping to calm her down, but instead I knocked my coffee over and it splattered onto my shirt.

HOT! I danced around, blotting up what I could with a fistful of napkins. Cin took advantage of my weakness and lunged.

Monique must have seen it coming because she plucked a jumbo muffin from the cake stand and shoved it in Cin's face without blinking.

Cinnamon tried to shake it off, but Monique smashed it in real good. Cin's vision was impaired, so when Tony tried to help her she didn't realize it was him through the bits of chocolate chips and muffin crumbs stuck to her eyelids. She punched him right in the jaw.

Or maybe she did know it was him, I couldn't be sure.

Tony flew back and brought down the rope that served to keep customers in line. The garbage can broke his fall.

I stepped over Tony, ready to pull Monique out of the coffee shop by her cotton candy hair, but I missed, and she darted out.

So instead, I leapt to my cousin's aid.

"Cin, are you all right?" I gently placed my hand on her shoulder.

"That bitch! Where is she?" She flung her head from side to side, sailing muffin bits into the air. "Did I get her?"

"No," Tony yelled, rising to his feet. "You hit me."

Cinnamon pried muffin chunks from her eyes. "Tony, what the hell are you doing here anyway? You know I come here every morning. Why is that so hard to remember?"

"Oh, so that means I can't be here then?" he asked.

"Um, actually," I interrupted, "that was part of the agreement." Cinnamon made me draw it up and serve as witness while they both signed off.

"Jeez. Fine, I give up." Tony threw his arms in the air. He straightened out the rope and righted the garbage can.

Cinnamon stormed off toward the bathroom.

Tony blanched like a scolded puppy.

"You okay?" I asked. His jaw was red where Cin had hit him. "You better put some ice on that."

"It's been a year," Tony whined. "She still hates me."

"She doesn't hate you." I hugged him. "She just hasn't forgiven you yet."

I helped Tony clean up the mess and apologized to Iris. Iris assured me that it was all worth it, thanks to the column she would get from the scene. Tony limped out the door, holding his jaw, and I went to see if my cousin needed help.

I knocked on the bathroom door. "Cinnamon, spice and everything nice?" I called, using my pet phrase for whenever she got into a scuffle.

Cin creaked the door open, her eyes downcast. Most of the muffin mash was gone. "That wasn't too smooth of me, was it?"

"Not your best moment," I agreed. "But hey, we all crack

up once in a while. According to my calculations, you were due."

I helped her clean up, gave her my best comforting hug and a pep talk. She seemed well enough for public consumption by the time we left the restroom.

Gus was in line when we walked back to the front of the shop.

"Hi, Cinnamon. Can I buy you a cup of coffee?" he asked.

He seemed oblivious to the crumbs in her hair and the chocolate stains on her shirt.

Cin held up her hand. "No thanks."

She was heading home to shower and change, and I was off to see Birdie.

"How's Birdie, Gus?" I asked.

"Oh, she's doing just fine. Scully's there with her. I'm just about to head back myself. I gave her extra pillows and blankets and everything. She's doing just fine. Honest," said Gus.

I asked if I could hitch a ride with him back to the station to see her, and he agreed.

Gus escorted me through the little gate back at the police station, steering me in the opposite direction as the interrogation room Birdie was in earlier.

My grandmother was sitting on a wide bench, her skirt spilled around her. Her right foot was propped up and her eyes were closed as if she were meditating.

"I thought you said Scully was with her?" I asked Gus.

Gus bobbed his head, blinking, "Shoot."

He spun around to hurry back down the hallway just as Leo rounded the corner. Scully shuffled in front of him carrying a six-pack of Budweiser.

"Gus, did you lose something?" asked Leo, hands outstretched. His face was hard and his tone sharp. I was glad it wasn't me he was mad at, although it did boost his sex appeal.

Scully sucked on a beer.

"Give me that." Leo yanked the can from his hand.

"Hey!" Scully shielded the rest of his beer.

"You let him just walk out of here." Leo glared at Gus.

I laughed and snorted a little.

"What's so funny?" Leo asked me.

"Oh come on. It's just Scully."

"I came back, though," Scully mumbled to Leo, hunched over and clutching the six-pack.

"Yes, and you brought back beer," Leo yelled. "You were in for public intoxication and you went on a beer run?"

He had a point.

"Don't matter. I came back." Scully did not see the problem.

"Get in." Leo thumbed toward the cell and held out his hand for Scully to turn over the six-pack.

Birdie chimed in then, "Don't you have somewhere else you could put him? No offense, Scully, but you snore."

Scully bowed his head. "None taken, ma'am."

I offered, "Why don't I pay his fine and maybe Gus could drive him home?"

"That sounds fair," Gus nodded.

Leo glared at Gus and turned to me. "When did you earn a badge?"

"Gee, Leo, you forgot to say, 'I'm the law in these here parts'." I pulled on imaginary suspenders.

Gus laughed and I joined him.

Leo clenched his jaw. "No. I enforce the law. I don't pull strings for anyone, unlike some people."

"What are you talking about?" I asked.

Birdie walked over to the bars.

"I just got a call from your friend the judge." Leo cocked his head toward the cell. "She's out if you can pull together ten grand. No bond hearing necessary."

"Anastasia ..." Birdie's eyes shot arrows at me.

Leo's gaze was still on me, giving me a look usually reserved for parents of wayward children. I had completely forgotten that I asked Cinnamon to find Birdie a lawyer. I guess she decided to skip the middle man.

"Gus, take Scully home." Leo stormed back down the hallway without another word.

Birdie grabbed me by my jacket collar and dragged me forward. She slid the door open and pulled me inside. Apparently, Gus had left it unlocked. I'd have to remember that if I ever got arrested.

"Ow, stop it," I cried.

"Sit down. You and I need to have a chat."

I sat on the bench and lifted my eyes to Birdie towering over me, completely confused. *What the hell did I do? She's the one in jail for attempted murder.*

"How dare you call Judge Kellerman," she spat. "Do you want to destroy your uncle's good name and the family's reputation in this town? The Geraghtys have never called in a favor. Not once. We take care of business on our own terms. And that includes abiding Celtic law."

Oh hell. Was she serious?

I decided not to throw Cin under the bus. "You'll have to forgive me, Birdie. I left my Celtic law book at home."

She was itching to pinch me, I could tell. Instead, she threw her arms in the air and leaned against the back wall. I followed her movement with my eyes. "Don't you remember the triads? Words of wisdom for every situation under the sun? Think, Anastasia."

I thought. I thought this whole thing was nuts. What on Earth did she want from me?

"Birdie, we are not in the Old Country. We are in the New World, and in this century, people who confess to poisoning their ex-spouses call judges and hire lawyers."

She ignored me, paced, and began reciting. "No law for the sake of law. Always do right. Responsibility for our actions."

Responsibility for our actions? What's she getting at? Doubt came knocking at the door again.

"Birdie, please tell me you did not harm Gramps."

Rolling her eyes, she took a deep breath that sounded a lot like a disappointed sigh. "If I were to poison your grand-father, believe me, he would be dead."

Nice thing to say while you're stuck in the slammer. No fear, this woman.

"Then why on Earth would you confess?"

"Because there is a danger lurking at our door, and the sooner it is drawn out the better off we all will be. What happened to Oscar was no accident, be sure of that. Should whoever made him so sick think that all eyes are on me, that person will grow careless, daring, perhaps try again. That, my dear, is where you come in."

Oh, this was not good. "What does that mean?"

"It is up to you to find out who hurt your grandfather."

"Birdie, I'm a reporter. I'm not Nancy Drew."

"Nonsense. People will talk to you here. They don't trust outsiders like Leo. But there will be more to it than just asking questions. You'll have to rely on that intuition you try so hard to shun. Use the magic you were born with."

The magic I was born with? I was born with a grand-mother who believed that singing to a pile of burning leaves before the first moon of spring would make the tomatoes grow bigger. "This isn't a game, Birdie. You are in trouble."

She clasped my jaw between her knuckles. "And you, granddaughter, can fix it. Follow the signs. Heed the messages. Remember what I taught you long ago, darkness—"

I finished for her. "Is drowned by three lights; nature, knowledge, and truth. I remember. Anything else you can tell me? Anyone you think would hurt Gramps?"

"Darling, if I knew that, I wouldn't be here."

On the way out of the police station, I passed Leo, who was filling out paperwork. I paused, but I wasn't sure what to say. So I said nothing and continued toward the door.

"She didn't do it," he said to my back.

I turned around.

"But she's mad as a hatter, so I feel safer with her locked up."

I laughed. "If that's a new law, you don't have enough cells for this town."

We locked eyes, and I wondered what it would be like to make out in a holding cell.

"Look, Leo, I didn't mean to offend—" I started.

Leo shook his head. "Let's forget it. I overreacted." He stood up and pushed his sleeves past his elbows. I imagined those Popeye forearms wrapped around my waist.

"Maybe you can make it up to me."

12

When I left the police station, dark clouds stained the sky and thunder clapped in the distance. I was on foot, and I really didn't want to get stuck in a downpour, so I made my way back to the Black Opal, in hopes of borrowing Cinnamon's car.

She didn't hesitate handing over her keys, but she asked if I could do her a favor.

"What do you need?"

I heard a high-pitched yelp and Cin glanced down. "Dammit, Thor, if you wouldn't sneak under there I wouldn't step on your tail." Cin looked back at me. "Lately, he hates thunderstorms. They never bothered him before."

I raised my eyebrows. Thor. God of Thunder. Hates thunderstorms.

"I'm aware of the irony," she said.

Leaning over the bar, I peered down. "Hey, Thor. How's it going, buddy?"

Thor's ears perked up and he hoisted his massive head. He scrambled to rise to his feet when he saw me, and his tail wiped out a shelf of tall glasses.

"Dammit, Thor," Cin grumbled.

"Hey, bartender," shouted a thin man a few feet down. "Can you stop gabbing and start pouring? I've been waiting for three minutes to get a drink." He adjusted his man-bun.

Cin eyed him. "Oh yeah? How long have you been waiting for skinny jeans to be in style?"

He glanced down at his pants, which clearly didn't slide on without a fight.

The man huffed away, and she turned back to me. "Stacy, can you do me a huge favor? Can you please take Thor home? He keeps getting under my feet. I don't know what the deal is, but he just won't go lie down. He's restless. I think there's a big storm coming. I'll pick him up later."

"Sure, I can do that." I scratched Thor's back. Thunder erupted, and he tilted his head toward the door. Funny. He didn't seem scared to me.

"Thanks. I better go." Cinnamon hurried away.

The crowd parted as Thor led the way and we headed for the back door.

I heard a noise near the dumpster and a voice. I loaded Thor into Cin's Trans Am and slammed the door. Then a head popped out from around the corner, and there was Pearl's niece puffing away on a cigarette, chatting on a cell phone.

I thought she's into natural healing?

"Hi there," I said. "Didn't know they made holistic cigarettes."

Gretchen forced a smile. "It's my one vice, what can I say?"

Something was nagging me about that woman, but damned if I could nail it down. I didn't have time to either when Thor began barking and clawing at the window. Lightning streaked the sky and thunder cracked.

"Nice seeing you again." I climbed into the car before Thor tore the seat apart.

A few drops of rain splashed the windshield as I headed toward the grocery store before going home. As soon as I pulled into the parking lot, the downpour began. I told Thor not to worry, that I'd be right back and hoped for the best.

He protested my decision to leave him in the car as I ran all the way into the store.

I dashed through the doors and headed for the produce section where I ran into Ed.

"Hi, Stacy." He was a little more rumpled than he was earlier.

He assessed his rain-slicked slacks and rumpled shirt, gave me a small smile. "Delivery came in late."

"Hope you have a mop." I pointed to the muddy mess accumulating around his black buckled shoes.

"Cleanup on aisle one, as they say." He ran a hand through his damp hair. "So, Stacy, how about we grab a cup of coffee and catch up?"

What was with this guy? We weren't exactly friends. Why was he acting so chummy? "Maybe some other time, Ed."

"Shot down again," he chuckled.

Good grief. "It's been hectic, that's all. I won't have much time to breathe today, let alone socialize. After I drop off the groceries, help out the aunts, visit Gramps ... I doubt I'll even get home before midnight." It was mostly true. "Look, I'm in a hurry."

Ed stepped aside and swept his arms out in a dramatic gesture. I rolled my eyes, hurried around him, and proceeded to power shop. Fifteen minutes later, I was at the checkout counter.

Gladys Sharp, Birdie's neighbor, and Geraghty Girls' groupie, was the cashier. I unloaded my groceries and pulled out my wallet, hoping she wouldn't ask about Birdie.

Gladys totaled up my order and her dentures clicked as she talked. "Shame about your granny," she remarked in her Polish accent, barely above a whisper.

"Yep," I whispered back.

"You come for tea later, honey, we talk. That cop come around the other day, but I don't tell him nothing." She swiveled her head and made a spitting gesture. "But you," she waved her finger at me, "*you* I tell."

Tell? Tell me what? Did Gladys know something about Gramps? Or was she just being gossipy? Either way, I decided to take her up on her offer and made plans to stop by her house when her shift ended. She handed me my change, and I grabbed the bags and rushed out the door into the rain. Thor seemed content as I shoved the groceries onto the passenger seat of Cin's car, and I wondered if he was really afraid of storms or my cousin. He lifted his giant snout into the air, sniffed once, then laid his thick head back down on the leather seat.

Back at the cottage, I made Thor sit and wait while I retrieved a towel to dry the both of us. I patted my legs and arms down first, then I ran it along Thor, vigorously rubbing his fur dry. He seemed to enjoy it. Moonlight came around the corner as I was wiping the mud from the dog's paws. He took one look at the Great Dane, hissed, and froze in place. His back arched. Thor woofed.

"Listen, you two, you're going to have to get along."

Thor considered this for a moment. Then he sauntered past me and into the bedroom. Moonlight relaxed a little and tentatively stepped in the direction of the dog.

"That's better."

GLADYS SHARP STOOD on her front porch waving as I approached her quaint little miner's cottage a short time later. The rain had stopped and the sky was trying to open up to the sun.

"Come," was all she said.

I folded myself into a wooden chair painted with daisies. The kitchen was small but charming, with red and white polka dot curtains and placemats to match.

Gladys set a tea tray down on the center of the table with cream, honey, two mugs, and a basket of lemon squares.

"I make myself." Gladys beamed. Her eagerness to chat hinted at few visitors.

I took a bite out of a lemon square and smiled at my hostess. "Delicious," I lied. They tasted like frosted cardboard.

She poured two cups of tea, and after we both spruced up our mugs, I sat back and smiled at Gladys.

"So what did you want to tell me?" I asked.

"I listen, you know. I hear things." She tapped her ear for emphasis. I didn't doubt that one bit. Her house was situated in such a way that she could see into half the bedrooms on the block.

She paused, milking her audience. I humored her and edged closer to the table.

"About a week ago, your grandfather, he come in and he say he want to talk to Mr. Entwhistle. So I get him. Ten minutes later I have question. Customer want to know where we get eggs. If the chickens are local. I say I never meet them, so I have to ask." Gladys paused and sipped her tea.

"So I try to call on the phone and no answer. I go back to the office and I hear shouting." She raised her eyebrows and gave a little nod. I wrinkled my forehead to let her know she had my attention. "So I stop. I listen. I want to know, you know?"

"Sure. What happened?" I reached into my back pocket for a notebook, where I usually carried one, but it wasn't there. A napkin served as an adequate substitute, and there was a pen Velcroed to the rotary phone on the wall. "May I?"

"Yes, yes." She made a welcoming gesture and I grabbed the napkin and pen. When I was ready, I nodded.

Gladys straightened her back. "So I hear your grandfather. He is angry at Mr. Entwhistle. He call him stubborn. Say cats have better business sense."

"Cats?"

"Ya."

Cats?

"Then Mr. Entwhistle yell back. He say your grandfather, he owe him. Pearl owe him."

"They owe him?"

Gladys nodded.

"Was that all? Did they say anything else?"

Gladys shook her head. "That was all I hear, then I have to go to register."

I tapped the pen. Could they have been arguing about the War Games idea? Cats. She must mean Wildcat. But why would Roy say that Gramps and Pearl owed him?

"Thank you, Gladys. That was very helpful." I rose from the table. I stuffed the napkin in my back pocket.

I thought about Birdie's words. Nature, knowledge, truth. At least I had some now.

It had stopped raining, although the sky was still gray

when I got to the driveway of the inn. The napkin was folded in my pocket and I pulled it out to review.

The last words I read were: *What don't I know?*

That's when I heard the scream.

I dashed up the steps to the inn and rushed through the door.

13

A cauldron rests on three legs. If those legs are all holding their own weight, the thing functions fine. You can throw chicken stock and herbs in it to make soup, burn some old love letters to release an old flame, or fill it with water, gaze at the liquid, and scry to invoke a vision.

Cut one of those legs off and the sucker falls apart.

That was the scenario unfolding before me.

At the moment, I had a guy about my age, 5'9", long nose, round eyes, and way too much hair gel, waving a piece of paper in my face and yapping like a terrier. "We are on our honeymoon. I asked for the Starry Night Suite. This says it's the Secret Garden Room. This is the most special day of our lives and I want the room I booked!"

"I'm so sorry ..." I asked him, searching for a name.

"Kyle." He crossed his arms and tapped his foot, daring me to do something about this mess.

I flashed my best hostess smile. "Look, Kyle, I will straighten this mess out, all right? I see that my aunts have spread out some lovely petite fours, and I believe I spotted a

Riesling in there with your name on it. Why don't you indulge while I fix this." I steered Kyle toward the parlor.

Kyle eyed the silver platter and crystal glasses lining the cocktail table. "All right. Thank you. Will you please see that our bags get to the room?"

"Certainly. Why don't you and your wife have a seat, enjoy the refreshments, and I will rectify this little problem."

Kyle's face lit with anger and his voice rose to a frequency only dogs would hear.

Uh-oh.

"Wife? I don't have a wife. I was told that this bed and breakfast was LGBTQ friendly." The other guests looked our way, waiting to take a shot at me.

I turned back around and ushered Kyle toward the parlor. "Indeed, we are LGBTQ friendly. My sincere apologies. It was presumptuous of me to assume." I reached for a glass of wine and handed it to him.

Kyle stiffened, eyebrow raised. "Yes, it was."

"There you are." A tall man with a tan and warm eyes came around the corner chewing on a spinach tartlet. "I've been looking for you." He stopped chewing and bent to kiss Kyle's cheek. "What's wrong?"

"I just wanted everything to be perfect." Kyle flopped into a leather chair.

"Everything is great. This place is terrific." He rolled his eyes at me and winked. I smiled in return. "Jeremy." He offered his hand.

"Hi, Jeremy, I'm Stacy. Sorry about the mix-up. We'll get it taken care of."

"No worries," said Jeremy. "It's been a bit stressful lately for us. You know ... *weddings.*" He put his arm around Kyle and spoke softly to him, trying to cheer him up.

Taking that as my cue to leave, I went to look for the aunts.

Angry voices drifted from the parlor. I darted through the pocket doors and into the room to find two young women yelling at a large, middle-aged man holding a bottle of wine.

Where were the aunts? Dealing with lunatics who did not share my bloodline was above my pay grade.

"No way, jerk, that's for everybody." A tiny brunette wearing a poncho was stabbing the air with her finger.

The man clutched the bottle to his chest and shook his index finger back at the woman. "Look, missy." Bread-crumbs spewed from his mouth. "This is the missus and mine's anniversary, see? We ordered the wino package, you got it? This is the wine and this is my package." He yanked at his groin and laughed.

I could have gone a lifetime without seeing that.

"Ewwwww," the ladies chirped in unison.

"Excuse me, folks," I called from behind them. Everyone ignored me, and the air was laced with tension.

"Well, we wanted the Wild Woman package." A skinny blonde with a ponytail and tight jeans piped up.

Wild Woman package? I didn't like the sound of that.

She took a step toward Captain Happy Pants. "But they said they give a wine and cheese hour, too. So that's for everybody."

"Excuse me." I tried again, louder, and forced my way into the room.

"Hey," said the little brunette to the skinny blonde. "Maybe he's part of the Wild Woman weekend? Maybe we're supposed to confront him?"

"Yeah, like assert ourselves." Nodded the blonde, a twinkle in her eye.

I didn't like where this was heading.

The women exchanged glances and jumped on the guy like two piranhas attacking a whale. An older woman, whom I could only guess was the missus, started swinging her huge purse at the two young women. The honeymooners tried to break it up, and Kyle got kicked in the shin. Screaming, he went for the blonde's ponytail.

I climbed on top of the piano that sat near the entryway, did a two-finger whistle, and bellowed, "*Enough!*"

Everyone stopped. Kyle had Blondie's ponytail wrapped around his fist. The brunette was hanging from the teamster like a cape while he chugged wine straight from the bottle. The missus stood with her purse over her head, ready to swing again, and Jeremy's hand clutched Kyle's shoulder. They all swiveled their heads to me, frozen in place.

I took a deep breath, and in my most authoritative tone went with this: "Everyone slowly and carefully release your hands and lower them to your sides." Kyle unclenched the ponytail. The missus lowered her purse and the teamster dropped the wine bottle. He gave me a sideways stare as it poured onto the carpet. "Pick it up and put it on the table." He did. "All of you take two steps back." Again, the group did as they were instructed.

Orders flew from my mouth as my hands waved like a traffic cop. "Girls, park it on the green settee. Kyle, Jeremy, have a seat on the gold sofa."

Just then Lolly wandered into the room in her bathrobe, walking backward.

"Lolly!" Her makeup was on in full-force. That was a good sign. But she wasn't wearing a ball gown so I assumed she needed a jump start. I pointed to the cocktail table. "Take that wine, drink it, and go put on your party dress."

Lolly grabbed the bottle and scurried away.

"You two," I shouted at the older couple. "Grab the brocade loveseat." Everyone shuffled to their corners. "Now you will all sit there and behave while I straighten this out." Mid-shout, the front door opened and in walked Fiona and Chance. *Thank the goddess.* Two people with some sense who could help with this Jerry Springer audience.

My expectations were over-shot. A dozen things were wrong with this picture, but Fiona noticed only one. "Stacy, honey, you're such a pretty girl. Why don't you comb your hair?" She breezed through the parlor and went to check on the registry.

Lifting my hands to my head, I attempted to smooth my mane into place.

Chance approached the piano, hands in his pockets, stifling a laugh. "You gonna sing a song?" He grinned, blue eyes dancing.

"Funny," I said.

He held out his arms. "In that case, let's get you down." I wrapped my arms around his shoulders, and he gently lowered me to the floor.

"Thanks."

The guests followed Fiona into the library.

"Anytime."

"You're not going to ask what happened?"

"Stacy, I've learned after all these years not to question the methods of the Geraghty Girls."

"I'm not technically a Geraghty."

A slow smile spread across his face and he raised one eyebrow. "Oh, yes you are."

Fiona walked over to us before I could argue with him further.

"Well, the room situation has been straightened out, and I gave the Giovannis their wine package." She put her index finger to her lip. "Now I still need some help with the credit card machine and the luggage. And, of course, the girls will need a little instruction for their Wild Women weekend. Birdie usually leads that."

"I'll take the luggage," Chance offered.

Damn. I was gonna say that.

He winked at me and ran to the stairs where several bags sat waiting to be carried up to their rooms. Chance grabbed two, and Jeremy gestured, indicating they belonged to him.

Fiona squeezed my arm. "Honey, I'm sorry things got out of hand. Chance had a question about the gutters on the roof of the cottage, and I thought Lolly could handle everyone for a few minutes alone. But I guess it was too much for her."

This bunch was too much for Dr. Phil. But it was odd I hadn't noticed them out there.

"It's fine," I said. "How about I handle the charges and you take care of the Wild Women?"

"Well, um, I can do that for now, but I may need you at some point."

"Why?" I asked.

"Well, sweetie, this business with your grandmother could take a while," Fiona replied.

"Don't worry about that. I'll take care of Birdie. This is all a big mistake."

Fiona touched her finger to my chin. "Your grandmother makes no mistakes, dear."

14

*I*t was after six by the time the guests all checked in and paid up, and I headed to the kitchen to hunt for food.

A warm hand slid down my back as I filtered through the fridge. "How about I take you out for a hot meal? You look like you could use a break," Chance said.

I faced him. A hot meal sounded great. And I could use a lot of things, but I wasn't sure he should be the one to give them to me.

He must have sensed my hesitation, because he sweetened the pot. "The way I see it, you have two choices. You can come with me and I'll treat you to a free meal, a few minutes of escape, and a shoulder to lean on, or," he looked around the room pointedly, "you can stay in this house and risk it."

Well, that settled it. If there was one thing I could depend on with Chance it was a quiet, drama-free evening. Plus, it would give me an opportunity to get some information from him.

"I do have one request, however." He joined his hands

together in a plea. "Can I use your shower? I haven't been home yet from working on the roof all day."

I wrinkled my nose. "Sure, Stinky."

He grinned. "Great. I think I have some clean clothes in my truck. I'll meet you back at the cottage."

Chance breezed through the kitchen doorway, and I grabbed my jacket to head out the back.

I stood on the stoop for a moment, watching layers of pink, gray, and blue paint the sky. It smelled like more rain was coming, but the clouds were far off. I had my key in the lock just as Chance ran up behind me.

We wiped our feet on the mat, and I shook out my hair and hung the jacket on a wall hook near the door.

"Towels and soap are in the bathroom," I told Chance.

"Great. I'll be with you in ten minutes." He took off his boots and headed for the shower.

I went to hunt for some fresh clothes in the bedroom where Thor was lazily snoozing on top of the queen-sized bed, Moonlight snuggled in his arms. I wondered if I should feed the dog, but then I remembered Cin hadn't given me any food. I decided to bring him home a doggie bag for dinner if he was still here.

The first garments in my suitcase were a red V-neck sweater and khaki pants, and I changed into them. A check in the mirror showed my makeup had smeared, so I dug into my bag of tricks to touch up. Then I ran a brush through the snarls in my hair and finished with a blast of hairspray before Chance called to me.

"Hey, Stacy? Do you have a blow dryer?"

"Yep. Hang on." I unplugged the dryer and shuffled from the bedroom to the bathroom where Chance was standing with the door open. I stopped short. His hair was wet and he wore nothing but a white towel, slung across his hips. A trail of chest hair led to his belly button and pointed downward. I was very familiar with that area and I was imagining what I used to do with it.

"Can I use it?" he asked when I didn't move.

I swallowed hard. "Sure." I stretched out my arm, dangling the hair dryer by its cord.

Chance reached for it and held onto my hand. We locked eyes for a minute and my breath caught.

The towel slipped as he pulled me into him, lowering his lips onto mine. Tiny drops of water trickled from his freshly washed hair onto my nose like dew dripping off a morning glory. Tension was replaced by a tingling all the way to my toes as I succumbed to the sweet taste of him.

Then he broke away and a brief look of regret crossed his face. He smiled, thanked me, grabbed the dryer, and closed the door.

My heart fluttered as I tried to conjure up one good reason why I shouldn't twist the handle and join him. I thought about it for a minute. Then I plopped down on the couch and scolded myself.

"Ready to go?" Chance asked after a few minutes, clean-shaven and spice-scented.

"Ready," I answered.

We drove to the restaurant in comfortable silence, and I stole a glance at Chance's profile, thinking of how it had changed over the years. Gone was the peach fuzz and freckles, replaced with a perpetual tan from working in the sun and a five o'clock shadow that never quite went away. One thing that remained steadfast over time was that strong jawline. I thought of how hard it would set when he was determined. Either in the classroom, on the football field, or working out a problem like how to get your best friend to stop crying when her father died. The answer, apparently, was to kiss her.

And boy did he know how to do that.

We slid into a booth at Pearl's Palace, and a waitress stepped up with two menus. "Hey, Chance, who's your new friend?" she asked.

I lifted my head, and the woman's eyes grew big. "Oh my heavens," she whispered.

I glanced at Chance. He shrugged his shoulders.

"Olivia, this is Stacy."

"You don't have to tell me who this is." She waved her hand. She had pale skin and ash-blonde hair clipped at her neck with a barrette. "Honey, you're just as pretty as your mama."

I smiled, still trying to place her. "Thank you."

She must have sensed my hesitation. "Your mom and I were pals in high school. Thick as thieves. A shame what happened to her." She shook her head.

Chance jumped in at the mention of my mother, protective as always. He never let me fight my battles and that irritated me. "Hey, Olivia, we're undecided yet. Could you please give us a minute?"

"Sure, honey, take your time. Something to drink?" Olivia asked, a pad of paper and a pen in her hand.

We ordered iced teas, and Olivia started away.

"Wait," I said.

She tossed me a look.

"Mrs. Malloy?" I asked. "Coach Harry Malloy's mom?"

Olivia smiled wide. "It's Locke now, honey." She winked and walked away.

I scanned the restaurant. "I wonder if Pearl's here."

"I haven't seen her since your grandpa got sick." Chance read over the menu.

The Palace, as it was known before Pearl bought it, hadn't changed a bit since I was a kid. It was a typical, old-fashioned diner complete with a soda fountain and rotating pastry display. Booths anchored the center of the room. The kitchen sat in the back where waitresses used a turn style to place their orders and cooks barked at them to write more legibly. A Formica counter with chrome stools dressed in turquoise leather hugged the left side of the building, and it always smelled like fresh brewed coffee, burger grease, and donuts.

The door chimed as I was looking around and in walked Shea Parker. I quickly buried my head in the menu and sunk down in the booth. He'd been at me to take over as editor of the Amethyst paper since before I left for college, never understanding the word 'no'. I didn't feel like discussing it tonight, so I pretended to be invisible.

"What?" Chance whispered.

"Shea Parker," I mumbled.

I slid farther into the seat, but it was too late. He spotted me like a hawk spots a field mouse. He charged over and scooted in next to Chance.

"I thought I'd find you here. I had a hunch." Parker wrapped his long, skinny fingers around my tea and took a sip.

"Sharp as ever." I yanked my tea away from him, removing the straw.

"Parker, do you mind?" Chance asked, annoyed.

"Not at all." Parker winked. "Olivia, I'll have the usual," he yelled without turning around. He wore an orange windbreaker, white pants, and pointy shoes. He looked like a candy corn with eyeballs.

Olivia walked over and asked, "You two ready to order?"

I opted for a chicken Caesar salad and a fresh straw, and Chance ordered a burger and fries.

"Parker, we were kind of in the middle of something," Chance said.

Parker ignored him and slumped over the table, staring at me with his little, round eyes, hands clasped.

"What?" I said.

"Do I get an exclusive?" he asked, blinking rapidly. Parker wouldn't take a hint if it were wrapped in a bundle of hundred dollar bills.

"You're kidding, right? You're the only paper in town." I didn't even ask what he was talking about or how he knew. Scanners, small town life, and an underground network of busybodies were the glue that held the town together. Word traveled fast.

"I'm not the only paper in the tri-state area. I just want your word that you won't grant any interviews to anyone else."

"I won't grant any interviews. Period." Granny poisons Gramps would be huge news for these folks.

"Oh, I see what you just did." Parker sat back and waved a finger at me. "Okay, smarty, no interviews to anyone except the *Amethyst Globe.*"

"Right, no interviews."

"Great, and you'll write it."

"Very funny. I said 'right'."

"Yes. You will write it."

"Stop it, Parker."

"Just repeating after you."

I kicked him in the shin.

"Not nice." He wagged his finger.

Olivia slid a white Styrofoam container in front of Parker.

"You know you want to work for me." He slunk from the booth and grabbed the container. "I'll hold you to it."

"I won't do it," I yelled to his back as he marched out the door.

Jeez, he was annoying. How did my dad ever put up with Parker and his awkward fashion sense?

Chance said, "You know, you might enjoy working for him. He'd give you whatever you want. A corner office, a secretary, maybe even one of those mini refrigerators."

I stared at him like he was having a seizure. "A story about who won the prize for the best pie at the county fair is not my idea of journalism."

"You know, Stacy, some of us hicks are pretty cultured. We discuss politics, films, current events. Heck, we can even read."

I didn't mean to insult him. But I guess that did sound snotty. I was batting a thousand today for miscommunication.

"I didn't mean it like that, Chance. You know that. Come on."

"What I know is you're trying to convince everyone that you've been running toward something since you left here. But I think you've been running away from something. Or someone."

I shifted in my seat. "Oh, really. And what, or who, might that be?"

Was he talking about himself? Did he think I was still in love with him? There was no denying that Chance was my first love, and when I was a teenager, I thought it would last forever and always with a big heart around it. Everyone thinks their first love will be with them their entire lives, and in a way, they are. But what I wanted out of life and what

Chance wanted were so vastly different, we may as well have been living on different planets.

Chance sat back, a crooked grin on his face. "You tell me." He was frustratingly cute with his hair tousled from the wind, eyes the color of rain clouds, and shoulders that filled out his shirt in ways that defied gravity. But he was still full of malarkey. Just because I didn't choose to live in this one-horse town didn't mean I was running away. What was so wrong about wanting more out of life than what you were born to? Like solving problems without chants and crystals.

I gave Chance a 'you're talking out of your ass' look and smiled. Shaking his head, he reached for my hand. It felt warm. Safe.

Olivia returned with our food, halting our conversation and saving me from saying something else stupid. She also produced a fresh straw and a bottle of ketchup. "Anything else?"

"Mrs. Locke, is Pearl around?" I asked.

"Call me Olivia, honey." She threw a glance over her shoulder. "Haven't seen her much since your grandpa fell ill. And I'm here all the time."

I nodded and smiled. "Thanks."

She smiled and walked to another booth.

I stabbed at my salad, and Chance attacked his burger. We ate in silence for a few minutes. Chance was watching a game on the television behind me, and I was wondering how I was going to spring my grandmother from jail. Then I wondered how many other women had this problem.

We talked about the family dinner at the Geraghty House. Chance had been working on the roof and Fiona graciously invited him to join them.

"I can't remember anything unusual, really." Chance

darted his eyes away as he thought about that night. "Well, there was one thing."

"What?"

"Birdie was cordial to your grandfather. She didn't threaten him one time."

That was disturbing. I couldn't remember a meal when Birdie hadn't needled Gramps for one thing or another. It was her true talent. She had taken the practice of empty threats and raised it to an art form. I did a case study on it once for a human development class.

"However," Chance dipped a fry in ketchup, "she did have a moment with Wildcat."

This was not surprising. "What happened?"

"Well, I'm not sure, but I think he pinched her, and the next thing I knew, his chair collapsed. She was across the room at the time, but ..."

"Got it."

"Any conversations stand out between Wildcat and Gramps? Anything about a business proposal?"

Chance shook his head. "Just stories about the war. Things like that. Pearl didn't seem to appreciate his presence. That was clear the minute they were introduced."

"Really?" This was news to me. "What makes you say that?"

Chance wrinkled his forehead for a minute, organizing his thoughts. "She was just quiet the whole night. She kept looking at him in the strangest way."

Everyone looked at Wildcat in a strange way, but it did pique my interest.

"How so?"

Chance considered it. "Like she thought he was full of it."

That was understandable. Sucking down my tea, I

contemplated my next move when something shiny caught my attention at the bottom of the glass.

Chance watched as I fished it out. Another penny.

"A penny? In your iced tea. That can't be good."

I had a feeling he was right.

15

I was hoping to see Gramps before visiting hours ended, so Chance dropped me back at the cottage after our meal. He had promised not to wake me before sunrise again.

Funny, I thought as I walked up the path, *could have sworn the porch light was on when I left.* Then I remembered I forgot to get food for Thor and wondered if Great Danes liked pizza. I had a cheese and pepperoni in the freezer.

A spider's web clung to the doorway, a sign that a visitor was coming. Careful not to disturb it, I unlocked the door and flipped on the hall light. It flickered, and a chill raced down my spine.

It was quiet. Too quiet considering my over-sized house-guest. Soon, I found the reason why.

It was as if I missed a hell-raising keg party. The couch appeared to be inside out, there was a lamp kissing the carpet, and the damn shoe chair's heel was busted. Even the desk was knocked over, phone book and menus scattered everywhere.

And in the midst of the chaos sat Thor, chewing on something.

"Thor."

He galloped over and nuzzled my hand.

"Did you do this?" I shook a finger at him.

Thor cocked his head, confused.

"Did you destroy this place?" I asked again, sternly.

Thor sat and harrumphed at me, displeased with my accusatory tone.

"Well who did? Pretty sure the cat couldn't make this big of a mess."

Thor took a step backward and sat down, stone-faced, admitting nothing.

"Go on." I flicked my hand back.

He plopped his huge frame down on the carpet and stared at me in defiance.

Damn, this dog had a mind of his own. "Fine."

I hauled the groceries to the kitchen, which appeared to be unscathed, and set them on the countertop. Resting my foot on one of the stools, I assessed the damage. Moonlight was sprawled across the top of the fridge like he had the best catnip buzz of his life.

"What did you do? Watch him tear the place apart?"

The cat yawned and rolled on his back.

I sighed and moved through the living room, replacing cushions and uprighting furniture. The shoe chair was a challenge. The heel fit back on the base, but I couldn't guarantee it was safe to use, so I tested it and fell on my ass. Hot glue might work. Where did Fiona get that thing anyway? I balanced the toe of the shoe on top of the heel and made a mental note not to sit on it.

Birdie's voice came to me as I was stuffing papers back

into the desk drawer. *"You'll have to rely on that intuition you try so hard to shun. Use the magic you were born with."*

Intuition. Messages. Magic. A lot of good that's done me. If it weren't for my intuition, my father would be alive today.

It was because of me he took that particular route to work that day. Because of my stupid dream that warned his head would crack against the fire hydrant, blood oozing from his skull. My screams were all it took to convince my father to drive rather than walk that February morning to work. I can still play the scene over in my mind when I close my eyes or gaze into a black mirror. Maybe if he had taken that route, maybe someone would have found him. Could have saved him.

Instead, he hit a patch of black ice on Highway 20 and crashed head-on into a tractor-trailer. He was killed instantly.

I finished tidying the living room and went into the bedroom to grab a notebook and pen from my suitcase. After the light blinked on, it was apparent that the party had continued in there. Not to my surprise, I might add.

If I hadn't known better, I would have thought someone just had the sex of a lifetime in that room. The mattress dipped off the bed, sheets were tangled, and the suitcase had spit all my clothes onto the carpet.

I crouched to pick up the garments.

"Dammit, Thor!" I yelled. Cin could have warned me he was like a tornado.

I was about to call her and tell her that when the lights went out.

hy does the electricity always go out at night?

I waited for my eyes to acclimate to the blackness before I stood. Thor's heavy panting wasn't all that comforting at the moment. He sounded like a hungry lion, and I once again realized I didn't have food for him.

Think. When Fiona gave the tour was there a flashlight, oil lamp, anything that would offer illumination? Wait a minute. My cell phone. That had a light on it. It was in my coat, in the hallway.

Moving forward, I heard, "Woof."

I apologized to Thor for stepping on his tail.

I felt around the bed, which was no easy task since it wasn't where it was supposed to be, and tumbled over my open suitcase, falling face first into the doorknob. Pain shot through my cheek. *That should leave a nice mark.*

Damn, it's dark. Even if clouds weren't shielding the light of the moon, the curtains were closed tight and thick as bricks. There weren't many street lamps in the residential section of Amethyst, and the back of the main house faced the front of the cottage. So no benefit of a porch light.

I veered left and kept going toward the front door until the floor changed beneath my feet from carpet to tile. Felt around for my coat and knocked it off the hook. Then I heard the phone slide across the foyer and smack into the wall.

I shifted to find two eyes staring at me, nearly glowing.

A scream ripped from my throat.

Then a tongue covered my face.

"Thor! You scared me to death!"

I felt for the phone, found it, and punched the flashlight app.

The illumination from the cell phone wasn't much, but it helped me maneuver through the cottage. Hey, so I wasn't Ben Franklin, but it got the job done. Now to hunt for matches and candles.

The empty grocery bags hung from the knob of the back door and a breeze made them rustle. Was there a window open? A draft around the frame of the door? I went to investigate and discovered paw prints on the glass of the door. Big ones. I eyed Thor, who was shadowing me.

"Were you trying to make a break for it?"

He nudged my hip and in that brief touch, a jolt shot through me. Static electricity? I gave the Dane a curious look.

Then the front door flew open, there was a crash, and something screeched by my ear.

I was still screaming when I realized the screech came from Moonlight, startled by the door. It must not have clicked shut. I picked him up to comfort him and screamed again. There was a man standing in the entryway.

17

*T*hor trotted right up to Leo and slobbered on him. "Hey, big guy." Leo scratched the dog's ears. I guessed Leo and Thor had already met judging from the friendly greeting. "Sorry, I startled you, Stacy. Are you all right? I heard a scream."

I pushed my heart back into my chest. "Fine. Thank you. Seems the storm took out the electricity, and I think Thor may have molested my couch while I was gone, but other than that ..." I made the okay sign.

"Fusebox?" he asked, pointing around the cottage.

"I'm not sure exactly."

Leo fired up a flashlight and asked if there was a basement. There wasn't, so he dug around in the utility closet until the lights came back on.

"Thanks, Leo." *Gotta love a man who's handy.* Handy and sexy were my two favorite combinations. Like peanut butter and jelly.

"No problem." Then he noticed my face. "What happened to your cheek?" He reached to lift the hair away from my forehead.

"Doorknob." It missed my eye, thankfully, but there'd probably be a bruise, but Birdie had a great bruise remedy.

His hand cupped my cheek for a moment. It was almost a caress and if I was a more graceful woman, I could have swooned. He went to find a towel and filled it with ice.

I asked, "So, what brings you by? More relatives to arrest?"

Leo dabbed the ice pack to my swollen face. "Wish it was that simple." His expression told me I wasn't going to like hearing this news and he wasn't going to like saying it.

"Oh please, things couldn't possibly get any worse."

Here's a tip: Do. Not. Say. This. Ever. It's tempting fate. Things can *always* get worse, and any idiot on the planet knows this. Except for me, apparently.

Leo pulled out some papers from inside of his leather jacket and passed them to me, still catering to my wound.

"What's this?" I asked, scanning the documents.

Sighing, Leo furrowed his eyebrows like they do in crime shows. "Motive."

I flipped through the papers, which had been signed by my grandfather less than a week ago.

It appeared to be a million dollar life insurance policy on my grandfather listing Birdie as the beneficiary.

"This can't be right." I pulled up a chair. I flipped back and forth through the papers. "It has to be a mistake. No one mentioned this to me. This has to be something that was never updated after the divorce."

"It's no mistake. It's a brand new policy. I checked."

Why would Gramps take out a policy for Birdie now? I'm sure the rest of his estate went to Pearl, Cin, or myself. But Birdie? Was there something I didn't know? Something between them? Was Birdie in trouble financially? And if she were, what would she do to get out of it?

I slapped my forehead for even thinking it. No way. My grandmother might have been a lot of things, but she was no murderer. Besides, what was that business with the spell if she wanted to do him in? There had to be another explanation. Unless ...

Was it a trick? Was the spell to seal the deal? I was missing a few pieces of the puzzle, but I was determined to find them.

"There's something else, Stacy."

"Of course, there is. What?"

"I spoke with your grandfather's doctor. He's certain it was ethylene glycol in your grandfather's system."

"Let me guess. That's the long answer for antifreeze."

Leo nodded, looking like he hated this conversation.

I shoved the papers into a drawer in the desk and ushered Leo through the cottage. "Thanks for stopping by, Leo. I appreciate everything." I needed some alone time to think this through.

"So I guess that means you aren't up for a drink?"

"Not tonight, maybe another time." *Please, God, let there be another time.*

I wondered if the aunts were still awake. All the clocks were off, thanks to the power outage.

"Leo, what time is it?"

He checked his watch. "After ten."

Cinnamon would still be working. Too late to bother the aunts, but I had my laptop.

I set the ice pack down on the entry table. "Really, Leo, thanks."

He turned suddenly and cupped my face in his hands. His eyes were an island. A base of sturdy brown flecked with green and gold. He kissed one eyelid, then the other. "Take care of that shiner." His lips fell to mine, and I was a puddle.

Leo pulled away slowly and didn't say another word as he slipped out of the cottage.

My head spun as it tried to process this latest development.

Thor had something in his mouth again when I closed and locked the door, which I planned to do religiously now. He spit it out when I walked over to him and I noticed it was chewed up fabric. Plaid. I bent to touch the frayed edges and a chill seized me again. What was it Birdie used to warn about chills down the spine? An unexpected presence? Uninvited guest?

The spider web. A visitor coming. But ... Leo had been here. Was someone else here before that? Before I got home? I picked up the fabric, rubbing it between my fingers. Immediate pain—as if I had been punched—shot through my stomach. Then a wave of nausea swayed me.

"He was in here." I circled slowly, the knowledge settling into my gut. No details, just ... a masculine presence.

Thor stood and leaned against me with all his weight and I felt the jolt again. Animal communication was never a gift of mine, but I knew this dog was trying to tell me something. He trotted to the back door and I followed. My sight trailed from the paw prints to the handle.

I twisted the latch and a slip of fabric, matching what Thor had in his mouth, fell to the ground. Red and black plaid.

The Great Dane sat, tongue wagging, looking ever so proud, and I understood what had happened to the cottage while I was out. I ruffled Thor's ears and promised him a juicy steak.

"He was in here, wasn't he boy? And you chased him away."

Thor held his paw up, and I shook it, knowing this was the beginning of a beautiful friendship.

"Well, buddy, at least I know what happened." I surveyed the cottage before heading to the fridge to find something tasty to feed my new pal.

The bigger question was—who was *he*? And what did he want?

Or was it a *she*?

18

*A*fter the realization that someone had broken in, I texted Cin, telling her I would keep Thor overnight, leaving out the part about the break-in. I didn't need her coming over here, guns blazing. That done, I found some forgotten meatloaf in the freezer and nuked it for Thor. He seemed overjoyed with the hot meal and I was grateful for the company. Moonlight ate hurriedly and escaped out the back door earlier and I hadn't seen him since, so it was just the two of us.

We stayed up past midnight researching on the Internet. I researched ethylene glycol poisoning and was surprised to find several news stories. A neighbor getting rid of a barking dog, a wife slipping it into her husband's drink, a suicide. I also learned, if not detected, it could cause kidney failure, renal failure, brain damage, and death. Sometimes in twenty-four hours, depending on the amount. Gramps was lucky his doctor recognized the symptoms in time.

I decided to do a search on Pearl, too. Her last name was Walker. I found some old photos of her scanned from a book on the history of carnivals. That was no surprise since

I knew that was how she had met Gramps. There were a few records on ancestry websites that may have been about her, although I couldn't be certain since I didn't know what city she was born in. The only other item was a newspaper article announcing the opening of the restaurant. I searched on Gretchen next and found several listings on Facebook and LinkedIn, plus an obituary from an East Coast newspaper, but none of the profiles or the pictures matched the woman who was Pearl's niece. Maybe Walker wasn't Gretchen's last name.

All I found on Wildcat was a mention in a military newsletter and a blurb on the website of a bar where he won first place in their dart league.

I filtered through the county records next for real estate transactions. Oddly, there was no record of Entwhistle on anything. Not even a residential sale. Gramps, however, held a lot of deeds in town. Maybe someone was behind on the rent and decided it would be easier if Gramps weren't around to collect. Or perhaps someone wanted to purchase some property that Gramps didn't want to sell.

Exhausted, I decided to call it a night and turn in. My head was throbbing by the time it hit the pillow.

THOR SLOBBERED me awake the next morning and trotted to the front door where I let him out to do his business. I went in search of food and started washing some pears before the doorbell rang.

Cinnamon was standing there when I opened the door. "Lovely. You don't even bother to ask who it is when there is a maniac running around trying to off members of our family?"

"Who is it?" I asked.

"Smart ass. Come on. I brought some pastries and coffee from Mom's shop. Thor," she called over her shoulder.

Thor trotted in after Cinnamon, and I shut the door.

She set the paper bag and the coffee tray on the counter and grabbed two plates from the cupboard.

"I tried to call but your phone wasn't working." She plucked the coffee from the nest and set it next to the plates.

"The battery's probably dead." I eyed the white bag Cin was digging through, mentally counting the sugar and fat grams. "I was just fixing some breakfast. I went shopping yesterday."

Cinnamon paused from unpacking the pastries to make a face at the fruit on the counter.

"That isn't food. This is food." She held a cream puff bigger than my head in her hand.

I chose a biscotti and grabbed a coffee.

"What happened to your face?" Cin asked.

"I fell into the stupid doorknob." I plugged my phone into the charger. Then I saw the time. "Oh crap."

"What?" Cinnamon had some cream on her chin.

"We gotta get over there." I ran into the bedroom to throw on some clothes and slap some makeup on the bruise.

"Where?" Cin called from the kitchen.

I was jumping into a pair of drawstring pants when I came out.

"Cin, you have to help me. I promised the aunts I would help out with Birdie gone. You have more experience with this stuff. These people will eat me alive."

"Stacy, I schlep booze, not breakfast. It's a little different atmosphere. Besides, Fiona can handle it."

"She can't do it all by herself. I'm telling you, without Birdie it's a freaking funhouse."

It took a little coaxing, but I finally got Cinnamon to agree to help at the B&B.

Which everyone will probably hold against me for the rest of my life.

"YOU GOT EGGS BENEDICT? I specifically requested Eggs Benedict," said the teamster whose name I discovered was Hal.

He was talking to Cinnamon, who had just set a plate of muffins on the table. A frilly white apron with pink gingham clung to her chest. Lolly insisted on it. Mine was lace. And lime green. We looked like 1950's housewife rejects caught in a time warp.

"I think the ladies are whipping up some delicious egg soufflé along with a few other tasty treats," Cin told Hal.

It was creepy how well she could fake polite.

Kyle, the honeymooner, and the Wild Women squealed with delight.

I was setting up the buffet with hot water and tea bags. I smiled and winked at Cin. I knew she hated every minute of it, but I was proud she was on her best behavior.

"I could really use some Eggs Benedict, boy." Hal's jowls shook as he spoke. He poured himself a cup of coffee, a napkin tucked into his undershirt.

His wife, Mary, chimed in, "It's his favorite. There's a little diner on the northwest side. Armitage, I think. They got the best Benedict." Mary slathered cream cheese on a croissant. Her rose print pants suit appeared to have been applied with wallpaper paste.

"Yeah, and they give you what you want. You want scrambled? You get scrambled" Hal slurped his coffee and a trail of it dribbled down his chin.

Cinnamon shot me a look that said, *You owe me big-time.*

Hal shrugged and gobbled a slice of pound cake. "It's all I'm saying'."

Cin opened her mouth. I held my breath. She decided on a smirk and floated into the kitchen, where I could hear the aunts banging pots and pans. The aromas of bacon frying, freshly brewed coffee, hot syrup, and melted butter mingled through the dining room.

"Well, whatever it is, it sure smells great," Jeremy remarked. He helped himself to a muffin.

"You'll have to do an extra half hour on the treadmill if you eat that." Kyle clucked his tongue.

"I'll risk it." Jeremy cut the muffin in half.

"If anyone would like some tea, I have it here on the buffet. Help yourself," I said.

The skinny blonde got up. "Do you want some, Melanie?"

Melanie spread jam on a biscuit. "I'll take peppermint if they have it, Trish."

"There's sugar, cream, honey, and lemon. So that should get everyone started." I gave the table one last assessment.

So far so good.

"That guy's a jackass," Cin whispered to me when I got to the sink with the empty tray.

"It's only an hour. Let's just get through it and then we're off to see Gramps."

I watched Lolly flip a pancake over and over again on the countertop. It wasn't cooked.

Yep. The coffee was in the basket, but someone forgot to turn on the percolator. And I don't mean the Columbian roast.

"I can't thank you girls enough for helping us out this morning. Your Aunt Lolly isn't the same without Birdie here." Fiona was at the stove draining bacon onto paper towels. She already had a platter warming with sausage links. Alongside that were a stack of blueberry pancakes, three different kinds of syrup, and butter.

"No problem, Auntie. Do you want me to take the pancakes into the dining room?" I asked.

"Oh, that would be lovely, dear," she replied.

I grabbed the food and nudged Cin. She shook her head. I gritted my teeth at her. She stomped her foot. I kicked her.

"I'll grab the syrup and butter." Cin stuck her tongue out at me.

"Very cute," I whispered, following her into the dining room. "Who wants one?" I asked the group, raising the platter.

Everyone raised their hands except Hal, who pouted like a kid who'd lost his balloon.

I went around the table and plopped two pancakes on each guest's plate. Then I placed the platter in the center. Cinnamon set the syrup and butter down and went back into the kitchen.

"So what's on the agenda for today?" I asked no one in particular.

"Jeremy and I thought we'd take a drive and check out the town. Then there's an art exhibit at the gallery on Main Street," said Kyle through sips of orange juice.

"We're continuing our Wild Women Adventure." Trish gushed. "We have a whole list of tasks to complete and then we report back here to the She-Woman Head Heathen."

Wonder who that could be? The problem was the Head Heathen might not be around for a while.

I wanted to ask them if they ever spent the night in the pokey. Now that's a Wild Woman. "Sounds exciting."

Kyle gulped.

Cin came back around with the hot bacon and sausage. She dished it out at the far end of the table, clearly avoiding Hal. I topped off coffee cups.

"You know what would go great with that bacon?" Hal asked as Cin approached him.

This guy was trying to break Cinnamon like a wild horse, and I wasn't sure how much she would take.

"A hot poker up your ass?" Cin replied with a smile, like she was suggesting activities for the day.

Here we go again.

Kyle dropped his fork. I got the feeling the guy still hadn't recovered from the night before. Jeremy massaged his shoulder.

Hal stared at Cin for a minute. I tensed. Then he busted out laughing.

Cin curtsied and went back into the kitchen, and I followed her.

"Cinnamon, come on. Just ignore him."

"What are you talking about?" she asked. Lolly had a cup of coffee in front of her and Cin was pouring Kahlua in it. "He loved it."

"Just behave."

Fiona took an egg casserole out of the oven. "Stacy, would you mind? This is the last hot dish. Take the oven mitts and hold the pan, and Cinnamon you scoop it onto the plates. It has to be hot or the eggs fall apart. Go, go."

We went.

"I'll try some of that." Hal was still laughing. I walked over to him with the dish. He pointed at Cin. "Hot poker. That's a good one."

If he only knew. I had never actually seen my cousin impale a person, but there were rumors.

Cinnamon smiled, softening like melted ice-cream. She turned to spoon up a huge portion of eggs.

"You're all right, kid." Hal smacked her on the ass.

I stopped breathing for a second. He shouldn't have done that. Cinnamon carried a little black book in her purse that contained the names of all the men who have touched her without permission. Many of them were never heard from again.

There was nothing I could do since my hands were occupied by a pan of hot egg soufflé. So I stood and watched Cin dump a huge, steaming pile into Hal's lap.

Hal bounced back from the table and jumped up. "Son of a bitch! What did you do that for?" He threw his napkin down and shook his pants.

I set the eggs on the table and ran for a towel.

"I'm sorry, did you want more?" I heard Cin ask, and before I could stop her, she scooped up another glob and lobbed it at his face.

I grabbed the spoon from her hand and handed Hal the towel. I was about to apologize and get Cin out of there when I heard Melanie yell, "Food fight!"

I whirled around to find the Wild Women facing off with the newlyweds.

The girls were dipping their pancakes in syrup while Jeremy and Kyle each grabbed a handful of greasy pork products.

I did a 'safe' sign with my arms and simultaneously screamed, "*Stop!*" in the deepest bellow I could muster.

Everyone stopped and looked in my direction. Then they all pitched their fistfuls of food at me.

In an instant, I was dripping with butter, syrup, sausage, and bacon. And I was hoping to get through one day without being sticky.

I tried to scrape off whatever the hell was stuck to my eyelids, but the syrup kept it glued in place. I feared I was making it worse because I could hear squishing sounds as I tried to pull the mounds off my forehead, cheeks, and nose. Real blueberries, too. Which were great on pancakes. Not so great on clothing.

Someone handed me a napkin, but that compounded the problem. Now I had bits of paper dotting my face as if I had sliced myself shaving my whole head.

I heard chairs moving and shoes clicking on the hardwood floors. I pried open an eyelid with my index finger and saw them all rushing from the room.

That pissed me off.

"Where the hell do you all think you're going?" I yelled.

No one answered me.

"Well?"

"I'm going to get some Eggs Benedict," Hal mumbled.

I snatched the napkin from his shirt and dipped it in his water glass, wiping my face with it. When I was through, I tucked it back in his shirt and grabbed his shoulder.

"You are going to sit your ass down and eat your breakfast." I shoved Hal back in his seat. Mary sat, too.

I snapped my fingers. "You four." Pointed to the chairs. "Sit!"

The Wild Women and newlyweds returned to their seats.

I surveyed the table. There was still plenty of food left. Although it was mostly in a big pile.

"Now. This is what's going to happen. You all are going to enjoy the meal that my aunt has prepared. Then you will help us clean up this mess. And for the rest of the weekend, you will act like people vacationing at a Bed and Breakfast, not a fraternity house on spring break."

.   .   .

AN HOUR later Cinnamon and I were back at the cottage. "That went well." She was scooping leftover bacon, eggs, and sausages into a bowl for Thor who watched with enthusiasm. A puddle of drool was forming at his feet.

"Don't worry, Cinnamon, I won't ask you to help out again." My voice oozed sarcasm.

"Good." Cin sunk into the couch.

"You know, an apology would be nice." I took off my shoes and proceeded to wring out my socks.

"For what?"

I stared at her. "Are you kidding? Look at me!"

"You can't think that's my fault." She feigned innocence.

Thor's giant head bobbed from me to Cinnamon, not sure whose side to take. He finally decided it was none of his business, belched and plopped onto the carpet.

I silently counted to ten. "Accountability, Cin. Some of it *is* your fault. Accept it."

Smiling, Cin curled forward. "You sound like Birdie."

I rolled my eyes, stomped to the bathroom, and slammed the door behind me.

The shower felt great. Hot water poured down my back, washing away the muck of the morning. I soaped all the food off my face and lathered my hair up twice. Scrubbed my hands until they reddened, but my fingertips were still pale blue from the berries. Maybe a little lemon juice would help. Nature had a way of providing solutions to every problem.

I turned off the water and reached for a towel when a thought occurred to me. Nature. Birdie said that nature would help me figure out what happened to Gramps. What was it? Nature, knowledge, and truth? If it weren't for the storm, Thor wouldn't have been here. And if it weren't for him chasing the guy, whoever he was, ripping off a chunk of cloth, I wouldn't have known someone was in the cottage at all. I guess nature had lent a hand.

Were any footprints outside? Or did the storm wash them away? Whoever was in here must have taken their shoes off because the carpet was clean.

I wrapped the towel tight, stepped out of the shower, glanced in the mirror, and yelped.

"Cin!"

"Yeah? What's up?" she asked through the door.

She was still here. Then how could I be seeing what I was seeing?

In the mirror was another message.

HOME AGAIN

Could the intruder from last night have taken the time to write it? Obviously, this was not left over from a previous guest.

But Chance took a shower yesterday, too. Had he seen it? Or was he the one who wrote it?

"Come here."

She stuck her head through the doorway and wrinkled her brow. "What? Something stuck?"

"Funny. Look." I pointed to the mirror.

"Home again." She looked at me. "Why yes, you are."

I rolled my eyes. "Smartass. Did you do that?"

"Well, I'm not a pervert and we are related, so no." She frowned. "Wait, what's going on?"

I didn't want to worry her so I said, "Maybe it was the previous guests who stayed here."

She didn't look too certain.

I wrapped a towel around my hair and puttered past her into the bedroom.

She followed. "Stacy, why did you want to keep Thor overnight?"

"I don't know. It was late."

After pulling on a clean pair of jeans and a green tee shirt, I blasted my hair with the blow dryer and donned my Cubs hat and a white hoodie. Why bother with makeup at this point?

Thor galloped into the room, and I scratched his ears.

"I know you're lying so you may as well just tell me or I'll tell Birdie about the time you used her crystals in your eighth-grade science project."

I wished I hadn't. They were fresh off a love spell and my teacher left his wife for the lunch lady that weekend.

Cinnamon sat on the bed as I told her about my uninvited guest. "What do you think he was after? I mean, it's obvious he didn't know Thor would be here."

I regarded her, not liking my next thought. But I said it anyway. "Maybe he thought I would be."

19

"*I*'m serious, Stacy, I want you to stay with me," Cinnamon said a short time later. "And you need to file a breaking and entering report."

We were in her Trans Am on our way to the hospital to visit Gramps. It was a decent day, so Thor decided to snooze on the porch, and Cin left him there with a giant bowl of water, telling him that Fiona would be around to check on him later.

"Cin, that's ridiculous. You aren't even around at night, you're at the bar. And Birdie made it clear that she wanted me to figure this out."

"Birdie didn't know the bastard would stalk you." Cin was convinced that whoever broke into the cottage was responsible for Gramps' illness. "But you're right about me. I'm not home much." She drummed her fingers on the steering wheel, thinking. "Well then, at least borrow Thor. That dog has taken to you. He won't let anything bad happen to his new buddy."

I must admit it gave me peace of mind to know that Thor, all one hundred-eighty pounds of him, chased whoever it was around the cottage and then took a bite out of him. What a badass friend to have.

"Deal. I'll bring him around once in a while to visit you. But you foot the food bill." I didn't even want to know how much that dog could put away.

"Done. I'll drop some off later. So what's our game plan?"

"Well, assuming Gramps is in good shape, which I think he will be, we get some info from him and ask for the money to bail out Birdie. Although she may not go before a judge until Monday since she won't let me call anyone to speed things up. Hopefully, he won't hold the reason she's in there in the first place against her. Then we get her out and hopefully she can help me figure this out."

"I hate to bring this up, but I have to get the bar open by noon."

I checked my phone. It was 10:30 in the morning.

"That's fine. I can get Birdie out on my own. I'll stop in later if I need to pick your brain. I've been out of the loop for a while, so I have no idea what business ventures Gramps has been up to."

"Check."

She swung the car into the parking lot, and we jumped out. The day was warm and windy with a few fallen branches littering the road from yesterday's storm. The sun shone through trace clouds and the T-tops were off the car. Cin straightened her hair in the rearview mirror and pushed her gold sunglasses up the bridge of her nose.

I zipped my hooded sweatshirt, tightened my ball cap, and headed for the doors. Cin was right behind me as we sailed through. My high school chum, Lynn, sat behind the front desk.

"Don't you ever leave?" I asked.

Lynn laughed. "Hey, Cinnamon. That was a great band at The Opal the other night."

My cousin affects people in one of two ways. Either they're afraid of her or they want to be her. I guessed Lynn fell into the second group.

"Thanks." Cin slid her sunglasses up on her head.

Gramps was watching the Bears lose when we got to the room. "What are you trying to do? Walk it into the end zone? For cripe's sake," he yelled at the television.

"You tell 'em, Gramps." Cin thumped the air with her fist. "They'll never be like the '85 Bears."

He shifted his head our way. "Hey, hey. My two favorite granddaughters." He sounded strong.

I leaned over to kiss his cheek. "You have another one somewhere we don't know about?" I joked.

Pearl came into the room then. "What a nice surprise. Hello, girls." She walked over to give us each a peck on the cheek.

We hugged her back.

"Sorry we didn't bring you anything, Gramps. We weren't sure if we were allowed to after, um," I wasn't sure how to finish that thought so I said, "the other day."

I was talking about Birdie's little stunt. I had no idea why I brought it up, but considering the response I got I wished I had kept my mouth shut. Pearl grimaced at the mention of "the other day" and reached for her knitting. Cin rolled her eyes and tapped me with the back of her hand.

"What do you mean? Your grandmother? Bah!" Gramps waved an arm. "Sweetheart, I have been putting up with her antics my whole life. She doesn't bother me. She's a little loopy, you know." He made a circle with his index finger near his temple.

"I've heard that." I nodded.

"She's dangerous," muttered Pearl from her chair.

"Now, Pearl, you know that's not true," Gramps said.

"Oscar, how else do you explain this?" She motioned to the hospital bed.

Holy crap. She thinks Birdie's guilty. Now how was I going to ask for the money?

"She should be locked up, that one." Pearl focused back on her yarn, stabbing the needle through it.

That would have been a nice segue. *Speaking of locked up, have you got ten grand I could borrow?*

Gramps made a 'what are you gonna do' face.

Cinnamon changed the subject. "Mom says she has a batch of cannolis with your name on it when you're better."

"You tell your mother, I'll be there in no time to take her up on that." And you," he pointed at me, "don't you have a job to get back to?"

"The news can wait." I shrugged. "You're more important."

"I'm fine." He leaned over, still staring at me. "Where'd you get that beauty?" Referring to the bruise from the doorknob.

"Bar fight." I grinned.

Gramps laughed. So did Cinnamon.

"Not you, I don't believe it. *You* maybe." He waved at Cin.

My turn to laugh.

"Hey," Cin cried, pretending to be offended.

"Where is that nurse?" asked Pearl. "It's time for your grandfather's medicine."

Cin walked over to the doorway and ducked down the hall. "Don't see anyone, Pearl."

Sighing, Pearl placed her knitting on the table. "I better go check." She rose from her chair. "Don't let him have any sweets." She strolled from the room.

Gramps waited until she was gone. "Okay, where is it?"

"Where's what?" I asked.

"Right here." Cin reached into her purse and produced two cookies wrapped in wax paper. She handed them to Gramps.

"Almond cookies. What are you doing to me? I need chocolate, sweetheart," he whispered.

"I know, but that's all Mom had ready this morning. I'll bring you chocolate chip later," Cin promised.

"I can't wait that long. You have to go to the gift shop or the vending machine or something. I need a fix." He had the look of a strung-out junkie. He wasn't kidding.

"Jeez, fine." Cin rolled her eyes.

Gramps relaxed. "Now, what is it you two want to talk to me about?"

Cin and I exchanged looks.

"Come on, let's have it before the warden comes back."

"Birdie's in trouble," I blurted.

Gramps sat up a little straighter.

I explained her arrest, her reason for confessing, and the insurance policy. Gramps shook his head and stared at the bedrail.

"She didn't know, you know." He sighed and the effort seemed to pain him. "No one did. I only told the police because they asked if I had any life insurance, and if I did, who the beneficiaries were. There are trusts, investments, but I wanted to do that for your grandmother."

"Are you sure she didn't know?" I asked.

"The only two people who knew about that policy besides the insurance agent were me and my lawyer. Not even Pearl."

"Gramps, why would you even do that? Why would you

take out such a huge policy and then put it in Birdie's name?" I asked.

"Yeah. Why wouldn't you just leave her a portion of your estate?" Cin questioned.

Gramps swiveled his head from Cinnamon to me. He sighed, then smiled. "Listen, the day I married your grandmother, I made a promise to her. I said that I would always take care of her, no matter what. I never break a promise. And knowing that stubborn woman, she wouldn't take a cent if she could grant her share to another family member. This way it was a windfall. A gift to her when I died."

The way Birdie talked, that would be gift enough.

I glanced at Cin. Did I see a tear in her eye?

Cin cleared her throat. "You're something, Gramps."

He laughed. "People can't always live together. Doesn't mean they don't love each other." He stared at Cin as he said that.

"Now, Stacy, you go to Stan Plough and you tell him that you need that money. He should be able to arrange for you to get a check today."

"Don't I need your signature or something?" I asked.

"Stan's a good friend. He'll do it," he said.

"Who will do what?" Pearl inquired as she entered the room.

"Stacy here wants a ride on Wildcat's Harley." Gramps squeezed my hand and winked. "Why don't you girls go grab those magazines I wanted?"

"We're on it." Cin yanked me through the door.

I smiled at a nurse carrying a tray into Gramps' room. Once we were outside of the room, I muttered, "Damn, I hoped to talk to him without Pearl."

"I'll take her for coffee when we go back up."

We hopped on the elevator to the main floor and

followed the signs that pointed to the gift shop. The shelves were filled with picture frames, greeting cards, magazines, books, and bouquets. A vanilla candle failed to mask the antiseptic scent of the rest of the hospital.

"What should we get him?" I approached a table loaded with candy boxes wrapped with shiny, white paper.

"I think he likes chocolate-covered cherries," Cin replied.

I read the stickers on the boxes. Chocolate-covered orange peels, caramel clusters, mint medallions, coconut haystacks, fudge, peanut brittle. No cherries.

"I don't see any." I scanned the other aisles. On the far wall, there was one lone box, covered in red paper with a matching bow. "Maybe that one has cherries."

We walked over, and I plucked the box from the shelf. Beneath it sat a penny. I picked it up and checked the date. It was newer than the others. I was in high school at the time.

Birdie's voice came into my head again. *"Follow the signs. Heed the messages."* I had four pennies now. And no clue what they meant.

"Are you still saving pennies?" Cinnamon asked.

"Yes. I've been finding them everywhere, Cin. It's the strangest thing. I used to just pick one up once in a while. If I was having a bad day, or something great just happened and I had no one to share it with, there it would be. A penny. And I would think, 'Dad's here with me.' But ever since your phone call, they're everywhere."

"Spooky."

I nodded and glanced at the candy. "It would look pretty funny if we don't come back with magazines."

"You're right."

I grabbed *Time, National Geographic,* and *Newsweek.* Cin

reached for *Car and Driver*. We paid for everything and headed back up to the room.

Wildcat was yelling at Dr. Gates when we stepped off the elevator.

"Now you listen to me, Dickless Joe." He poked him, and Gates shrunk back a bit. "I'm not leaving until I talk to my friend." The two men stood in front of Gramps' door.

"What's going on?" I asked.

"This jockstrap thinks he can order me around." Wildcat took a step forward. "I got socks older than you."

Gates didn't bother to hide his agitation. He turned to me. "The nurse is taking your grandfather's vital signs, and administering his medication. We asked him to wait out here for a moment." Gates walked off.

"Wildcat, relax." Cin patted his shoulder. "In a minute, you can go in and see him."

"No, I can't. Pearl doesn't want me in there," Wildcat grumbled.

I told Wildcat, "I'll talk to her."

I couldn't see why Pearl would want to keep Gramps from his friend, but the fact was she wasn't family. She had no right to make those requests.

The nurse threw the door open then and yelled, "Doctor, come quickly."

Gates jogged back, and we all followed behind him. Gramps had his eyes shut. I couldn't tell if he was breathing, and Cin grabbed my hand.

"What happened?" the doctor asked. He flashed a light in Gramps' eyes. They were vacant.

The nurse was talking too fast for me to make out what she was saying. Then the doctor yelled, "Pentobarbital!" He darted his eyes at us. "Get these people out of here and get a crash cart."

The nurse ushered the three of us through the door and yelled down the hall.

We all stood there in silence for a minute, staring at the door.

Cinnamon was the first to speak. "He's a tough old goat. He'll be fine."

Wildcat didn't say anything.

Two thoughts ran through my mind. The first was, *If Gramps dies, how will I ever clear Birdie?*

The second was, *What the hell is Pentobarbital?*

20

*W*e had been sitting in the lobby for an hour waiting for someone to give us an update when Cinnamon pulled me aside.

"Take my car and go get Birdie." She handed me the key.

I shook my head. "No." A little because I felt I should wait and see how Gramps was, but mostly because if anything happened to her car Cinnamon would kick my ass.

"Stace, it's all right. Someone has to get Birdie out of that cell, and Gramps thought you should be the one to talk to Stan."

My gaze fell on Pearl. She was flipping through a magazine, frowning. I wondered how she felt. Couldn't be easy what she was going through. "You'll stay with her?"

Cin nodded. "I'll call Bay. He can open the bar, and Wildcat can drop me there later. I'll take Pearl to the cafeteria and we'll get something to eat. Take her mind off of things."

"Did you call her niece?"

"Pearl said she was by this morning. She's doing some work at the Palace now."

We glanced sideways at Pearl for a minute.

"Listen, something's not right with Gretchen," I whispered.

"What do you mean?"

"Well, I don't know exactly. I get a weird vibe from her."

"I know what you mean. She seemed to show up out of nowhere, and now she's in their business, doing their books."

"Their books? I thought she was just helping out with paperwork at the restaurant."

"Yeah, that's what she told me, too, but Pearl said she's an accountant so she was coaching Gramps and her on some investments. Pearl sounded happy about it, but I thought it was strange."

Me too. Why lie? Unless you're hiding something.

"I'll leave my phone on. Keep me posted." I walked over and bent down to kiss Pearl on the cheek. "I have to go take care of some things, but Cin's going to stay here with you, okay? I'll be back as soon as I can."

She lifted her face and squeezed my hand. Her eyes were weary, dark. Like she had been locked in a closet for a week.

"You're good girls." Her voice was thin.

I wanted to ask her Gretchen's last name, but I didn't think it was the best time. Maybe I would just head to the Palace and find out a few things myself.

Lynn was still at her post when I reached the exit. "Hi, Stacy." She glanced over her shoulder.

"Hi, Lynn," I called, rushing past her.

"Wait." She reached out.

I stopped and looked at her. "I'm kind of in a hurry."

Lynn fired her words at me. "You know that nurse? The one who was looking after your grandpa?"

"You mean the highly incompetent one? Yes, I remember her."

"No, that's just it, see. She isn't." Lynn glanced around again.

"She isn't what?"

"Incompetent."

"What are you saying?" I asked. I felt like I was playing charades.

A visitor approached us then and asked Lynn if he could speak with her.

"Certainly." She turned to help him, paused, and peered back over her shoulder at me.

The look on her face made me shudder.

21

I thought about what Lynn said as I carefully maneuvered Cinnamon's car down the highway. She was trying to tell me something, but what? That this latest setback for my grandfather was also no accident? If that were true, I needed to get some answers fast.

Sliding up next to the curb in front of Stan and Bea Plough's house a few minutes later, I glanced at the Geraghty Girls' house.

The Ploughs' lived in a boxy brick house, with a sprawling front yard and an apple tree. I hurried up the walkway and rang the doorbell.

Bea Plough, Stan's wife, answered the door. "Yes?"

"Hello, Mrs. Plough, I'm Stacy Justice—"

"I know who you are, Stacy." Mrs. Plough taught Sunday school at St. Mary's Catholic church. Rumor had it that anyone who didn't recite a Psalm accurately got whacked with her wooden paddle. That was one blessing of Birdie's house. I never had to sit in Mrs. Plough's class.

"Of course, excuse me. Would it be possible to speak with Mr. Plough? It's rather urgent," I pleaded.

Pursing her lips, Bea smoothed out her gray skirt. Her hair was knotted in a bun that rested on top of her pink scalp, like a dollop of whipped cream on a scoop of strawberry swirl. "I'm afraid Mr. Plough is indisposed at this time." She shut the door in my face.

I cranked the bell again.

After a moment, the door creaked open.

"Yes?"

"Please, would you happen to know where I could find him?"

"No." Slam.

Gave the bell another turn.

"*What*?"

"May I please wait here for your husband? Mrs. Pl—"

"No." Slam. Lock.

Oh, this bitch is asking for it.

Ring, knock, ring, knock. Ring! Knock!

The door opened again. "Stop that!"

"Look, lady, I can play this game all damn day, so just let me leave a message for your husband or tell me where he is so I can speak with him myself."

"What's going on out here, Bea?" Stan asked from behind her.

Lied to by a Sunday school teacher. Wasn't that the definition of hypocrisy?

"It's nothing," Mrs. Plough said over her shoulder.

"Mr. Plough," I called.

"Who is that?" Mr. Plough came forward, and his wife stepped aside. "Stacy?"

"Hello, Mr. Plough, may I please have a word with you?"

"Certainly. Come in, come in. Bea, would you please get Stacy an iced tea?"

I held up my hand. "No. I'm fine." She'd probably spit in it. "I would just like a moment of your time."

"Why don't we go into the study?" Mr. Plough outstretched his arm toward double pocket doors to the left of the entry hall.

I nodded and followed his lead. "Thank you."

The parquet floors were laid in a geometric pattern with a sundial star in the center. Law books filled floor-to-ceiling bookshelves, and two brown leather chairs faced a long, cherry wood desk. The room was warm. A stark contrast to the foyer.

"Have a seat." Mr. Plough closed the pocket doors behind him.

I sat in one of the leather chairs and waited for him to do the same. He moved slowly; his blue suit hung from his thin frame like a towel draped over a shower rod.

Mr. Plough settled in a chair behind the desk.

"You'll have to excuse my wife, Stacy. She's a little over-protective of my time, but she means well."

No, she doesn't, but hey, whatever floats your boat.

"Now, how is Oscar?"

I sighed, "Not so good, I'm afraid. He's had a little relapse."

"Oh, I'm terribly sorry to hear that." Mr. Plough frowned. His brown eyes drooped a bit at the creases.

I smiled at that. It was nice to know that his lawyer cared about Gramps that much. Now I was sure he would help.

"Anything I can do?" he asked.

"Actually, there is, I hope." I took a deep breath, organizing my thoughts before I spoke. "Well, I'm sure you may have heard about the initial cause of my grandfather's illness."

Mr. Plough clasped his hands. "I have." He shook his head. "Still can't believe it. Poison, they say."

"That's what they say." I sat there a few seconds.

"Go on," Mr. Plough urged.

"Well, the thing is." I chuckled softly and put my hands on my thighs. "Somehow, my grandmother has gotten herself ... tangled up," I made some weird hand gesture that even I didn't understand, "in all of this ... and, not that it's true, you know, but—"

"But what?" asked Mr. Plough.

I had to spit it out. "Gramps has asked me to come to you to arrange for ten thousand dollars to bail out Birdie."

Stan sat back in his chair. "I see. Well, you certainly don't need an explanation to run an errand for your grandfather."

I smiled. *Yippee.*

"Just give me the signed request, I'll notarize it, and the bank will cut you a check."

I stopped smiling.

"Oh, don't worry. I trust you. No one will know Oscar wasn't present." Stan winked.

"That isn't it. I don't have a signed request."

Stan pursed his lips briefly. "Well, we can work around the formalities. Do you have a note in Oscar's script?"

I shook my head.

"Oh. Well, I'll just phone him at the hospital."

I shook my head again. This was going downhill fast.

Mr. Plough mimicked me, shaking his head. "No?"

"He was unconscious when I left."

"Unconscious? Then how did he ask you for the money?"

"That was before the nurse gave him some barbie something and he passed out. Come to think of it, you may have a lawsuit there." Jeez, I wasn't making any sense.

"Stacy, without Oscar's authorization, I can't grant you access to his funds."

I felt a lump rise in my throat, but I was determined not to cry. "Mr. Plough, my grandmother is in jail for something she had nothing to do with. The only person with enough money to get her out of jail is my grandfather, who may or may not be in a coma, and who is also the one person who can lead me to who put him there. I don't know what's going to happen to either of them. And I don't know if I can help, but right now, you're the only one who can at least give me some peace of mind about one of my last remaining family members."

Mr. Plough stood up and circled around to the front of the desk. Taking a seat in the chair next to me, he leaned forward. I didn't like the expression on his face.

"Stacy, I can sympathize with you, I can. And I would like to help you, but my hands are tied."

It was strange but I felt we had a common bond. We both had to deal with nutty women and we both played by the rules.

One of those commonalities was about to change for me.

I rose to my feet and wiped my face with a tissue. Then I remembered something about trusts.

"Wait, Gramps said there were monies in trusts. Does that include me?"

"Certainly. But that only gets activated in the event of his death."

Back to square one. It was ironic really. Now the only way I could help Birdie was if Gramps were actually dead. Birdie and the aunts worked hard, but they barely made ends meet. Same with Pearl. She made a modest living. If Gramps kicked the bucket, the two biggest winners would be Birdie and Pearl.

Wait a minute.

"Miss Justice?"

I looked at Stan. "I'm sorry. I was lost in thought there."

"That's quite all right. I was just asking, did you say Oscar was in a coma?"

"I'm not sure. He was unconscious when I left the hospital."

"Well, that would certainly change things."

"Why?"

"Should he be incapacitated, Oscar did appoint a power of attorney to guard his estate and oversee his health decisions."

"Is that you?"

"No, no. Let me see. I have the paper in his file."

My knee betrayed my nervousness by bouncing up and down. Mr. Plough opened a large, cherry wood file cabinet and rifled through it. He pulled out a piece of paper and examined it.

"Yes, here it is. The first one is ... oh, I see, it's your mother."

My mother? She's been gone for years. A lot of good that did me now. Why wouldn't Gramps have changed that? "Well, if he has her listed, that doesn't do me a lot of good."

"There is a second." He walked the paper over to me.

"Who?"

"The man's name is Chance. Chance Stryker."

I laughed. "Oh no, that must be a mistake. Chance isn't a relative of Gramps."

Stan placed the paper on the desk. "That may be, but, you see here, there's the name." He tapped the page.

I scanned the document. Stan was not mistaken.

I pushed the paper back toward Stan and rose. "Thank you for your time." I hurried toward the door.

"These things have a way of working themselves out, you'll see. You're a smart girl. You'll figure it out," called Mr. Plough.

That didn't make me feel better.

I crossed the hall wondering what the hell was going on with Gramps and why Chance was listed as power of attorney when I heard, "Serves her right, you know."

I tipped back to see Mrs. Plough standing at the top of a wide, curved stairway, looking down on me, her lips puckered into a twist. "Excuse me?" My stomach wrenched. Jeez, she was scary.

"Devil worshippers receive the Devil's due."

It was such a ridiculous statement that at first, I thought I had misunderstood. "My grandmother does not believe in a devil. Let alone worship one."

"My god condemns those who ignore His words."

I was about to open my mouth again when my head started spinning. Feeling dizzy, I grabbed the banister to steady myself. Then a picture of a thick, black belt with a gold buckle flashed in my mind. Welts. Blood. A boy sobbing, crying for his mother.

And the scene was clear.

I raised my eyes up at Mrs. Plough. "And what does your god do to child abusers?" I didn't wait for an answer as I opened the door.

22

I stood on the porch for a second trying to figure out what just happened to me. I didn't feel dizzy anymore. I shook my head. *That was strange. Where did that memory come from?* Did I see Mrs. Plough take a belt to a student once? If I did, I couldn't remember.

The biscotti was not enough to get me through the day, so I decided to head to the coffee shop. Iris usually stocked ready-made sandwiches, salads, and soups, and I needed some fast nourishment.

I climbed into the car and screamed my fool head off when I noticed someone was in the backseat.

"Thor, how did you get in here?" I asked.

The dog blinked, made a weird sound that sounded like exasperation, and rested his head on the passenger seat.

"Okay then. I guess you'll be joining me for lunch."

He chuffed in approval, and I fired up the engine.

A few blocks from Main Street, the windshield wipers switched on, flapping from side to side at warp speed. I flipped them off, and the dash lights started flashing. Then the radio blared, the cigarette lighter popped out, and the horn went haywire.

Oh, please, not Cin's car. Anything but her precious car.

I pulled up to Muddy Waters and cut the engine for a minute, wondering what method of torture my cousin would employ if I broke her car. It had to be a fluke. I cranked the engine again.

Honk, blare, swish, swish, "la, la, la," pop!

Oh no.

My phone rang then, adding a nice chorus to the mix.

"Hello?"

"Hi, Stacy, it's me," said Cinnamon.

"What the hell is that noise?"

I cut the car off. "Nothing."

"So, here's the scoop on Gramps. The drug he was given was Pentobarbital. It's a sedative. The dosage he got is usually given to brain injury or brain surgery patients to protect the brain by putting it into a temporary state of unconsciousness. Turns out there was a head injury patient on the same floor that was supposed to get the shot."

"A temporary state of unconsciousness. That sounds like—"

"A coma. But the good news is it shouldn't last longer than a few days."

That was a relief. "How's Pearl?"

"Better now."

I chatted with Cin a few more minutes and made arrangements to meet her later to pick up some food for Thor. I didn't mention the car. Clicking the phone off, I shoved it in my sweatshirt.

I turned to face the Great Dane. "Now listen, buddy, this is our secret. What say you don't tell Cinnamon that her

Trans Am is possessed, and I'll get you a giant roast beef sandwich?"

Thor snorted and bopped my hand with his nose.

I suddenly had a craving for potato chips, though I didn't really like them. I tilted my head at the dog. Maybe *I* wasn't craving them. Maybe *he* was.

"Chips too?"

Thor woofed, his tongue slapping the headrest.

"You drive a hard bargain, Big Man."

I rolled the windows down and hurried into Muddy Waters. Iris was behind the counter when I walked in. She wore the same canvas apron as the last time I saw her, but her shirt was pink and the pants were blue.

She waved a finger at me. "You were holding out on me."

She must have heard about Gramps. "I thought Pearl would want to tell you, Iris."

"That's what I figured." She smiled. "What can I get you, honey?"

I scanned the glass case. There were sandwiches, muffins, pastries, cookies, and chips. It all looked good. I couldn't decide where to start.

"Not sure what I want yet, but I'll take a roast beef to go. Extra beef."

"Take your time, honey." Iris turned to collect a large sandwich from the cooler.

The door chimed, and Monique waltzed in, which would have stunted my appetite on any other day.

She walked over to the counter. "Iris, give me a large caramel latte to go." She was in another leather get-up with a bustier so tight I thought she might pop a lung. "I'm glad you're here, Stacy, I need to talk to you."

The tone in her voice led me to believe she wasn't about to invite me to a dinner party.

"What is it, Monique?" I asked, still studying the menu. Turkey on rye looked good.

"Look, we both know your cousin and I have never seen eye to eye, but I've always considered you a friend," she said.

Raising one eyebrow, I tilted my head to the side. "Oh really?"

Monique stiffened. "Well, maybe not a friend, but I don't want to hit you with a shovel every time I see you."

"Charming, Monique. You should host a game show."

Monique didn't say anything as Iris came back to the counter to hand her the coffee. "You ready to order?" Iris asked me.

"I'll take that turkey sandwich and a bag of chips. To go please."

"Coming up." Iris grabbed a white paper bag and stuffed the two sandwiches inside of it. Then she reached for the potato chips.

"Look." Monique grabbed my elbow.

I circled to face her and shot her a glare.

She let go.

"I just thought I would give you fair warning that I'm going after Leo and I would appreciate it if you would stay out of my way."

That explained the mirrored sunglasses. She thought she was in an episode of *CSI*.

"And why exactly are you telling me this?"

Monique jutted out her hip. "Because the word around town is that you and the good cop are rather chummy. I just want you to know that he's mine. So back off."

"Here you go, Stacy." Iris had my order at the register.

I pulled my wallet out and walked toward her, Monique close behind.

Now, I didn't know if anything would develop with Leo.

Considering the fact that he thought I couldn't stand erect and that my family was the reason they invented Prozac, I'm sure he had mixed emotions about me. But I'd be damned if Monique Fontaine was going to tell me who I could and could not spend time with.

I threw my shoulders back and smiled. "Look, Monique, I realize that you have this unfettered desire to mark your territory when there's a new female in town, especially during mating season, so feel free to squat wherever the mood strikes." My smile dropped and I leaned into her. "But don't *ever* threaten me."

Her bravado slipped as I settled the tab with Iris, who snorted.

Then Monique touched my wrist as a pain shot through my head. She said, "I always get what I want, Stacy. Just ask your cousin."

Putting my finger to my temple to steady the dizziness, I lifted my eyes to watch Monique walk out the door. As she did, an image of Tony passed out on a couch popped into my brain.

"You okay, honey?" Iris asked as she peered at me.

I nodded. The pain subsided. "I'm fine, Iris. What do I owe you?"

She rang up the food, and I paid her. I was just about to leave to share lunch with a handsome, furry friend, but since my universe is run by Loki, that didn't happen.

If karma existed, I must have been a real asshat in a previous life.

"Hey, Sunshine." Shea Parker stood in front of me.

"Parker, I don't have a lot of time." I picked up the bag of food.

Parker grabbed my bag, opened it, and reached in for the chips. "Then we'll talk fast."

I snatched the Ruffles out of his hand, and he shot me a wounded look.

"What do you want from me?" I asked.

"For you to work for me at the paper."

"Not gonna happen."

"Then what do you know about your grandfather?"

"Nothing."

"Baloney. Oh, that sounds good." He winked at me. "Iris, can I have a baloney and Munster on rye with ketchup?"

"That sounds disgusting."

Parker gave me a frowny face. "You promised me a scoop."

"What do you expect me to tell you?"

"Whatever you know."

"My grandfather is sick."

"I know that."

"So?"

"What?"

"What more do you want?"

Iris slipped Parker his disgusting lunch, and Parker bit into it and started talking with his mouth full. "Here's the deal. I ask a question, then you ask a question."

The idea of my family misfortune sprayed across the local paper was less than thrilling, although the thought of accessing Parker's database did hold some appeal. The thing is, even though Shea Parker acted like a drunk toddler at times, in my mind he would always have one redeeming quality. My father trusted him enough to go into business with him. News was Dad's life, and he wouldn't put an important responsibility like that in any idiot's hands. Just this particular idiot.

"Go," I said.

"Who's the Harley rider?"

"Bill 'Wildcat' Panther. Gramps' war buddy. What's with Gretchen?"

"Gretchen who?"

"Pass. What do you know about the Entwhistles and the store?"

"Turns a hefty profit. Rents from your grandfather. Son is an odd duck. Which war?"

"Vietnam, I think. What do you mean rents?"

"I mean he doesn't own the land or the building. Why is the Harley guy here?"

"Business proposition. Did he sell it?"

"Who?"

"Entwhistle's son."

"No. The old man never paid the note. It was a land contract. Fell behind on the payments. What kind of proposition?"

"Gaming. So Roy is making a bundle and no mortgage. He has it pretty good."

"Ed would have it even better if your Gramps kicks it."

"Why?"

"Because the entire plaza and the land would go to Ed."

Parker explained that after a few beers one night at the Elk's Lodge, Ed was bragging about how he got into my grandfather's pocket. Why Gramps would leave a perfectly prime piece of real estate to a monkey in a suit was beyond me. And if that were the case, what was Roy grumbling about at the hospital, and why would he say Gramps owed him? Unless …

Gladys said Mr. Entwhistle. I assumed she meant Roy, but could she have been talking about Ed when she overheard that argument? I made a mental note to ask her. Then I put that aside for a minute and sucked up my pride.

"Listen, do you have any friends at the DMV?"

Parker smiled wide.

23

*T*hor and I ate our sandwiches on the curb outside of Muddy Waters. He happily scarfed down the roast beef as I prayed to the automobile fairies to fix my cousin's car.

When I turned the key, it sounded like a garbage can quartet.

Honk, honk, flash, pop, scrape, swish!

"Son of twatwaffle." I banged my hands on the steering and bent down to tinker with the knobs.

Pretty sure that made it worse.

There was only one place to go.

I didn't have to honk the horn as I swung into the parking lot of Tony's garage because it was still honking itself. Tony was bent over the hood of an old muscle car, a red towel waving from the back pocket of his jeans. When he heard the noise, he unfolded himself from the hood and looked behind him.

Throwing the car into park, I yelled out the window, "I have a problem."

Tony wiped his hands on the towel and shouted

something.

"What?" I asked.

"*Turn it off!*"

I nodded and cut the motor.

A wide grin spread across his face as he approached the Trans Am. He gave Thor a pat on the head, and the dog nuzzled his hand. "What did you do?"

My head was shaking vigorously before I even stepped out of the car, and Tony lifted the seat forward so Thor could jump out.

"Oh no. This is not my fault. You restored this thing."

"Yeah, and it's not all paid for yet, so what did you do?"

I crossed my arms defiantly. "That thing is possessed, I swear. It has a mind of its own."

Tony laughed. "You're pissing yourself, aren't you?"

I smirked at him. "Just fix it."

Tony could identify what was wrong with a car in less than ten minutes. I was confident he could fix the demon mobile and my weekend from hell would resume in no time.

He stuck his head through the window and examined the dashboard. "Probably a short in the wiring. Shouldn't take long. Tell me what happened."

I explained to him how the car decided to test out all its own parts.

"Let me pull it into the shop." Tony got behind the wheel and fired up the engine.

I plugged my ears. He sat there with it idling for a minute. Then there was sweet silence.

"So it comes and goes?" he asked, still looking at the dashboard.

"Uh, I don't know. It just happened twice."

He pulled the car into the garage and left the door wide open. Then he grabbed a few tools from a long, metal workbench and anchored himself on the front floorboard. I dragged a rickety stool over, sat down, and watched.

"So how's my ex-wife and my ex-dog?" he asked.

I laughed. "The dog is good. He's keeping me company for a few days. The wife is the same."

"You talk to her yet?"

"Not yet, Tony. But I will." *As long as she lets me live after this.*

"Thanks."

He fiddled with the wires for a while.

"Tony, Cin told me that Thor drank some antifreeze once."

Tony moaned. "That dog. He would eat his own toes if you let him."

I'd have to remember that.

"How did you know what was wrong with him?"

"I saw him do it." He unscrewed the dashboard.

"Oh. So you knew it was lethal? That it wouldn't just make him sick?"

"Yeah, I knew I had to get him to the vet. It tastes sweet, so they like it. Now they make it where it's safe for pets, though."

"They do?"

"Sure. There was even an article on it in the paper."

"There was? When?" I would have to ask Parker about that. Wonder who wrote it.

"Last week." He popped his head out. "Listen, Stacy, I can't find a thing wrong here. I'm going to drive it around the block. See what happens."

"Go for it."

Tony maneuvered into the driver's seat and backed the car out of the lot. I stood in the garage and watched. I didn't hear a thing as he drove away.

If there was an article on the toxicity of antifreeze in the newspaper, then anyone could have thought to slip it to Gramps. It probably listed the symptoms, too. Stumbling, disoriented, slurred speech, nausea. There were a handful of people at dinner that night. I didn't know if Gramps went anywhere after. What if he did? Somewhere he didn't want anyone to know about?

The fumes in the garage began to strangle my thoughts so I stepped out for some air. The aroma of motor oil made me want to vomit, but to Cinnamon it was perfume. I was wishing she and Tony could work things out as he coasted back to the garage.

"Nothing." He exited the car.

"What do you mean nothing?"

He shrugged. "Seems fine now." Thor was sitting next to me, and we exchanged a look. He seemed as perplexed as I was.

"Let's see." I hopped in and twisted the key. The engine revved and that was all. No other action. What if I drove it? I backed down the driveway and onto the street.

More fireworks.

A U-turn got me back into the lot. Tony was leaning over the silver car when I got there.

"It's your problem now. I'm leaving it here." I tossed the keys on the seat.

"Oh, she won't like that." Tony shook his head.

"She won't like *that*." I pointed behind me. "What are you working on by the way?"

Tony turned to look at his project. "*That* is a 1968 Oldsmobile 442 W30 convertible." He grinned. "Your cousin's dream car. They're insanely expensive, but I finally found one that was in bad shape on Craigslist. I'm gonna restore it. Sold my Camaro to do it."

The body was rusted, it had no tires, and the windshield was cracked. Looked like a piece of junk to me, but, what did I know?

Tony's eyes misted for a moment. I placed my hand on his. "I'll talk to her, Tony."

He nodded. "You're going to leave the Trans here?" He wiped his fingers and nodded to Cin's car.

"Yep. I'll drive her over later to pick it up. Thanks for your help." I took a few steps in the direction of the sidewalk, and Thor trotted alongside me.

Tony called, "Wait a sec, I'll give you, er, two a ride."

I looked at Thor. "What do you think, big guy? Want to ride with Tony?"

Thor woofed. "I guess that's a yes. Thanks."

A few minutes later, I climbed into the passenger seat of an SUV. Thor leapt into the back seat and stuck his head out the window. "So do you use that safe antifreeze now?"

Tony nodded and fiddled with the radio. He took the back exit out of the garage, and we were headed down an alley when I saw a familiar face. Two, actually. Gretchen and Doctor Gates.

"Stop the car." I sunk down into the seat. "Tell me what you see."

"What the hell are you doing?"

"Just tell me what you see, Tony."

"I see two people talking. A man and a woman."

"Just talking? Anything else?"

"No. Can we go? This is kinda freaky."

"Get the license plate on the car, and then yes, we can."

Gretchen was sitting in the driver's seat as we sailed by, so maybe it was her car. I quickly snapped a pic of the plate and texted it to Parker, asking him to call in a favor to his friend.

Tony pulled up to the police station, and I asked him to take Thor to the cottage, explaining he could get the key from Fiona. I thanked him and he drove off, Thor's large, brown eyes staring after me. The Great Dane gave one loud wail of protest before the car faded from view.

I took the steps two at a time and pushed through the door.

There was no one at the front desk when I got there, so I rang the bell.

A few seconds later, Birdie circled around the corner.

"Hello, Anastasia." She frowned. "You have a bruise. I may have something for that in my chambers."

Chambers? "Birdie." I swung through the little half-gate. "What are you doing? You can't just walk around the place like you own it."

She was eating a chocolate donut. "Why not?"

Why not?

"Because you are … Ugh! Never mind. Come on." I tugged her elbow, leading her down the hall to her cell.

When we got there, I thought I was staring at a mirage.

It could have passed for a suite at the Hilton. A fern stood in the corner, books were scattered across the nightstand, there was a blow-up bed adorned with a duvet and throw pillows, a painting of the moon phases on the wall, and a tufted bench on the side of the bed. It was nicer than my apartment in Chicago. All she needed was a wet bar and a disco ball.

I didn't realize my mouth was wide open until she said, "Don't gape."

I slowly swiveled all the way around. "How did you …"

Ignoring my question, Birdie sat on the bench. "Did you bring me a change of clothes? I asked Fiona to send you with a change of clothes." She licked the frosting from her donut.

"No, Birdie, I'm sorry. Fiona was a little busy this morning."

As were we all.

"I could use a change of clothes. It would brighten up my day. I've had this thing on forever." She frowned at her blouse and skirt as if they had been fished from a dumpster.

I sat on the bed. "I'll bring you some clothes later. Right now—"

"But, I could use some freshening up *now*." She punched her lip into a pout. "Perhaps you could run to that new boutique that opened up next to the bakery?"

I rolled my eyes. "You want me to go shopping? Forget it. Listen, Birdie—"

"I think it is the least you could do for your grandmother." She polished off the pastry and reached into the nightstand for a napkin.

She sure knew how to lay on the guilt. "All right. Stop with the clothes. Here." I stood up, unzipped my sweatshirt, then tossed it on her lap. The tee shirt came off next. Birdie smiled.

"You happy? Now give me your damn shirt so I can talk to you."

Birdie unbuttoned her blouse and handed it to me. Just as I turned to slip my arms through the sleeves, I heard, "Afternoon, ladies."

I glanced up at Leo.

And me, shooting him a full frontal in my white lace bra.

Could a person actually die from embarrassment?

Spinning around, I buttoned the shirt as fast as I could. I think Leo must have been a little shocked because I heard him say, "Um, sorry, bye."

I shook my head at my grandmother. "Every time I see that man you make me look like a lunatic."

"Don't be ridiculous. You look fabulous." She filtered through the nightstand drawer again and produced a satin pouch.

I rubbed my eye so it wouldn't twitch. "We need to talk."

A quick peer down the hall revealed we were as alone as we were going to get. I went back to the bed and sat down. Birdie added some water to the pouch.

"Did Ed deliver groceries that day of the dinner?"

"He delivers on Tuesdays and Fridays."

Another dizzy spell washed over me. I closed my eyes, but there were no pictures this time.

"Are you all right?" She dabbed the pouch against my bruise, squinting.

"Are you kidding? No, I am not all right." Although my bruise felt better already. I stood up and walked to the wall. A picture of a woman holding the Earth in the palm of her hand caught my attention. "I'm worried, frustrated, confused, scared. Plus, crazy things have been happening to me." I turned around. "And not par for the course crazy, either. Really weird stuff." Leaning against the wall, I put my hands behind my head.

"Like what?" Birdie asked softly.

"For starters, Cin's car is going bonkers on me. I'm afraid to drive it. The lights go on, wipers start up, radio blasts."

"Electrical surges?"

When she said that I thought about the blackout at the cottage. "I thought so, but Tony couldn't find anything wrong with the wires."

"What else?"

"I've had a few dizzy spells. And I keep seeing flashes of distant memories. Except I don't remember them."

"Visions?"

My eyes popped open. I was falling right into her trap. "No, Birdie, not visions."

She stood up and took a step forward. "Dreams that seem all too real? Feelings in the pit of your stomach, like you *know* something. Physical discomfort?"

"Cut it out." Now I'd done it. There was no backing up this train.

Grasping my shoulders, Birdie stared into my eyes. "My dear, this is what you were born for."

"What's behind door number two?"

24

"*B*irdie, please." I grabbed her hands. "We need to discuss some important business. Not this hocus pocus, abracadabra crap." I waved an imaginary wand.

Birdie slapped her palms on her thighs and shot arrows at me with her eyes. "How can you still deny what you are when it is staring you in the face?"

I crossed my arms. "What? What am I? A psychic witch? Because I gotta tell you, if that's what you think, I suck at it."

Birdie's face grew red and a tiny vein on her forehead throbbed. "Witches are *not* psychics. And magic is not mysterious. You know that. A witch is simply a person who practices magic. And what is the definition of magic?"

She planted her hands on her hips and waited for my response. I wasn't getting anywhere until I passed this test.

"Magic is the culmination of Energy and Will to bring about Change," I parroted.

"And who aids us in that?"

Us? What us?

She held her chin up and tapped her foot.

"All Nature and the Spirits," I said.

I toed the rug. Spirits. The pennies. I completely forgot about the pennies.

Birdie smiled. "To answer your question, Anastasia, no you are not psychic, not yet anyway. You are *sensitive*. Attuned to nature, the forces of energy and our spirit guides. If you want the responsibility," she added. "Turn your back on it and it dissipates."

Dissipates. Disappears. Like my mother.

My mother. I had to find out why she was still power of attorney for Gramps.

I met my grandmother's stare. "Turn my back on what? What responsibility?"

Birdie grabbed my hand. I could feel the warmth of her fingers penetrating my skin, my flesh, my bones. Her voice was steady, her eyes bright. "There exist only three, who avail their people. The Guardian of sacred truth, the Warrior in the heat of battle, and the Seeker of Justice, wherever she be."

I stared at her. So she didn't think I was the Ghost Whisperer. She thought I was Joan of Arc. "I'm guessing you think I'm the Seeker of Justice?"

"I know you are." Her voice was low and scratchy, like a casino junkie.

"How?" Best to humor her.

"It was in the Blessed Book my mother kept. A third generation child of the New World. I knew the minute your mother brought your father home."

I shook my head. "Simply because his name was Justice—"

Birdie held up her hand. "That's all for now." She walked over to the bench near the bars and sat down. A brown satin cushion was fastened to the top. "Now, what business do we need to discuss?"

I joined her and explained how I was still working on the bail money. She didn't seem to care one way or another. We discussed a few business dealings of Gramps' but she didn't know much about what took place after their divorce. She was surprised to hear that my mother was still named as power of attorney, but Gramps had always believed she would come home one day. Perhaps, Birdie said, that was his way of holding onto that faith. Then I asked what she thought about Roy and Ed Entwhistle, hoping to gain further insight into their relationship with Gramps.

"Your grandfather took in every stray dog, helped whomever he could and I didn't object until that moron, Roy, nearly ruined us." She fluffed her hair with her hand.

"What did he do?"

"What did he do? Nothing." She threw her arms in the air. "The man had no ambition, no drive. He was willing to sit and watch his ship sink, and he tried to talk your grandfather into staying on deck with him. I never interfered with Oscar's business until then. If I hadn't, we would have lost everything."

But instead, Gramps gained a fortune. Maybe he thought he owed his success to Birdie. Perhaps that was the reason for the policy. And it was also possible that Roy resented Gramps and Birdie for his failures early on. He was doing fine in recent years, but what if Wildcat's proposal threatened his livelihood? Maybe Gramps was planning to kick Roy out and rent the space to his old war pal.

"Birdie, did you know that Gramps granted Ed the plaza and the land it's on in his will?"

She shook her head.

"Any idea why he would do that?"

"You'll have to ask him, Anastasia."

I decided against telling her the state he was in now. I

asked about Gretchen, and Birdie had never met her. Never even knew Pearl had a niece.

"What's Wildcat's angle?"

Disgust fell over her face like a veil. "I don't even know why Oscar keeps in contact with that beast. He saved your grandfather's life once during the war, but other than, he has no redeeming qualities."

Seemed she and Pearl agreed on that.

"You want to elaborate?"

Birdie rolled her eyes. "He has always been jealous of your grandfather. Wanted whatever it was he had and wasn't ashamed to take it. Success, money," she looked at me pointedly, "love."

I didn't like where this was headed. The last thing I wanted to hear about was the love lives of my grandparents. It was right above how a toilet functions as Things I Don't Want To Know.

"What are you talking about?"

"Haven't you ever known someone who weaseled their way into people's lives, sucking their souls out little by little?"

I had, actually. When I was a little girl, a playmate of mine would get so jealous of anything I got that she would steal it. I spent hours casting spells to find my lost things until I dreamt that she had taken them and buried them in her backyard. Being an only child, I took matters into my own hands and dug up her mother's freshly planted tulip bed. There, in the earth, was a Barbie doll, a slinky, a pair of clogs, and my pet rock. Actually, now that I think about it, that might have just been a rock. She wasn't allowed to play with me after that.

"Yes."

Birdie just blinked.

"So he's untrustworthy?"

She didn't respond.

If there was ever a question I never thought I would be forced to ask my grandmother it was this: "Did Wildcat try to steal *you*?"

Birdie balked. "Please. He couldn't handle me."

Who could?

So that left Pearl. Or some other woman.

Birdie wasn't positive, but she had her suspicions. And frankly, it would explain Pearl's attitude toward Gramps' old friend. We shelved that discussion, and I told Birdie I'd do everything I could to find the truth and promised to get the money to bail her out.

"Really, dear, don't bother. It's rather like a vacation. Besides, this will all be over soon enough."

Only Birdie would view jail like a vacation. Although, judging from the guests at the inn this weekend, I couldn't blame her.

The guests. That reminded me.

"Birdie, what's the Wild Woman package?"

A sly smile spread across her lips. "Why?"

"Because you have two of them tearing the place apart, and I'd like to channel their energy into something constructive. Or at least far away from me."

"Don't worry. The girls should have plenty of tasks to keep them busy the rest of the weekend. It's all in their packet in the room."

"Okay, but they said they had to report back to the She Woman Head Heathen. I'm guessing that would be you. So, then what?"

"Lolly or Fiona could take my place," Birdie said.

I thought about that. In theory, it sounded great. It was the application that concerned me.

Birdie saw my eye twitching. "Sweetheart, I'm not sure you're quite up to the job."

"What job?"

"Reintroducing a woman to her pagan roots."

She was right about that. My résumé listed absolutely no experience in pagan roots revival. That was a job for professionals.

Thank the Goddess. I kissed my grandmother's cheek and rose to leave.

Birdie grabbed my hand, deadly serious. "Learn to recognize the signs. There are no accidents. Every feeling you get, every inclination, every physicality has specific meaning." She clutched my hand tighter. "And if you ever feel nauseous, I want you to be extremely careful."

"Why?"

"Because that signifies harmful intent."

"Good to know."

I made my way to the gate and turned to wave good-bye. Birdie waved back. Just as I was about to curve the corner, she called me, "Oh, and, Anastasia?"

I turned back around. "Yes?"

"Follow the pennies. They hold the truth. Find the truth, find the perpetrator."

"How did you ..."

Birdie smiled like a woman who's fortune cookie just came true.

Around the corner, I bumped into Gus carrying a Dungeons and Dragons game. "Oh, hey, Stacy."

"Hey, Gus, whatcha got there?"

"Dungeons and Dragons. Your grandma and I have been playing'. She's real good."

"I bet she is. Have fun."

Somehow I couldn't picture that scenario in any Chicago precinct.

Leo was at his desk when I reached the lobby. He looked up and smiled when he saw me. "How'd the fashion show go?"

"Very funny," I said.

"I didn't know you could be so ... cat like. Very agile, that move back there." He grinned at me and waggled his eyebrows.

"That's right. But I have sharp claws."

He drank me in and scratched his head.

"Um, you've got things a little mixed up there." He waved a finger at the blouse.

Looking down, I discovered two buttons weren't fastened at all and the rest of them were out of order. Cripes, now he thought I couldn't even dress myself.

"I was going for a new look. Bag lady chic. Do you like it?" I curtsied.

Leo laughed. "Why don't you come over here and have a seat. I'd like to ask you a few questions."

I crossed to the desk and pulled up a chair.

"Can I get you some coffee?" he asked.

I shook my head and sat.

Leo's tee shirt hugged his skin, and his face was freshly shaven. He looked good enough to eat.

"So, how's the investigation going?" I asked when he didn't say anything.

"That's what I was gonna say." His fierce gaze drilled into me and my toes curled. Damn, he was sexy.

I sat back, pretending to be disinterested. "What do you mean?"

"Look, I know you and the Grand Poobah are cooking up

something and I want to know what it is." Leo hinged forward and folded his hands together.

"I don't know what you're talking about."

"Well, something's going on."

I gave him my Little Bo Peep stare.

He stared back, holding my gaze, and I wanted to crawl across the desk and straddle his lap. "Don't play innocent with me, Stacy, I've seen your caped crusader costume."

No denying that.

"Halloween's coming up," I lied. "Just trying out the ensemble."

Narrowing his eyes, Leo drummed his fingers on the desk. I folded my hands in my lap and beamed like an influencer getting paid more than she's worth.

"Fine. The truth is, no one in this town will talk to me, and the few who do talk claim your grandfather is a saint, your grandmother is a martyr, and I'm an asshole."

That was Amethyst for you. Single out the most normal person in the crowd and ostracize him.

"Leo, I feel for you, but I don't know what I'm supposed to do about that."

"For one thing, you could stay out of this. We're looking at an attempted murder and whoever did it might not be too thrilled at some reporter asking questions."

I clamped my mouth shut.

"Stacy, I want to get to the bottom of this. And I want your grandmother out of my jail cell. She's turning the place into a sleep-away camp and she doesn't listen to a damn word I say."

"Then let her go."

"I can't do that. She signed a confession and bond has been set. It's up to a judge at a preliminary hearing now."

"And how long can that take?"

"A few days, maybe more."

I took a long, hard look at the chief of police. He didn't grow up in Amethyst. Didn't understand which way the wheels spun in a small town, let alone a small town that should be located in the middle of the Bermuda Triangle. But maybe that was a good thing. Leo was smart, I knew that. He could probably be objective. If anyone could take in the big picture and paint it with a fresh perspective it was him. But what if he screwed up? It was my family on the line. My future. My past. What did he care if it all went to pot?

Leo studied me like a lion studies an injured gazelle. He knew I was deciding which path to run down. He was deciding when to pounce.

He softened then, took my hands in his. The heat generated from that simple gesture made me feel, if only for a moment, safe. We locked eyes, and I tried to capture the emotion behind his. I saw a flash of frustration, and then, sincerity. "All I want is to catch the real baddie."

Perhaps it was because I felt I could trust him. Or maybe it was because he had sexy, kissable lips and I had been going through a dry spell. Either way, I took a deep breath and told Leo what little I had learned so far about Ed and Roy Entwhistle, Wildcat, Pearl, the policy, the power of attorney. Most of it, he already knew, but he wrote everything down anyway. I also told him Gramps had been given the wrong drug.

Leo sat back and shook his head. "None of this adds up."

"There's something else."

"What?"

"Well, I think someone was in the cottage that night you came by."

"Someone broke in?"

I thought about that. I didn't lock the door, so technically, there wouldn't be a sign of a break in.

"The door was unlocked, but someone was there. Ransacked the place."

"How can you be sure?"

I saw a spiderweb on the door and chills ran down my spine.

"Well, the place was a mess when I got home the other night. I brought Cin's dog home with me, and I went out and—"

"Wait a sec. Don't you have a cat?"

"Yes."

"You left a strange dog and cat together alone on the first night?"

"Well, I bought them drinks first. What's your point?"

Leo ignored that last comment. "Couldn't that be why the place was trashed? The dog was chasing the cat?"

I wrinkled my nose. "Well, that's what I thought, but I also found a scrap of clothing on the back door. Like it had torn from someone's shirt. And Thor was chewing on a piece of it, too."

So there.

"Uh huh." A skeptical look crossed his face. "Don't you have a carpenter over there fixing a roof? Maybe he went in for a glass of water one day and tore his shirt."

I never thought of that. I hadn't even opened the back door of the cottage before that. I wouldn't have thought to look there if it weren't for Thor's paw prints.

Leo asked, "Did you see footprints? It was storming the other night."

"No." But I knew what I felt. Or had Birdie finally gotten to me?

I feigned interest in a hangnail. *Was* someone there? What about the mirror? Guess it could have been Chance.

But why would he screw around like that? Now I felt like an idiot.

Leo walked around the desk and leaned against it. "It just seems strange that someone would go into the cottage when you weren't there just to mess it up. Nothing was taken. Right?" He folded his hands in his lap.

I nodded.

"But, seriously, I do want you to be careful. Don't make any moves without talking to me, agreed?"

"Agreed."

"And if you hear anything, I would appreciate it if you kept me in the loop." He pulled out a business card and handed it to me. "Call me day or night. For anything."

"Actually, I am concerned about something else."

"Shoot."

"Pearl's niece. There's something about her."

"How do you mean?"

"I get the feeling she's up to something, that's all."

"Well, I can't go around arresting people on feelings, Stacy. But if you hear or see anything concrete, let me know. If it eases your mind, I did question her. She wasn't anywhere near your grandfather Wednesday night."

"Thanks." I stood up and held out my hand.

Leo shook it. Then he put his other hand over mine. "Why don't I come by later and check out the cottage? We'll see if someone really did break in. I'll even bring dinner. You like pepperoni?"

Was that a double entendre? I raised my eyebrows. Hmm. Maybe I had another reason to stick around town.

"I do."

25

*I*t was still warm when I left the station, but the sun was hidden behind a massive cloud. I hadn't been home in a while, and I suspected if I didn't show up with some food for Thor, I would regret it.

The Black Opal wasn't far from the station, so I footed it over to Emerald Avenue and weaved around to Main Street. I needed to touch base with my cousin. Fill her in and get some dog food. What did a dog that size eat anyway? Tuna fish? Chicken? An entire side of beef? I also planned to call Chance and ask why the hell my grandfather trusted him with his estate. And why didn't anyone think to mention it to me?

The streets were full of tourists enjoying the fall colors. On the corner was an acoustic guitar musician singing a Bob Dylan tune, and the nutty scent of fresh popcorn drifted through him.

Scully was sitting at the bar when I got there. No sign of Cin, just two guys shooting pool in the back room.

"Hey, Scully." I slid onto the stool next to him. "You keeping out of trouble?"

Scully cocked his head toward me, his face wrinkled up like a tree trunk. "What?" He sounded like a drunken pirate.

"I said, are you keeping out of trouble?" I asked a little louder.

"Am I sleeping with Mrs. Dougal?"

Yeah, that's what I asked.

I leaned in closer and shouted, "Are you keeping out of trouble?"

"Jeez, Stacy, I can hear you all the way in the back," Cinnamon yelled as she rounded the corner.

"I'm not deaf," Scully grouched.

Cinnamon unloaded the case of beer she was carrying onto the cooler and parked a hand on her hip. "So what's the latest?"

"Our grandmother thinks that I can single-handedly figure out who tried to poison Gramps *and* wrangle her out of a false confession because I am—get this—the Seeker of Justice."

"Well …" Cin skirted around to the front of the bar, "aren't you?"

"Are you trying to send me over the edge? Because I am this close to losing my cool." I made a measurement with my thumb and index finger.

Cin laughed. "Well, you are a reporter, right? Don't you try to seek justice through your work?"

"That's different."

"How?"

The two guys shooting pool waved to her as they walked out. She waved back.

"Because there I use facts, interviews, records. She wants me to use 'magic'." I held my hands up and made quotation signs with my fingers. "Oh, and of course, the spirit guides."

"Spirit guides?"

"Yes, apparently they never heard of inflation because they're leaving me messages in pennies."

"Well, you said you've been finding them everywhere."

I gaped at Cin. "Since when are you on her side?"

She shrugged.

Sighing, I ran my fingers through my hair. "This is too important, Cin." I met her gaze and wrinkled my brow. "I couldn't save my father. And when he died, I lost a little bit of my mother every day until she took off with no forwarding address." I cast my eyes down at the floor. "What if I can't save Gramps *or* Birdie?"

In that moment, I realized I might be in Amethyst longer than I thought.

Cinnamon was about to say something when the door swung open and in walked a skinny man with long, curly hair carrying a life-sized stuffed gorilla. The guy took a seat at the bar and pulled one up for the gorilla. The gorilla didn't sit down. This seemed to agitate the man who forced the gorilla into its seat.

My mouth dropped open. "Are you freaking kidding me?" I stared at Cin.

She lifted a finger. "Hang on."

She approached the man who ordered two Jack and Cokes. Cinnamon made the drinks and slid them in front of the guy who passed one to the gorilla.

She didn't bat an eyelash as he handed her some bills. She rang up the drinks and walked back over to me.

"Regular?" I asked.

"He cooks over at the Palace."

"Must cost a fortune in hair nets."

She looked at me, and we erupted with laughter.

The guy didn't seem to notice as he sipped his drink.

I tapped the bar. "Hey, I need dog food."

"I just bought a forty pound bag. It's in the back."

I wrinkled my nose.

"I'll help you carry it," she said.

"Well, I walked here."

"Okay. So go get the Trans Am, leave it here, and I'll bring the food by later."

I was so not looking forward to this conversation.

"That might be difficult."

"Why?" Cin questioned, narrowing her eyes at me.

Maybe if I spoke fast she wouldn't hear me. Or hit me. "So here's the thing. The car was acting a little funny and I—"

"What do you mean 'funny'?" Her face was pinched like she had eaten a lemon slice.

"I think it has a wiring problem. Anyway, I took it to Tony and—"

She put her hand right in my face. "Whoa, whoa, whoa. Say that again?"

I slapped her hand away, annoyed. "What was I supposed to do? He can fix it."

"I would have taken care of it."

"You know what? That man loves you. Yes, he made a really big mistake, but he would do anything to make it up to you. Doesn't he deserve a second chance?"

Cinnamon shook her head. "I can't believe you're saying this. After what he did."

Before I could answer her we heard a loud crash.

We both turned to find the skinny guy on top of the gorilla, beating the crap out of it.

"Pete," Cin shouted, and ran over to the scene.

I followed.

Cin reached down to grab Pete's arm, but he was really wailing on the thing. "When I buy you a drink, you better drink it," he screamed to the gorilla.

I went over to help, and my head started spinning. Cin saw this as an opportunity to continue our argument.

"How could you take his side?"

Black nylon fur flew all over the place.

"I'm not taking his side," I tried to grab Pete's other arm, but the guy was quick.

Scully moved two seats down and snagged the Jack and Coke from the bar. The other one was splashed across the floor.

Pete was wiggling in Cinnamon's grasp.

"After what he did. And with her," Cin yelled at me, wrestling with Pete. She seemed to be winning over on that side.

My side wasn't going so well. He was scrappy for a guy with the girth of a toothpick. He got in a good eye poke, and I yelped before I slammed his shoulder forward, knotting his hands together. Cin stuck her knee in his back. The face of the stuffed animal was mocking me, but then it became Tony's face. His eyes were closed, asleep. And then Monique's face, laughing.

These partial visions were starting to grate on my nerves. Didn't the spirits understand that I would figure out their message a lot quicker without having to buy a vowel?

Pete stopped squirming, and I loosened my grip. "Just talk to him. Go there and talk, Cinnamon. You owe that to yourself."

We both yanked Pete off of his friend and hoisted him to his feet. Cin was sweating, and my borrowed blouse was torn and still mis-buttoned.

Cin glared at me. "Fine. I'll talk to him." She wiped her forehead with the back of her arm.

I walked over to her and gave her a hug. "Cinnamon spice and everything nice," I sang and patted her head.

"I hate it when you say that."

Pete sat back on the barstool. "Hey, who took my drink?"

Scully scooted farther down, chugging the Jack and Coke.

And before I could fill her in on the latest in the family news, twenty people walked into the bar.

"Aw hell. Stacy, call Bay. His number is next to the phone, top of the list. Tell him I need help. You go take care of Thor and we'll talk later. There's some canned food behind the bar, too."

The food had a picture of a gray wolf and the size of the can told me that just one might piss off a dog the size of Thor, so I grabbed eight of them. The bartender said he'd be at the Opal in ten minutes, and I headed back to the Geraghty cottage.

A LONG "MEEEEOOOOOOOOOOWWWWWW" followed by a deep "woof" greeted me.

Clearly, I was neglecting my roommates. I scratched Thor behind the ears, patted Moonlight on the behind, and made a pit stop in the bathroom.

After washing up, I ran a comb through my hair, and went into the bedroom for a fresh shirt. I wiggled into a turtleneck that hugged my chest. I hadn't had any run-ins with pork or pastry products today, so I thought I'd risk applying a little makeup. I ran eyeliner on my lids, brushed on some blush, layered mascara on my lashes, and painted my lips. I had to put the hat back on because my hair was flattened to my head.

Moonlight jumped on the counter and demanded food,

so I popped open a can of tuna and spooned it into a small bowl. He didn't even wait for me to finish before scarfing down the fish.

Thor licked his giant snout, waiting for his turn. His huge eyes were glued to my every move as I rifled through the cabinets, searching for a bowl the size of a hot tub.

Thor wagged his tail as I emptied three cans into a ceramic bowl and placed it on a side table. Then I poured him fresh water and set it on the porch so he could take care of business. After that, I hopped into the Jeep and pointed it toward the hospital.

26

*N*o one was at the front desk when I entered the revolving door, which was disappointing. I wanted to speak to Lynn about what she had said earlier. Maybe I could catch her later.

The door to Gramps' room was closed. "Hi, Pearl." I knocked softly, and she invited me in.

Pearl glanced up, her face drawn like she hadn't slept in days. "Hi, sweetheart."

"How is he?" I asked, nodding to Gramps.

"Oh, well, he's still sleeping, you know," she said. "He should wake up soon, they tell me."

I walked over to the bed and leaned in to kiss my grandfather's cheek. Then I lifted my head to meet Pearl's eyes.

"Can I buy you a cup of coffee?" I asked.

Pearl hesitated. Then she brightened. "I suppose I could use a pick-me-up."

We traveled down the hall to the elevator and walked toward the cafeteria. There were two registers in the center of the room. The coffee bar was closest to the door and we headed toward it.

"Pearl, I want to talk to you about Gramps. There are some questions I have that I'm hoping you can answer."

"Sure, dear. What would you like to know?"

Grabbing two paper cups, I poured hot coffee into each, then handed one to Pearl.

"For starters, I was wondering where he might have gone after the Geraghty dinner."

"Home, I suppose."

"You mean you don't know?"

"I like to check in at the restaurant. Close things up. Do paperwork. But Oscar always goes straight home after those meals. Your grandmother has a way of zapping his energy." She made a visible attempt not to roll her eyes, but one of them went rogue.

"About what time did he get sick?"

Pearl watched me as she poured cream into her cup. "I know you don't want to hear this, Stacy, but the only person who would do this to your grandfather is your grandmother."

I sighed. "Please, Pearl."

She sighed. "About ten o'clock I noticed something was wrong. We made it downstairs, and I called Eddie. He helped me put Oscar in the car."

"Eddie?" *Holy hell.* "Ed Entwhistle?"

Pearl licked her lips nervously. She skipped a beat before responding.

"Yes. He helps out from time to time. Delivers supplies to the restaurant whenever I run out of something. Ed would be closing the store, at that time, you see, so I thought he could just swing on by."

"Why wouldn't you call an ambulance?"

"I didn't think it was that serious," she said softly. "I thought maybe he had too much to drink at dinner. But I wasn't certain. Maybe he ate something that disagreed with him. So I thought it best to get him checked out, but it wasn't as if he was unconscious or anything."

"I understand that Ed is in Gramps' will."

"Where did you hear that, dear?"

I noticed it wasn't a denial. I didn't answer her. Just waited.

She gave a little nervous laugh. "You know Oscar. Generous to a fault. Hands out dollar bills like tissues. The man sure knows how to make a buck, he just has no idea how to save one." Her tone held a hint of bitterness.

That explanation didn't satisfy the question. I got the feeling there was something more to the relationship, but Pearl wasn't willing to enlighten me. We sat down at a small table and sipped our coffee.

"So this deal with Wildcat. How does Gramps feel about it?"

She frowned. "I couldn't say. Your grandfather's business is his own."

Behind her, the big bay window showed the sky darkening. Another storm brewing.

"Is there anything else you can think of that might help?"

"I already told the police everything I know."

"What about an insurance policy or another property he might have willed to someone?" I asked as nonchalantly as I could.

Pearl's head snapped up. "Why would he need an insurance policy? He had plenty of money to leave to his family."

Unless his family couldn't find that money. Or someone else got to it first. Or it was all gone. Pearl's response led me to believe that she didn't know about the policy for Birdie. I wondered if she knew about Chance being listed as the power of attorney. I decided it might not be a good idea to tell her since her behavior was curious to me. At that point, I wasn't certain who to trust.

"It sure is lucky your niece was able to get away and help out. Where did you say she was from?"

"Oh, um, she's from out west."

"And what does she do?"

She glanced down at her coffee. "Accounting."

"So she's helping with scheduling, placing orders, that kind of thing?"

"That's right."

"What about the finances?"

"A little bit."

"Is she your sister's daughter?"

Pearl scooted her chair out, and as she did her coffee tumbled, but I managed to upright it. "Stacy, I should get back to Oscar."

As she hurried away, I wondered why she was lying to me.

27

J left the hospital with little more information than I went in with and it was beginning to concern me. The more questions I asked the less answers I got. The clouds were threatening to unleash rain at any minute as the Jeep engine turned over. There was no umbrella in the backseat, just a rumpled bag from the fast food place I stopped at on my trip out here.

Next on my list of things to check into was the loft Gramps shared with Pearl. I had to find out what she was hiding. No one else seemed to know anything about this niece of hers, and if she was elbow deep in my grandfather's finances, you bet I wanted some details. Plus, I figured it was safer to find out what hand Ed played in all of this by digging through their files rather than ask him directly. Pearl, clearly, was not offering up any information on his relationship with Gramps. Stan might know more if I asked the right questions. I hated the thought of stepping back into that house with Cruella de Vil guarding the door, but Gramps did mention that Stan was a good friend, not just his lawyer.

I snapped the windshield wipers into play as the rain swooshed down. The wind rocked the Jeep, and I pumped the gas, hoping to get home before the storm hit.

That was when my tire blew out.

The Jeep bumped and bounced along the side of the road before coming to a stop. Climbing out, I saw that the right rear tire was like a deflated balloon. There was no spare.

I started back around the car to climb in and call for help as a semi blew past at sixty miles an hour, showering me with rain water, mud, and moldy leaves. I used my hand to squeegee my face, said a few curse words, and opened the door. Sticking to the mud that covered the handle was a penny. The date was more recent.

I piled back in the car, reached for my cell phone, and dialed the Opal, hoping my cousin or her bartender, Bay, would pick me up.

"Black Opal," Cinnamon answered. I could barely hear her over the roar of the jukebox and the chatter of the crowd.

"Hey, it's—" Beep. Click.

I checked the phone. *Low battery. Terrific.*

Dialed again.

"Black Opal."

"Cin, hi, it's—" Beep. Click.

Why? Why was this happening to me?

I tried one more time.

"Who the hell is it?" Cinnamon shouted.

I tried to talk fast. "Stacy—" Beep. Click. Dead.

Perfect.

Well, this was a small town. Any minute now someone would drive by and stop.

I fumbled for a towel in the backseat and came up empty. Then I waited. And waited.

Any minute now never came.

The nearest gas station was half a mile down the highway. I could walk there, maybe borrow a phone and get someone to pick me up. I flipped the penny over in my hand. It was the year I graduated from high school. The year I lost my virginity to Chance.

But what would that matter?

Thunder cracked the sky and lightning illuminated the Jeep. Uh-oh. Thor was probably digging a hole underneath my bed right about now.

I sat there for a few minutes, working up the courage to brave the wind and rain. Tucking the penny in the pocket of my jeans, I gave myself a pep talk.

It's just a little rain, Stacy. You won't melt. Suck it up.

I grabbed my keys and locked the Jeep, then trotted down the road as quickly as I could.

Within five minutes I was soaked to the bone and I still couldn't see the damn gas station. A carload of kids drove by, beeping and honking, hanging out the window and making obscene comments. Great. Saturday night before Halloween. Every college student was on the road, looking for trouble.

And I was sporting nipples that could cut glass.

I hugged my arms around my chest and walked faster.

Tires screeched behind me then, and a car skidded on the gravel, pelting me with tiny rocks.

I turned around.

"Hey, baby, need a ride?"

The guy hanging out the window acted like he'd just won a beer-guzzling contest. His face was pockmarked and his words slurred. He couldn't have been twenty years old, and from the inflection in his voice, I figured he wasn't aiming to win a Boy Scout badge.

"I'm okay. Thanks." I turned around to run.

Which might have gone fine except for the ditch. I did a nose dive right into it.

A car door slammed behind me as I extracted myself from the mud. I was pretty sure I had landed in a used wad of gum, but I had bigger problems as I heard a second door slam and realized the only place to hide was a plowed down cornfield.

"Come on, baby, we just want to party. Don't you like to party?" asked the beer guzzler.

I turned. Three of them now, coming toward me.

"Yeah," said another guy, built like a tank. "We know a great place to party.

My stomach did a two-step. I felt sick. Nauseous. Birdie warned about nauseous. Harmful intent.

Oh, hell.

I backed up carefully like you would if you met a rattlesnake.

Years ago, I had learned enough martial arts and self-defense to apply for an Avenger position. But after I turned my back on magic, and all that came with it, those skills faded, too. Although I hadn't tested them out recently. So this could go either way, but I wouldn't have bet money on me.

My cell phone was still in my coat, so I pulled it out. "Actually, boys, I was just about to call the police. See, my Great Dane is loose and I came out here to look for him. He likes to hunt the coyotes that live in the hills. Here, Killer," I called, looking around and whistling.

"Man, I hate dogs," grumbled the tank.

"Shut up, Jim," hissed his friend. "If that phone worked she wouldn't be out here by herself in the rain."

The little jacknut was smarter than he looked. I glanced around for a rock, a stick, anything to use as a weapon.

They all stepped closer.

I didn't know if these creeps had it in them to hurt me, but they were young, big, and drunk. And I was cold, dirty, and waterlogged.

I summoned my deepest, scariest goddess voice and blared, "Back the hell up!" I fumbled in my pocket for a bluff. "I swear I'll mace you so damned fast you won't be able to find your dicks in the dark for a week."

Cinnamon was rubbing off on me.

Keys. I did have keys, and if I jammed them just right, I could take out an eye, an eardrum, or a scrotum. I tucked the keys between my fingers, one by one, still in the jacket. Improvised brass knuckles. I was about to brandish my fist when, to my surprise, two of the punks held their hands in the air.

"Take it easy," one of them said. "We're just playing." He thumbed behind him. "Want a ride."

"Not even a little."

No one moved until a truck barreled over the center divider. We all swung our heads toward it. The driver did a U-turn and careened onto the shoulder in front of Monkey See, Monkey Do, and Monkey Dumbass.

I didn't recognize the vehicle, but I recognized the driver.

Chance hopped out, a wrench in his hand. "I'll give you all precisely two seconds to get in your car and get the hell out of here before I scatter little pieces of you across the highway." His voice was totally calm. Like he wouldn't hesitate to impale any one of them. I was impressed. And a little turned on.

The boys chose option number one.

I couldn't blame them. Chance resembled a bull when he was angry.

"You okay?" he asked.

"Yeah. Thanks."

"Come on. Get in the truck and I'll take you home." He guided me to his pickup, opened the door, and helped me in.

"Here, put this on." He reached into the backseat and pulled out a warm, flannel shirt and draped it around my soggy shoulders.

I thanked him and slid my hands through the sleeves.

"Do you know those guys?" I asked.

"No. Must be tourists."

I nodded.

"Stace, you're shaking. Let's get you into some warm clothes."

Chance looped around Route 20 and headed for the cottage.

"Want to tell me what happened?" he inquired.

I sighed. "I was on my way home from the hospital when the stupid Jeep got a flat."

Chance shifted his eyes to me.

"Don't say it," I warned. He must have told me a hundred times to replace that spare when I bought it.

That was the thing with Chance. He was always right. It was his most irritating quality.

"How's your grandfather?" he asked as he pulled onto Lunar Lane.

"He should come out of it any day."

"I'm glad." He coasted up the driveway, and I noticed the rain had let up a little.

"You want a cup of coffee?" I wondered how I was going to approach him about the power of attorney thing.

"That would be great." He cut the engine, and we both got out of the truck and walked to the cottage door.

I didn't see Thor when I let us in.

Moonlight was snuggled on the couch. Everything else seemed in place.

I put a pot of coffee on and told Chance I'd be right back. I washed my face in the bathroom, removed my soiled shirt and hat, and wrapped the flannel back around me. I grabbed some sweats from a hook behind the bathroom door and slid into them.

When I came out, the radio was playing and Chance handed me a steaming mug.

I decided to get right down to business. "Chance, why didn't you mention that my grandfather named you as power of attorney to his estate?"

He tilted his head, raised his eyebrows. "I guess it never came up. Why? Does that bother you?"

"I just wondered why you didn't mention it."

"I didn't think it was important. It was a long time ago."

Didn't Stan imply this was a recent decision?

"How long ago?"

Chance shrugged. "A few years. You were still in college, he thought Cinnamon was too young for that responsibility, Pearl wasn't even living with him yet, and Birdie ... well, they have their own special relationship, so he didn't mention anything to me about why he didn't appoint Birdie."

"So you're saying that when my mother never returned home, he decided you should be the one to control his estate should anything happen to him?"

Chance darted his eyes away, took a sip of coffee. "I think

he assumed you would come back here after you got your degree. That ..." He dropped his thought, hesitated.

"What?" I asked.

"Jeez, you're going to make me say it, aren't you?"

"Say what?"

Chance let loose a heavy sigh and cast his eyes down as he spoke. "Oscar had this idea that you and I would end up together. He figured by the time it would matter, I would be ... family."

An incredibly uncomfortable silence followed as we stood there listening to Led Zeppelin.

"Well, there's a light in your eye that keeps shining, like a star that can't wait for night. I hate to think I been blinded, baby. Why can't I see you tonight?"

Chance, thankfully, changed the subject. "You going to the festival tomorrow?"

Halloween was bigger than Christmas in Amethyst. Thousands of people showed up for the two-hour parade down Main Street, and the locals celebrated long after. I hadn't given it much thought. The aunts were likely cooking up something for the Samhain celebration since they personally hosted the event. It was held in the thick woods behind the house.

"I'm not sure." I sipped my hot coffee. Cream, one sugar. He remembered just how I liked it.

"Well, if you decide to come, look for me. I'll be dressed as Zorro."

I smiled at that. "Maybe I will if I can figure out this mess with Gramps."

Chance set his coffee down. "Stacy, I don't think it's a good idea what you're doing. Poking around into people's business. It could be dangerous."

"Well, I'm sure you don't, but you don't get to make those decisions for me anymore."

Chance looked shocked. "What do you mean, 'anymore'? If anything, you were the one who was always trying to protect me."

A memory flashed through my mind. A little boy picking on another little boy. Chance sticking up for the victim. The bully punching Chance in the stomach. Me bespelling the bully's locker so that when he opened it, he would stick to it the rest of the day. They had to call the fire department. A lot of the kid's victims took advantage of his immobility.

"I don't need rescuing."

He raised an eyebrow at me.

"Okay, so I needed a little rescuing today, but, you know, in general."

Smiling, Chance walked around the counter. He put his hands on my shoulders.

"Is it a crime to care about what happens to you?" His voice was soft, but his hands were strong. The combination made my knees tingle.

"Is that why you've been leaving me notes?" I said. "Because you care about me?"

Pulling me to him, Chance buried his head in my hair. "What notes?"

"The other day. When you took a shower. The mirror."

"I didn't leave you any notes."

Before I could process that, Thor came trotting around the corner and broke between us.

He pawed at my shin.

"Do you want to go outside?" I asked.

Thor sat, grumbling about something.

"I guess that's a yes." I looked at Chance. "Duty calls."

"Wait, what note?"

I didn't want to give him the details until I could analyze it more. What had it said? HOME AGAIN? "Just a scribble on the mirror. Probably something left behind by a previous guest."

Either he was playing a game, lying to me, or it wasn't Chance who wrote on the mirror.

I opened the door, and Thor darted for the grass as I stepped onto the porch.

Chance joined me, reaching for my hand. "Call me if you need anything."

I nodded. He kissed my cheek.

Another song came on the radio then, and Chance smiled. "Remember this song?"

"Don't run back inside, darlin', you know just what I'm here for. So you're scared and you're thinking that maybe we ain't that young anymore."

"'Thunder Road'."

Chance stroked my hair. Leaning in, he whispered in my ear, "We made love to this song. Our first time."

Then he put his mouth over mine and kissed me, long and deep.

I can't say I fought too hard, but I did have enough sense to pull away first.

When I did, Leo was standing in front of us holding a pizza box.

28

I broke free from Chance and smoothed my hair back.

"Leo, hi," I said.

Chance and Leo stared at each other like two roosters gearing up for a cockfight.

"This is Chance. He's fixing the cottage roof. He's an old friend."

Chance flashed me a wounded look.

Neither of them made an attempt to shake hands.

"Chance, this is Leo."

"I know who he is." Chance tilted his chin to Leo, his hands shoved in his pockets. "Hey."

"Hello." Leo nodded, staring at me.

Thor came over and lifted his leg on the porch railing. I was hoping neither of them would do the same.

The enormous dog galloped inside, and that seemed to break the trance.

"You like pepperoni, Chance?" Leo handed him the box and walked away.

"Leo, wait a second." I trotted after him.

"I gotta go, too." Chance headed for the truck, leaving the pizza on the porch swing.

I turned around. "Oh. Okay. What about your shirt?" I asked.

Leo turned back. "His shirt?"

"Keep it," Chance replied. He climbed into his truck and shut the door.

I jogged after Leo, whose legs were a lot longer than mine. "Wait a second."

He kept walking down the path. "You don't owe me an explanation, Stacy. It was just a date. No big deal."

"But I want to explain." I talked fast, spilling the story about the thugs.

Leo stopped when he reached his car on the street. Turning to face me, he held up a hand. "Look, I didn't have high expectations."

Whew, that's a relief.

Hey, wait a minute. What did that mean?

"Whoa." I held up my index finger. "This is just a misunderstanding."

Chance backed out of the driveway, spitting up mud and soggy leaves in his wake.

"I'm just saying it's too much." Leo got in the car.

"What's too much?" I asked.

He shut the door. "All of it."

I tapped the hood. "You're right, Leo." I crossed my arms and stepped back from the car. "You couldn't handle me."

Leo pulled the car off the curb. "Wrong. I couldn't share you." He stared at me for several beats.

I realized my mouth was open as he drove away.

I slogged back to the porch, picked up the pizza, and went inside.

There were napkins in the kitchen, so that's where I

headed. The radio was still playing the song as I shared lukewarm pepperoni pizza with my borrowed dog on a couch that wasn't mine. Needless to say, this was not at all how I anticipated the evening to play out.

The DJ came over the airwaves offering the only human companionship I was getting that night. "You've just been listening to the Rock Block hour. That was The Boss with 'Thunder Road'."

I sat up.

"Thunder Road". The lyrics started playing in my head. *"Hey, that's me, and I want you only. Don't turn me home again. I just can't face myself alone again."*

The messages on the mirror. I want you. Home again.

I stood up slowly, Birdie's words rushing at me. *"Recognize the signs."*

Okay, how did I feel? Not too bad. No dizziness, no chills. No stomach pains.

I went to the bathroom to get the penny I collected from the side of the road. Removing it from my jean pocket, I glanced in the mirror.

That's when I noticed the red and black plaid. The shirt that Chance lent me seemed awfully familiar.

I ran to the kitchen, yanked the drawer open, and pulled out the scrap of fabric that Thor had ripped from whoever broke into the cottage.

It matched the shirt.

That's when the nausea started.

My stomach roiled as I held that scrap of fabric. Why hadn't I felt it before? I was wearing the shirt now.

I ripped it off and turned it around.

There was a chunk missing from the back on the bottom. I held the cloth to it.

Except for what Thor digested, it was a match.

I sunk to the floor and dropped the shirt and the piece of fabric. The nausea subsided, but my heart ached.

Chance broke into the cottage. But why? Was he looking for something? Trying to scare me? Why would he do that? I put my head in my hands, not sure who to trust anymore.

The shirt was crumpled on the floor. He must not have realized that Thor took a bite out of it or he wouldn't have loaned it to me.

Call me crazy, but I think I'd notice if Cujo tried to eat the shirt off my back.

Thor came over and nuzzled my hand.

But there was something curious. "Hey, buddy. How come you let him in tonight?"

Thor thumped his tail and flopped on my lap.

Moonlight decided to join the party then, nuzzling Thor's paw.

I handed out some scratches and belly rubs before hoisting myself off the floor. A robe hung on a hook in the bathroom, and I donned that then poured a glass of wine. Moonlight jumped on my shoulder, and we curved around the counter and sat at the desk. I lined up the pennies and grabbed a notebook.

The coins clinked like wind chimes as I arranged them in chronological order. There were six total. The first one was the year I was born. That was easy enough. There was one that was a year before that. Then the year I graduated high school. Another one with a date I couldn't make out. And another one with a date that held no significance that I could decipher.

I sipped the wine and flipped over the other coin. The one that was in my iced tea when Chance and I ate at the Palace. Again, the year I was born.

The year Chance was born.

Is that why he wanted me to stay out of this? He was at dinner that day, according to Birdie. Did Chance try to hurt my grandfather?

Thor harrumphed, reminding me that I had work to do. I called Shea Parker to see what he may have found out about Gretchen.

"The car is a rental. Lucky for you I have a buddy there who owed me a favor. He said the name on the license was Gretchen Swanson."

"Did you get the license number?"

"Sure did. Last known address was a facility in North Carolina."

"What kind of facility?"

"Some kind of mental health center."

That gave me pause. "Was she a patient?"

"Well, here's where it gets tricky. There was a patient there by that name, but she died five years ago."

"What?"

"Yep. I don't know what this woman is up to, but you better be careful."

"What's the name of the hospital?"

"Sunnyvale Sanctuary just outside of Durham. On Penny Lane."

Penny Lane. Follow the pennies.

I thanked Parker and was about to hang up when I thought of something else. "You think you can find out if a Dr. Gates ever worked there?"

$\mathcal{M}$rs. Plough greeted me in her own special way.

"Get out of here."

"Pleasure to see you again, Mrs. Plough." Kill her with kindness. That was the plan.

"What do you want?"

A house to fall on you. "I need to speak with your husband again, please."

"Can't you understand I don't want you here?"

"Can't you understand I don't care?"

Her face snarled at me. "You're all alike. Crazy as loons."

She was about to slam the door, but I pushed her back and barreled through the doorframe.

"I'm calling the police. They should lock you up along with your grandmother."

"That's quite enough, Bea," said Mr. Plough behind her. He ushered her aside gently and turned to face me. "Stacy, what can I do for you?"

"I have a few more questions for you, Mr. Plough."

He escorted me into his study, leaving his wife with an

angry expression on her face. I was tempted to flip her the bird. Instead, I flashed the widest smile I could muster. That made her more mad, and I couldn't help but grin.

Mr. Plough sat behind his desk. "Don't pay any attention to Bea, Stacy."

That was like telling a mouse to ignore the hawk circling his field. But I shoved it aside anyway.

"I have a question about my grandfather's legal documents."

"Very well." He clasped his hands.

"You said my mother was listed as power of attorney, as well as Chance."

"That's correct."

"When was Chance added?"

Mr. Plough tapped his forefinger to his chin. "Some time ago. I can't recall the exact date."

"But you said it was altered only recently."

"That's correct. It was your mother who was recently added."

That didn't make any sense. "My mother has been gone for years, Mr. Plough. That can't be right."

The old man turned to rummage through a large, wooden cabinet. A minute or two passed before he retrieved the file. Settling back into his chair, he flipped the folder open. His fingers were crooked from arthritis as he turned page after page. Finally, he handed me a slip of paper. "It was my understanding that she's been in town recently."

I took the crisp page and glanced down. There was her name, in black and white. Her. Name. "Did you notarize this?" I asked.

"No. I wasn't the one who drew up the paperwork. Oscar brought it to me last week. Asked that I keep a copy in his file."

My head stung behind my right eye and a vision of my mother flashed in my mind. Sobs. A hand on her shoulder.

It was gone in an instant, but my head was still spinning from the news. *My mother was here? In Amethyst?* My stomach was churning with a mixture of excitement, confusion, and anger. Why hadn't she tried to contact me? Or Birdie? It made no sense. On the one hand, I was happy that she was alive. That she had made it home. Because the truth was, up until that moment, I had my doubts. There was no telling what had happened to her. She had disappeared without a trace, and I never knew if she was still breathing. I hadn't felt her connection in so long.

Another thought slammed into my skull. *Why hadn't Gramps told me? Why hadn't Pearl? What possible reason could they have to keep me from my own mother?* But the worse thought of all was this: *Maybe she doesn't want to see me. Maybe she blames me for my father's accident.* Just like I blamed myself.

I hurried out of the Plough home, avoiding Bea on my exit, and was nearly to the curb when I heard someone yell.

"There she is!"

I spun around. Wild Women.

Terrific.

"Stacy!" The little brunette stumbled forward. Melanie was it? "We're going to the Black Opal to complete our final task."

"Yep." Trish nodded. "Then we report back to you." She pointed at me.

I shook my head. "Oh no, ladies. I am not the She ... whatever it is." I waved my hand.

"She Woman Head Heathen," they chimed in unison, giggling. It sounded like the party had started before they left the guest house.

"Right. That's not me."

"No, but you are the ..." Melanie took out a piece of paper and handed it to Trish to read.

"The Celtic Goddess Imperial."

I couldn't wait to find out whose idea *that* was. "Ladies, you have been grossly misinformed."

Trish jingled car keys in her hand. "Maybe we weren't supposed to say anything. Like, maybe it was a secret mission." She frowned at Melanie.

A secret mission didn't sound half bad. There was something I needed to take care of at the Black Opal anyway. Something that had been bothering me about a couple of the visions. These two just might come in handy. Plus, I didn't want them driving. Double plus, I had no car.

I walked over to them. "Okay, Wild Women, listen up. You have deduced the course thus far. Now, I shall drive you to the next destination on the roster where you shall complete your mission forthrightly." I stuck my palm out.

"Why are you talking like that?" Trish inquired, handing me her car keys.

I mentally slapped her. "Get in the car."

After parking across the street from the Opal, the three of us headed to the door.

"So what are we supposed to do?" asked Melanie. She hiccupped.

"Just wait for my signal," I replied.

The ladies nodded, and we all walked in.

The Opal was packed with people. Many of them in costume for Samhain. Many of them intoxicated. Cin was dressed as a pirate wench. She wore a patch over one eye, her dark hair fell in loose curls, a tight, black skirt amplified her generous booty, and her short legs were stuffed into leather boots.

She tipped her chin toward me and asked Trish and Melanie what they were drinking.

Scanning the room, I spotted Monique. Cin and she have an understanding that basically states Cinnamon will take nobody's crap but anybody's money.

Monique moseyed over to me, teetering on platform heels. She plopped her plastic boobs on the bar. "You look like shit."

Now I admit I have had better days. But I did manage to squeeze in a shower, a blow dry, mascara, and lip gloss. However, my wardrobe was seriously depleted so it was either a worn-out Snoopy tee shirt and my high school gym shorts or black slacks and a halter top. I went with the latter.

Did I make the right choice? Debatable.

Monique was shoehorned into a Marilyn Monroe dress, life-threatening cleavage spilling over the top of it. She wore a rhinestone choker with matching earrings and enough Channel N ∘ 5 to marinate a horse. Her makeup was slathered on with a putty knife, and I could have made my own Monique mask out of the excess.

I grinned. "Aren't you supposed to leave the makeup when you graduate from clown college?"

She smirked. "Did I see Leo's car parked in front of your house?"

"I can't imagine you can see anything through fifty-six layers of mascara."

"You're just jealous." She waved her double Ds in my face.

I considered sticking a pin in one, but was afraid it would erupt and blind me. "Can I help you with something? Get you a drink? A bottle of turpentine for your face?"

"I warned you not to go out with Leo." She poked me.

"Did you just poke me?"

She smiled. There was red lipstick on her teeth. "Don't make me take him from you like I did Tony." The bitch poked me again.

I gave her a hard stare. "You better put that finger away before I confiscate it."

It hit me then, as I hoped it would. A pain shot through my head as she touched me once again. And then that image fizzled into view, full size this time. Tony sleeping on a couch I didn't recognize, clothed head to toe. Monique frowning, then laughing. It was clear to me at that moment just what it meant. I smiled.

30

I took a step toward Monique. She planted her hands on her hips, defiantly.

"You sneaky little rodent," I hissed. "You never *had* Tony. Did you?"

Monique stepped back, confusion clouding her face.

I advanced.

"Y-You know what happened," she stammered, twisting her purse strap.

I nodded. "I do now. And when I tell Cinnamon you better pray to the god of plastic surgery or whoever it is you worship that she doesn't mow you down with her car."

"Tell Cinnamon what?" She seemed nervous now. Her brow began to sweat.

"That Tony never slept with you. That he was so drunk he didn't remember what happened so you filled his head with a baloney story, knowing he would confess to her."

"That's not true." Shaking her head, she backed away farther.

I stepped forward. "It *is* true. And if you don't admit it, I swear I'll break your arm." Grabbing her elbow, I marched her to the back room.

"Ow, stop it. That hurts, Stacy." Her face was a mixture of confusion and fear. She was probably trying to figure out how I discovered her little secret.

I swung her around and pinned her up against the wall. "Talk."

"Are you crazy?"

"It runs in the family."

"Stacy, really. This is absurd." She gave a weak smile.

"I'll get the turpentine, I swear to God, Monique."

"Okay, okay."

I crossed my arms, and she licked her lips and sighed.

"I thought your cousin was the violent one," she muttered, straightening her dress.

"I've picked up some pointers from her."

I stared at Monique with raised eyebrows. We were standing near the wall that divided the bar. Monique was against the brick and I was facing her.

"I made it up, okay!" She sobbed and the tears started flowing. "Tony was drinking at the Elk's Lodge. He was upset because your cousin had left him all because of a stupid argument. She didn't answer her phone, just totally abandoned him for like, *three days*." She stabbed the air with her finger. "You know, she's the one you should be mad at. She should have treated her man better."

"Hey, every day Tony wakes up without a bullet in his leg is a good day. Especially after your stunt." Although she did have a tiny point. "Go on."

Monique sniffled, and I wondered if she thought Cinnamon was going to literally kill her for ruining her marriage. I couldn't blame her. The thought had crossed my mind, too. "I offered to drive him home, only I took him to my place. Nothing happened. He slept on the couch." She bowed her head. "I just wanted to hurt her like she's hurt me over the years, you know? She can be so *mean*. But I never thought it would go that far. I never dreamed they'd get divorced. Honest. You have to believe me, Stacy." When she lifted her head she looked like a Picasso left out in the rain. "I tried to tell the truth a hundred times, but she wouldn't give me a chance. And then it was too late."

I ran my fingers through my hair. What a complete and utter cluster fluff. Cin threw away her *marriage* because of this. She was not going to take this new development lightly, and I certainly wasn't going to be the one to tell her. On the other hand, maybe it would be a relief. To know that Tony had been loyal all along. One could hope.

"You *will* tell her."

Monique nodded.

"Tonight."

More nodding.

I couldn't look at her anymore. "Go fix your face."

She stepped around me, shielding her forehead, and hurried to the bathroom.

Now all I had to do was hide all the firearms in the tri-state area.

I walked over to the bar. Cinnamon was slinging drinks next to Bay. A curly-haired kid was refilling napkins and straws. My cousin glanced up as I squeezed my way through the crowd. "You drinking?" she asked, shaking something up in a tin.

"No. I need to talk to you."

Cin surveyed the bar. "Can't do it, Cuz. I'm slammed."

"It's important."

"Stacy, look around. I'm six deep."

I rubbed my temple. Then I heard some squeals and giggles to my left.

"I'll get you two bartenders. Just grab the key to the office and I'll meet you back there."

Cin poured some reddish drinks into two icy glasses.

I walked over to the Wild Women. "Ladies, I have a task for you."

Melanie clapped her hands. "Goodie."

Trish's eyes widened. "Is this it? Is this the last Wild Woman hurrah?"

I considered that. Cin wouldn't be too happy if I unleashed these two all over her customers. She preferred the abuse come straight from her.

"No, this is simply an endurance task. For exactly thirty minutes you will man this bar. You will not consume any alcohol. You will mix drinks and charge everyone accordingly. You will be cordial and polite. There's a price list near the register, and a bartender's bible near the bottles."

"Please tell me you're not serious," Cin said when I went back to her with my plan.

"It's just for a little while. What's the worst that could happen?"

Cin sighed and told the other bartender that the ladies would be assisting. Then I followed her to the back office.

"Okay, what couldn't wait? I know it isn't Gramps because I just called the hospital."

"Actually, it *is* Gramps."

I explained about the power of attorney document, my mother mysteriously making an appearance, and Ed's little inheritance. My suspicions about Chance were on the tip of my tongue, too, but I wasn't sure Cin would believe my theory.

Her eyes burned through me. "What else? I can tell you're holding back."

The pennies were tucked in my pocket. I still wasn't sure what reason Chance would have for breaking in or hurting Gramps, except for the money. He did have a brand new truck. There was no use holding back from Cin. I pulled the pennies out one at a time. I went through the dates with her, explaining what I thought they meant.

"So you think Chance has something to do with this?"

"Maybe." *Probably*.

"You've gone over the edge."

"There's more."

Cin folded her arms. I told her about the shirt, the notes, and the song.

Her face grew darker with each word.

"Oh my God," she whispered. "Chance broke in?"

I sighed. "Looks like it."

"But, that doesn't mean he's the one who poisoned Gramps. Chance makes great money. I can't imagine him hurting anyone, let alone our grandfather. He wouldn't do that, Stacy. Besides, it's not like he'll inherit from the will."

"No, but he has access to everything right now since Gramps is incapacitated."

"What about this Gretchen? If she's Pearl's niece, maybe those two are in on this together."

"Funny you should you mention her. Seems she might not be Pearl's niece." So I told her about the information Parker relayed to me

Cin put a palm to her forehead. "Let's backtrack. What's this about your mom?"

I shook my head. "I don't know. Have you seen her recently?"

"No. Of course not." She thought a moment. "What

about Wildcat? Have you noticed how he rubs Pearl the wrong way?"

"I have, but he has that effect on a lot of people. Where is he anyway?"

"Probably at the Elk's. He doesn't like my weekend crowd." She glanced at the clock. "Stacy, I gotta go. The crowd is going to get bigger."

When we stepped out of the office, Ed Entwhistle was standing near the door.

"Hey, I was just coming to get you," he said to Cinnamon. He was dressed as Dracula.

"What do you need, Ed, a pint of blood?" she asked.

Ed laughed. "No, but you might want to step back behind the bar."

Cin and I looked at each other and ran to the front of the building.

The place was even busier than when I first got there. Bay was running back and forth, shoving beers in front of customers. Trish was dancing on top of the bar with her shirt off. A few drunks were bent over the rail backward, and Melanie was pouring shots into their mouths.

But what caught Cin's eye was Monique making out with the DJ in the corner as "Monster Mash" skipped over and over again.

She started toward them when a woman in a French maid's costume stopped her. "Hey, where have you been? I've been waiting for a drink forever."

"Really? I'm sorry." Cin cocked her head. "Why don't you download a free drink coupon from my website."

"What's the website?"

"LikeIGiveAShit.com."

The woman stomped off, and Cin started for Monique.

I stopped her. "I'll take care of it. Get to work."

Cin hesitated, then grudgingly stepped behind the bar. The DJ caught her from the corner of his eye and unhooked his lips from Monique.

"Wild Women," I called.

Trish and Melanie stopped the debauchery and met my eyes. I pointed to Trish and then to the floor. She stumbled off of the bar. Melanie stopped pouring shots into customer's mouths.

"Ready for the signal?" I asked the two women.

They nodded in unison like Bobblehead dolls.

I thumbed at Monique, who was re-applying lipstick. Then I made a gunslinger gesture with both hands.

Melanie put the tequila bottle down and grabbed the soda gun. Trish went for a cheap bottle of champagne. They waited for a signal, and I nodded.

Within seconds, the champagne was uncorked and showering Monique. Melanie rinsed her off with Diet Coke. The pair high-fived each other, and I slipped around to the front of the long bar.

Monique screamed, "You bitches!" Then she lunged for Trish.

"No fighting in my bar," Cin shouted.

Monique stopped in her tracks. She slid her eyes to me, then Cinnamon. She must have deduced that I hadn't told my cousin the truth. Yet. I would if I had to, but there was enough on my plate, and since this particular monkey was not a member of *my* circus, I figured I'd let her clean up her own mess.

Trish bounced over to me, Melanie on her heels. "We had such an awesome time," squealed Trish.

"Of course you did. Tell your friends." I have no idea why I said that. I didn't think this was the kind of crowd *I* wanted in the Geraghty Girls' House.

"We can't wait to come back," gushed Melanie.

I didn't want to encourage that idea so I said nothing and headed for the door. I caught a smarmy look on Monique's face as I rounded the corner, and I knew she wasn't going to 'fess up to Cinnamon. I just could not have my cousin thinking for one more minute that the love of her life betrayed her trust. So on my way out into the October night, I called to her, "Monique lied about everything. It never happened."

Cin met my gaze, and I nodded. Her eyes narrowed for a second, then flashed with a murderous gleam.

Monique stopped wringing out her dress and looked up. "Oh shit."

The last thing I heard was Cinnamon bounding over the bar.

31

*T*rish and Melanie were in that wonderful drunken state when you're loud and obnoxious, but you don't give a flying fig if anyone can hear you. I decided to catch up with Wildcat at the Elk's and to load them into a cab the first chance I got.

The bar had floor-to-ceiling windows, and I spotted Wildcat before I entered, slumped over a boilermaker. To my surprise, Gretchen was there, too, finishing up a martini at a corner table. She put the glass down and picked up her purse to leave.

I shoved the girls into the doorway of the next building and told them to be quiet.

"Is this another test?" Melanie asked.

"Yes," I whispered.

I watched as Gretchen filed through the door and headed up the street toward the Palace, and I suspected, Gramps and Pearl's apartment.

I really needed to get in there, but that would have to wait.

The Wild Women and I hurried into the tavern, and I

instructed Melanie to pick up the martini glass and hide it in her purse. If Gretchen had a record, maybe her prints would reveal her true identity.

Trish ordered a Coke at the bar, and I sat next to Wildcat.

"Hey, kid." His speech was steady. "What are you doing here?"

"Looking for you."

"Well, you found me."

I jumped right to it. "Wildcat, what's the deal with you and Pearl? Why doesn't she like you?"

He just looked at me and swayed a bit. "I rub people the wrong way is all."

The bartender walked up and asked me for ID.

"What're you nuts? This here is Oscar's grandbaby." Wildcat clapped my back so hard I stumbled.

"No kidding." The bartender leaned on the bar. "How is the old coot? Hope it wasn't nothing he drank in here Wednesday."

"Excuse me?"

"Paul," Wildcat growled.

"My grandfather was in here Wednesday?"

Paul swung his head from Wildcat to me, decided Wildcat could rough him up better than I could, and walked away.

"Okay." I stepped off the stool. "Listen to me, old man. I've had enough of the bull. I want some answers."

"Okay. Don't get your panties in a bunch." He swigged his beer. "I took your Gramps out after dinner. Wanted to talk about my business proposition."

"Just the two of you?"

He hesitated. "Well, Ed came along. It concerns his building after all."

"And you left out this detail, why?"

"Don't look at me like that, Stacy. I don't know what the hell happened after that. He had a hot chocolate, we talked, and he went home."

I wanted to believe him. "Why didn't he tell the police this?"

Wildcat shrugged. "Guess he didn't want his old lady to know he was out with me."

Melanie and Trish were at the jukebox, wailing on the thing. Apparently it had swallowed a dollar without delivering. Paul reached for the phone.

"Why would Pearl care?"

Wildcat thought for a long time. Then he turned to me and asked, "You know how your Grandpa met Pearl?"

"At a carnival."

He nodded. "She was a knife thrower. Looked pretty darn cute in those fancy costumes."

I smiled. "Really? I didn't know that. That's interesting. I always thought she ran one of the booths or the cotton candy machine or— Wait a minute. How did *you* know how she looked?"

He took a deep breath. "'Cause I met her first. A long time ago."

Oh, this just keeps getting better.

"It was a long time ago. She came through town looking all sexy, and ... well, we had what you might call a relationship." He curled the label off his beer. "I left shortly after that. She didn't know I knew your grandpa 'til just this week." Then he added, "And I didn't know she ever got pregnant."

32

*T*rish and Melanie were gone by the time I finished talking to Wildcat, so they must have grabbed the one cab that ran through town, or a local gave them a ride because I still had their keys. I decided to take the liberty of driving their car back to the Geraghty Girls' House, thinking of what Gramps' old buddy had told me.

Apparently, Pearl placed the baby up for adoption and left town for several years after that. Wildcat didn't even know if it was a boy or a girl. I wasn't sure what any of that had to do with what was happening today, but I intended to find out.

THE NEXT MORNING, I took care of my four-legged friends before heading over to speak with the aunts.

I could see Fiona through the screen door swirling crepes in a pan, a bowl of sweet cherries and fresh whipped cream next to it. She wore a navy sheath dress and matching flats, her fiery hair pinned into a chignon. The back door was open, so I let myself inside.

"I thought you might need some help." I heard chatter drift from the dining room.

"Oh, isn't that nice, but your Aunt Lolly is doing well this morning. Birdie called and she had a nice chat with her." Fiona winked at me.

I helped myself to a cup of coffee and reached in the fridge for the cream.

"Good," I sighed. "Not sure I have the energy this morning."

"Would you like some breakfast?" Fiona asked, folding a crepe onto a plate.

"No thanks."

Fiona stuck her head in the fridge. "I'll have to call Ed for a special delivery today."

That led me to my first question. "Does Ed have a key to the cottage?"

"No." Fiona glanced at me sideways. "Why do you ask?"

I still didn't want to believe it was Chance who had broken into the place.

"No reason."

I grabbed a piece of toast from a platter and slathered it with butter and strawberry jam as Lolly sashayed into the kitchen. Her attire this morning was a black, strapless, full-length ball gown with pink tulle peeking out from the hem. Black kohl liner rimmed her eyes, and her copper hair was punked out in all directions. She looked like Madonna.

"Stacy, what a pleasant surprise." She planted a kiss on my cheek, branding me with orange lipstick.

"How are you doing today, Aunt Lolly?"

"Oh, I'm always excited on Samhain. The parade begins at 5:30. The bonfire starts at 8:00 so don't forget your cloak for the ritual."

I pretended not to hear that as I scanned the paper and tapped my foot, trying to figure out a way to ask them about my mother. Why had she *really* been in town? And why had she left again?

Unless ... maybe they didn't know after all. My eyes slid to Lolly as she hummed around the kitchen gathering plates and napkins, her gown sweeping the floor. Maybe it wasn't the best time to bring it up. I didn't want to upset her today, especially before breakfast.

The doorbell rang as I was rinsing my plate in the sink. Lolly was setting the table, and Fiona was elbow deep in crepes, so I went to the front of the house to answer it.

It was Gus. "Hey, Stacy. Would you come with me down to the station?"

My heart fluttered. "Something wrong with Birdie?"

"No, your granny's just fine. Beat me at chess today."

I didn't doubt it. "Well, what do you need?"

"The chief wants to talk to you, and he asked me to pick you up."

He sent his errand boy for me? Who does this guy think he is?

I folded my arms over my chest. "Gus, if you want me to ride in that squad car you'll have to arrest me."

Gus shuffled like a puppet. "Aw, gee, Stacy. Don't do this to me. He gets real mad when I don't follow instructions."

"Gus, if he wanted to speak with me, why didn't he call me?"

"I don't ask. I just do." He bit his upper lip.

"Fine." My phone was in the kitchen, so I grabbed that and told Fiona I would see her later. That's when I noticed the text from Parker. **CALL ME.**

Gus opened the back door of the squad car, and I shook my head. "No." He puttered up to the front passenger door and opened that for me. A few minutes later we were at the police station, and I was on the phone with Parker.

"Gates started his career in plastic surgery on the East Coast. He was at the same practice for a few years before he was persuaded to leave."

"What does that mean? Persuaded how?"

"Basically, his partners forced him to resign. I couldn't get the details, but either the guy was performing unnecessary surgery or he was padding bills for the insurance companies. He wasn't ever convicted of a crime, but my guess is that they threatened his license if he didn't leave quietly."

Parker gave me the dates and the name of the clinic. "What about after that?"

"He was a staff doctor at Sunnyvale."

The hospital where "Gretchen" stole her identity.

I called Lynn next at the hospital. She put me through to the department head I needed to reach in order to request that Gates be pulled off my grandfather's case. I cited personal reasons, and the woman didn't put up much of a fight when I threatened to sue them for administering the wrong drug to Gramps.

Leo was propped on the dividing gate when I finally made my way into the building. He didn't look happy, but I was getting used to that.

"Is this how you get all your dates?" I questioned.

No smile.

"Come with me, please." His voice was clipped.

I followed him into a tiny room with a metal table and one chair.

"Have a seat." He motioned to the plastic chair.

"I think I'll stand."

"Your Jeep is at Panzano's Auto Body."

"I know that." *What's this about?*

Leo scrubbed a hand over his chiseled face. "First, I wanted to say I was sorry. Obviously, you *did* break down along the side of the road and I didn't believe you."

He left out the part about Chance kissing me and I was grateful. "Apology accepted."

"Now we have a new problem."

"Lay it on me."

He gave me a hard stare. "You broke our arrangement and you're coming dangerously close to impeding this investigation."

He was right, but I didn't have time to check into headquarters every few minutes. "I can explain."

"Explain what? That you swiped a martini glass from a bar and sent a drunk girl to drop it off last night?"

Oh. That.

Crap. I didn't know she did that. I was going to get it from her myself before Barney Fife came calling. Someone was so not going to receive her Wild Woman certificate.

"I didn't tell her to bring it here. I was going to do that."

"Good. So maybe you'll leave the police work to me then?"

"Maybe." I smirked at him, walked to the table, and scooted on top of it. I told him about Gretchen, even though something was still knocking on my brain and I couldn't grab the last piece of the puzzle. I also let him know about Ed, the pow-wow meeting, Wildcat, and Pearl.

Leo jotted down some notes as I spoke. Then he nodded. "I'll run the prints."

"Ed delivers groceries to my grandmother's bed and breakfast. He could have maybe slipped something into the food or into a drink at the bar."

"Why would he do that?"

"Because if Gramps dies, he stands to inherit not just the building, but a pretty good chunk of land." I explained how Roy and Gramps had been in business together once upon a time, and Gramps' guilt about Roy losing everything.

Leo stood up and walked around the table to face me. He touched my shoulder, sending a tingle down my spine. "If anything changes, anything happens, you call. Understand?"

"Right, Chief." I saluted him and headed for the door.

Birdie wasn't in her cell when I popped my head around the corner. I assumed she was out shopping or grabbing a coffee or whatever the hell it was Leo allowed her to do, so I decided to get my car first.

The short walk to the garage felt good. I needed to stretch my legs and think. There was still a lot I didn't understand, but I knew that somehow Gates and Gretchen —or whatever her name was—were in cahoots. I just didn't know why. Or how either of them would stand to gain anything by hurting Gramps.

Cin's car was parked in the lot as I headed up the drive to the garage. I didn't see the Jeep, but I heard voices.

"You know you should thank my cousin for getting us back together," Cinnamon said.

Tony said, "It's on my list."

Then I heard kissing noises and debated if I should come back later. I didn't want to interrupt the reunion, so I started away.

"I think she's taking this all personally. Like she's responsible if anything happens to Birdie or Gramps. She said something about her mother. It about broke my heart."

I backed away, not wanting to interrupt their reconciliation.

Tony said, "I can't believe no one ever told her about what happened. It may help her, you know."

I stopped. *Told me what? What happened?*

"It's not my secret to tell, Tony. And besides, I was just a little kid when I heard that. I don't even know if it's true."

What secret?

"Well, if it is, I think she has the right to know that her mother was committed."

My heart skipped and my knees faltered. What was he *talking* about? It couldn't be true. It just couldn't. This was a small town. If my mother had been institutionalized, surely I would have known. Unless ... Is that where she had been all these years?

I had to get to Birdie. I needed to know the truth. I turned to run and skidded on a hubcap, sailing through the air like a lawn dart. My cousin's car broke my fall.

Cinnamon and Tony ran out to see what the commotion was.

"Stacy! Jeez, are you all right?" Cinnamon rushed toward me.

Nothing seemed broken except my pride. And maybe my heart.

Cin helped me to my feet as Tony rushed up behind her. My hip throbbed and I stared at Tony.

My cousin slid her eyes from me to Tony. Realization dawned on her, and her face twisted into a grimace. "Oh, crap. Stacy, hold on. It's not what you think."

I just kept staring at Tony, because I understood in that moment that my weakness fell with my family. I couldn't see their emotions or feel their thoughts.

But Tony I could read like a billboard. Guilt, embarrassment. Pity.

"Where's my car?" I asked him.

"In back," he answered.

Cin slapped his shoulder. "Stacy, wait."

I ignored her and jogged to the back of the lot where I found the keys in the ignition of my patched up Jeep. Cinnamon was calling, chasing me, but I didn't blame her. It wasn't her fault.

There was only one person I blamed.

33

I charged into the police station madder than I had ever been in my life. I hit the door so hard, a piece of art fell off the wall. Gus stood up as if he were going to reprimand me, but he took one look at my face and thought better of it. He sat down and pretended to talk on the phone. Leo was nowhere in sight.

I marched down the hallway and into Birdie's cell, which still wasn't locked. My attempt to slam it shut was futile because it was so freaking heavy. This ruined my entrance, but fueled my anger.

Lifting her head up from the book she was reading, Birdie smiled. The smile faded when she saw my expression.

My fists were balled into knots at my sides. I felt a vein in my neck throb.

When my voice came it was tight and small. I was expecting to roar like the Lion King, but instead, I squeaked like a kitten.

"How could you?" was all I could manage.

"How could I what?" Birdie removed her reading glasses

and placed them at her side. She folded her hands in her lap.

She was always calm. How did she do that? Sit there, without a care in the world, when I was running around with a dustpan cleaning up her mistakes.

Frustration took over and I yelled so loud I think I rattled the shade on her lamp. "Nature, knowledge, and truth. Wasn't that what you said? What you used to teach? Well, *Grandmother*, it's a shame you don't practice what you preach."

"What on earth are you talking about, child?" She stood and stared at me, confusion painted all over her face.

I paced, trying to organize my thoughts and control my anger. "Did she abandon me, Birdie? *Did* she? Or did you have her committed?"

A shocked look fell over my grandmother's face, and her shoulders hunched ever so slightly. She stilled for a few beats. When she lifted her head, her eyes were soft, like wormwood leaves.

"Don't you dare lie to me," I seethed. "Not now."

Birdie walked toward me. "Whatever it is you heard, whatever it is you *think* you know, I can assure you, it isn't the truth."

I backed away. "Then what is?"

Birdie sighed and her eyes slipped away from me to a place I had never been. Somewhere far off in the distance that she alone guarded. I think I knew, even then, that secrets would always be woven into my family's fabric.

"It was a long time ago. Before your father passed," Birdie began. "You were special, right from the start." Pausing, she smiled at me. "I knew who you would be the first time I laid eyes on you."

The lump forming in my throat tasted like acid.

"Your mother knew it, too, and she did everything in her power to prepare you for it. And to protect you."

"Protect me from what?" My words were a whisper.

Birdie's emerald eyes met mine. "Our family is special, Stacy."

She never called me by my given name, and it rattled my core.

"We have gifts that other's dare not dream about. We have ..." she searched for the right word, "responsibilities. You more than any of us."

I sighed. "Right. Because you think I'm the Seeker of Justice."

Birdie grasped my shoulders. "That and oh so much more. In time, you will learn just how powerful you are. How important your role in the world is. And when you have that kind of status, there are those who wish to take it from you. Who wish to do you harm."

"What does that have to do with my mother?"

Birdie bit her lip. She was weighing how much to reveal to me, I could tell. It was the same look she gave me when my father passed away. The same look she gave me whenever I asked if my mother was coming home. "You developed so quickly, so fiercely, that after a while, it depleted something from her. And she needed to get it back."

"What did I take?" Mist formed in my eyes as I waited to hear how I had destroyed my mother. Just like I had destroyed my father.

"Her gift, but believe me, child. You didn't *take* it. She gave it willingly. But as it faded, so did her defenses. And she needed all of her power if she was going to raise the next Seeker of Justice."

I absorbed that for a moment. "What was her gift?"

Birdie sighed, shaking her head. She closed her eyes and

thought for a while. Finally, she said, "Your mother's talent was complex. She had a magic that only *she* understood. What is important for *you* to know is that it was a short time she was in that facility. She had to be grounded, balanced, and there were people there that understood the ... uniqueness of her condition. People like us. She came right back to you after a full moon cycle."

I racked my brain, trying to recall my mother being gone for a month before she was ... gone forever. "Wait ... there was a class she took. Out of state ... somewhere. On herbs and healing properties. But that was just a week."

Birdie cast her eyes aside. I didn't like the vibe I was receiving.

"Oh, she didn't." I shook my head, incredulous.

My grandmother raised an eyebrow.

"She zapped my memory? Bespelled me?" How could she *do* that to me? It was the worst invasion of privacy.

"It was for your own good."

Seriously? What was *with* these people? "My own moth — Never mind. We'll stick a pin in that one for now. So where is she now?"

Birdie averted her gaze.

"Where *is* she?" I repeated, louder.

Birdie shifted her eyes to me. They were filled with sadness. Regret. "I haven't heard from her since after your father died. Since she left. Same as you."

Now I was really confused. "Hasn't she come to see you recently?"

Birdie's face crinkled. "Why would you think that?"

I wanted to scream. *Why does every answer lead to another question? Mom contacted Gramps and not Birdie? What's going on?*

"Because Stan Plough said—"

A feeling of dread seized my heart. *Oh no. Oh crap.*

I spoke quickly. "Birdie, what was the name of the facility where she stayed?"

Birdie lifted her head to the ceiling. "It was a long time ago. I don't know off the top of my head."

I grabbed her hands. "It's important, Birdie. Think."

She tapped her mouth for a minute. Her eyes met mine. "Sunnyside?"

"Sunnyvale?"

She blinked, nodding slowly. "Yes, that sounds right."

34

I apologized to Gus on my way out of the jail and asked him where I could find Leo.

"He got called out to the Shelby Farm. Someone tie-dyed all their goats."

Naturally. "Well, have Leo call me ASAP, okay?" I wrote down my cell number in case he forgot it.

Gus nodded. "Stacy, you going to the parade tonight?"

I paused for a minute. "I'm not sure, Gus." I started back out.

"Uh, hey, which costume do you think Cinnamon would like better?"

Gus held up a Mr. Incredible costume and a Spiderman suit. I didn't have the heart to tell him that she was back with Tony. Or that Leo would fire him for patrolling incognito at a parade. "How about something from Smokey and the Bandit?" I suggested.

"Hey, yeah, 'cause of her car. I could be Smokey."

"And you've already got the costume."

Gus looked down at his uniform. "Yeah."

I skated out of there, jumped in the Jeep, and pulled

away from the curb, backtracking down Lunar Lane. After turning left on Main Street, I parked a few doors down from the Pearl Palace.

The place was hopping when I walked in. Tourists, churchgoers, college students, and families were either finishing up breakfast or ordering lunch. I managed to grab a stool at the counter. The clock above the soda machine read 12:02.

I flipped over a coffee cup as a young waitress with a long, French braid approached me.

"Coffee?"

"Yes, please. Is Olivia around by any chance?"

"Sure. She's in the back section. You need something?"

"No. I just wanted to say hello."

"Okay. I'll send her over when she has a second."

I smiled. "Thanks." I dressed up my coffee and glanced around the room.

The kitchen was behind the counter, and I could see the cooks' arms sliding platters of omelets and potatoes, tuna melts, and club sandwiches through the pass. It had been a long time since I'd been to the apartment, but if I remembered correctly, the office was behind the swinging doors that led to the kitchen. The stairs that fed into the second floor were beyond that.

The waitress came over with a pad and pencil, asking if I wanted to order food. I didn't and told her so. A minute or so later, Olivia strolled over. "Hey, sweetie, how are you?"

She put an order up on the wheel and spun it back to the guys in the kitchen. Someone snatched the ticket, and Olivia turned back around to face me. She leaned against the counter.

"I'm fine. Gramps is improving."

"Oh, so happy to hear that. So I guess the boss lady will

be back around, huh? She hasn't been by all day." She tapped my arm and winked. "And I guess in no time, she'll be back to sneaking off to kiss your granddad goodnight."

"She does that?"

"Oh sure. Brings his dinner up to him if he doesn't want to come down."

A cook rang the bell on the stainless steel passthrough. "Order up."

"That's me." Olivia reached for a plate of toast and plopped a packet of grape jelly on top of it.

I watched the servers fill coffee cups and take orders as I gulped down my coffee. It was still pretty busy in the restaurant. I might be able to sneak in and out of the studio without even being noticed. Besides, if I got caught I was just the concerned granddaughter.

I tossed some bills on the counter as Olivia came back around to place another order. "Olivia, do you think I could use the phone?"

"Sure, hon. Just ask Mary at the hostess desk."

"Actually," I glanced around the busy dining room, "maybe I could use the phone in the office. It's a bit loud out here."

"Well, sure. Go on."

"Will I disturb anyone? Is Gretchen here?"

"No, honey. She had some errands to run." She smiled at me, and I made my way toward the kitchen.

Pete, the gorilla tamer from the Opal, greeted me with what might have been a machete, although I'm sure it was just a butcher knife.

"Hello, there." I approached carefully, praying his crazy was locked away for the moment.

"The bathroom is that way." He pointed toward the

doors with his knife. His voice was gruff, his apron stained with grease and what I hoped was barbecue sauce.

"Yes, that's true. Actually, I'm not here to use the bathroom."

"Can't come back here." He wagged his head for emphasis.

"Well, I can, actually. You see Pearl—"

"Pearl said no one comes back here. Just workers."

Okay. This was getting me nowhere. Obviously, Pearl was using this guy as a makeshift bodyguard and he took that seriously. What was I afraid of anyway? All I ever saw him do was take down a stuffed gorilla.

He stared at me like a lion watches a gazelle.

That big ass knife, that's what I was afraid of.

I peered past Pete's shoulder and I could see the little door to the office and the stairs that led to the apartment. I could also see through to the back door. It was one of those heavy metal numbers with a long arm that locked when it swung shut. I didn't have a key. So the back door was not an option.

"Listen up." I flashed my wallet and my driver's license. "I'm from immigration."

Three Hispanic men ran out the back door. A Caucasian man plastering the ceiling also took off.

Pete swung his head from side to side, confused.

"Order in," a waitress called.

"Pete, get in here," a young male voice called. "I'm backed up on fries, man."

Pete glanced at the door, shifted toward the grill, and glared at me. He raised the knife. I stepped back.

"Pete!" three people shouted in unison.

He shuffled back to the kitchen reluctantly.

I scurried into the office and shut the door.

35

J pulled out my phone, took out Leo's card, and dialed his number. "Come on, answer." But he didn't, so I ended the call and set the phone on the desk.

Pearl's office was compact but orderly. I rummaged through the drawers first, looking for anything that might tell me if she were partnering with Gretchen.

I found a ledger that seemed to be in the black. Some bills had been paid by Gretchen. Electric, water, phone. Nothing incriminating there, since Pearl did mention that Gretchen was helping out with the accounting.

I went to the file cabinet. Employee records, vendor accounts, licenses. Again, nada.

That meant that whatever clues, if any existed, would be in the apartment.

There were a few sets of keys in the desk, so I grabbed those, hoping one would unlock the loft, and stuffed them in my pocket. I quickly scanned for Samurai Pete, but he must have been cooking his heart out in the kitchen.

The stairs were steep, forcing me to take them two at a

time. After several attempts, I finally found the right key and unlocked the door. I poked my head inside.

"Anyone home?" Better safe than sorry.

No answer.

My eyes drifted around the expansive loft. I had heard that Gramps had it refurbished when he moved in with Pearl. The floors were smooth and stained a dark walnut color, the walls painted in soothing beige tones, and bay windows overlooked the town. There were just a few rooms. The kitchen was to the left, and the living room melted into the bedroom. A service elevator Gramps had installed when his knees wore out was off the far wall near his office.

I went straight to the back of the space and into Gramps' office. It was open.

The desk held pens, pads of paper, a laptop, and a few photos. Next, I went to the barrister bookcase. There were books on every subject from Winston Churchill to traveling Ireland. I flipped through several of them, found a scrapbook of my articles, and an early photo of Birdie, but nothing more. There was no closet, no filing cabinet.

Where does he keep important papers?

A few end tables in the living room held nothing I was looking for, so I circled back through the bedroom where there was a chest of drawers on the far side of the bed. Men's socks, boxers, undershirts. On the other side was a hefty wardrobe that anchored the wall. Belts and scarves hung on the back of the thick door. Dresses, skirts, blouses, and slacks hung along the top bar. Above that, a shelf lined with shoeboxes.

I moved in farther. Behind the everyday clothes, on a second bar, were a few sequined costumes in red, blue, and purple. All short, strappy things, like you might see a magician's assistant wearing. Or a knife thrower.

I stepped on the little ledge to reach for the shoeboxes. Inside were shoes.

As I hopped down I heard a slight pop. It sounded … hollow. I knocked around the wardrobe until I found the noise again. It felt like a built-in secret compartment. There was a keyhole, but no key on the ring would open it, so I searched for a screwdriver in the kitchen and found one in a junk drawer. I pried it open, and in the box, I found what appeared to be a slew of letters. I sat on the bed to read the first one.

36

Dear Dad,
I realize it has been a long time since you've heard
from me. I truly am sorry for that. I can
explain all of that soon, but I'm writing to
you now because I need your help. A
devastating car crash has left me in dire
straits. Physically, I am fine now, but the cost
of medical treatment has crippled me
financially. I know I don't deserve it, but if
you could find it in your heart to lend me the
money to get back on my feet, I would be
eternally grateful. You should know, too, that
I look drastically different. This is part of the
reason the cost of treatment was so
exorbitant. The wreck disfigured my face so
much that reconstructive surgery took almost
two years. I have attached the records, the
photos (so you won't be shocked, should you
decide to meet with me) and a copy of my
birth certificate. I would prefer that we keep

*this between us. For reasons, I am sure you
understand, Birdie cannot know.*

*I*t was a typed letter, signed in my mother's name, in what could have been her handwriting. There was no mention of me. No envelope. No return address.

Flipping through the box, I found the records mentioned, a few more letters, and photos of a woman's face that appeared to be badly beaten and then patched back together.

Could this be true? Was this one of the reasons she had stayed away so long? The records and bills were so convincingly detailed, the photos so graphic, so real. But Gates could have falsified the records and photos can be altered.

Was Gretchen parading as my mother?

Or *was* she my mother?

But Parker told me the real Gretchen Swanson died five years ago. Not that the name was uncommon.

I shoved the papers back into the box and tucked it inside of the compartment. As I did, I felt soft velvet brush my fingertips. I pushed some garments aside and found a black cloth, folded, thick and heavy. After setting it on the nightstand, I unfolded it gently. Buried inside were knives nestled between satin ribbons. Pearl's, I presumed.

My head was spinning with so much confusion, I almost missed the twist of the doorknob.

In a mad dash, I shut the wardrobe and dove beneath the bed.

Someone entered and closed the door. Soft beeping sounds floated from the living room and a voice said, "It's me."

Gretchen. Or whatever the hell her name was.

"I say we just cut our losses and get out of here. We have enough. I'm telling you, it's getting too sticky."

A pause.

"No. I don't care about that. This granddaughter is a pain in the ass. She's like a bad penny that keeps showing up."

Interesting word choice.

"Don't you dare put this on me. This is not my fault. How the hell was I supposed to know she had a kid?"

So she *was* posing as my mother.

"No, *you* were supposed to do recon when you got here, remember? Not shack up with that skank while I was doing time. This was supposed to be the big payoff. I mean it was perfect, especially after she blew town and never came back."

There was a brief pause, and then she said, "You better wake him up soon. I am not taking the rap for that old man's death." Another pause. "What do you mean you're off the case? Goddammit."

Gates. She was speaking to Gates.

"No. No way, Norman. I'm a con artist, not a killer. Let's just leave this one. We've still got Cincinnati."

Norman Gates? Are you kidding me? People should really be more careful what they name their children.

Gretchen was still arguing with Norman when a Daddy Long Legs joined me under the bed. I wasn't exactly afraid of spiders, but in my experience, these guys like to climb and I wasn't too thrilled about an arachnid using my face as a sidewalk.

Gretchen swore again. "Fine. I'll take care of it."

Her footsteps came closer to me as the spider camped out on my cheek.

Please leave, please leave, please leave.

I didn't know which one I was talking to, but it didn't matter since they both appeared to have made themselves at home for the time being. I heard the con woman filtering through drawers as my eight-legged friend waltzed down my neck.

I heard the wardrobe open and the shuffle of papers.

Mr. Spider decided to explore my mouth then, and I blew him off of me.

Gretchen stopped whatever she was doing. She crossed to the bed and peeked under.

She smiled wide. "Come on out."

I played dead.

"Come out or I will drag you out by your scalp."

I didn't like the choices, but I rolled out from under the bed anyway.

"Hi, Mom," I said.

37

*G*retchen paused, unsure if I was serious. Then she rolled her eyes. "You realize I have to kill you now."

"You can't kill me. You're a con artist, not a killer. You said so yourself," I pointed out.

She frowned. "I can kill you. I can kill you if I want to."

The elevator slid open at that moment and the imposter thought fast. She grabbed me in a bear hug as Pearl stepped through the doors.

I wriggled, but she was stronger than she looked. "Ew. Stop it, Psycho Sally."

Gretchen hissed, "If you say one word, I swear to you she dies."

"Oh my," Pearl gasped. "Does this mean ..."

"That's right, Pearl." Gretchen held her arm around me. Tight. Like she wears Powder Fresh deodorant tight. "Stacy knows who I am now. No more pretending."

Pearl clapped her hands. "I'm so relieved. No more secrets." She gazed at me with love, and there was no doubt that Pearl had nothing to do with this situation. "Wait right there. I'll get the camera."

Perfect, because I really want to remember this moment.

Pearl left, and I shoved Gretchen off of me. "Leave now and I won't take you down. I won't say a word."

"You expect me to believe that?" she scoffed.

"No one got hurt. Let's keep it that way. You and Dr. Doom just get the hell out of my town and stay away from my family."

"I wish I could, but you see, I need enough to get gone for good." She regarded me, probably assessing the threat level. I was without a weapon, had forgotten a lot of my fight training and most of my witchiness. But I was pissed off as all hell and a good deal younger than her, so this thing could go either way.

However, I wanted it over. "I'll pay you. I'll get the money from Gramps as soon as he wakes up. I'll tell him it's for my grandmother."

Gretchen considered this for about two seconds. "You know, I almost lost my lunch when I found out you existed. What kind of a mother doesn't talk about her own kid?" She shook her head.

"Yeah, the nerve of her, omitting information like that. She could have screwed up this whole diabolical plan you've got going on."

Gretchen glared. "So I told them I didn't want to alarm you. That we should lie about who I was for now until we spent more time together. I was only thinking of my *precious* daughter. I wanted to spare *her* further pain and embarrassment. Pretty clever, don't you think?"

"Genius. You're like a Bond villain."

"Shut up," she snapped.

"Wow, you *are* clever, what with those snappy comebacks and all."

She moved toward me just as Pearl appeared.

A camera hung around Pearl's neck and she was carrying an old photo album. She insisted I sit next to Mommie Dearest on the sofa and started snapping pictures. I felt like I was in a Stephen King novel.

Worst family reunion *ever*.

After a few minutes, Pearl said, "Boy, you two *do* have the same eyes."

We regarded each other. Her eyes were the same color as my mother's, same shape. Only my mother's eyes had once held hope, happiness, love. Gretchen's were full of greed.

I cleared my throat. "Pearl, why don't you show Mom some of your old tricks from the carnival days?"

Gretchen jabbed me in the rib, still smiling at Pearl.

"Oh, no, dear, I couldn't do that. Don't even know where my props are." Pearl slapped her knee. "Hey, how about I make some tea?"

"Pearl," I emphasized my words, "I think *you* should show off *your* talent." I eyed the knife set on the nightstand.

Unfortunately, Wilma Whackjob saw what I was doing.

We exchanged the briefest glance, and then both lunged for the velvet case at the same time. She was closer and got to it first. Before I could blink, Gretchen was waving a nine-inch blade at me.

I clamped onto her wrist with both hands, wrestling the knife away from my neck.

"Girls! Stop that right now," Pearl clapped at us like we were two twelve-year-old girls goofing around.

Why do they give convicts access to weights? I wondered as she fought me step for step, her biceps rock hard through her top. I managed to stay her off, guiding her toward the bed. We wrestled and grunted as we each fought for control of the blade.

"I mean it now. What is wrong with you two?" Pearl shouted.

Just one more step and I could gain leverage.

"Oh, for Heaven's sake," Pearl cried. "Stop."

Almost.

"Please, stop that, girls."

A few more inches.

Gretchen pushed back slightly, and I gripped harder. The tip of the knife was aimed at my eye now. I reached my foot forward to trip her, but my foot had other plans as it met the velvet case. I slipped and my legs went with me.

I landed flat on my back, the wind knocked from my lungs.

Gretchen hesitated, holding the knife high. For a moment, I wondered if she had second thoughts.

Then it plunged directly into my chest.

38

*M*y breath caught in gurgles. I gasped, coughed, fought for air.

Gretchen's eyes widened.

Then I realized the blade hadn't broken my skin. In fact, I felt nothing at all. Not an ounce of pain.

"What the hell?" Gretchen looked at the knife, puzzled.

"Are you two about done?" Pearl inquired, and I bucked my attacker off me.

"You mean to tell me these knives aren't real?" I asked.

"Absolutely not. What do take me for? You think I used to practice with real knives? They're prop knives." Pearl launched into an explanation. "You see, in a show, the knives pop out from behind the wheel and—"

"Shut up," Gretchen yelled.

"Well, I believe I do not like your tone, young lady." Pearl parked her fists on her hips. She glared at Gretchen.

"I can't take this anymore," pseudo-mom mumbled, and went for her purse.

I tackled her and shouted for Pearl to call the police. "She isn't my mother, Pearl, she's been conning you!"

"Stacy, you just don't recognize her. It's all in the paperwork. Where is the paperwork?" Pearl asked the imposter. "It will explain everything."

Gretchen kicked me in the stomach before she belly-crawled away from me, planting a parting shot in my head that made me see stars. I scrambled to hold her down, and wound up with one red pump in my hand. It made a nice dent in her cheek as I spiked it at her, but she got to the purse anyway. She fumbled around inside it for a second, but lost hold when the end table I lobbed at her knocked her sideways.

The contents of the purse skidded across the wood floor in all directions. Lipstick, a pen, gum, and needles. Big, juicy ones. Pearl took one look at them, and she must have realized that something was wrong, finally. She darted from the room as I dove for the needles. I didn't know what was in them, but I didn't like this chick's track record. That reminded me. Had Leo ever run her fingerprints?

"I can't find the cell phone!" Pearl yelled.

"Use the landline!"

Gretchen pounced on me before I could get to whatever poison she was toting around town. My hand grazed the pile and the needles skidded under the bed. Flipping over, I belted her in the jaw. Then I landed a jab to her eye for good measure.

"We don't have one," Pearl cried.

"Then leave! Pearl, go get help!"

Gretchen yowled and slugged me right back and it hurt like a mother. She must have split my lip because blood filled my mouth. She tried to get up, but I kicked her in the ribs and she sailed back, smacking into a wall. I peeled myself up as the doorknob twisted.

Good, Pearl. Very good.

I was hoping the kitchen had real knives.

When I turned to race toward them, I saw Gates standing over Pearl's motionless body. A dripping needle in his hand.

I ran to her. "No! Oh God, Pearl."

"She won't feel a thing, I assure you. She'll just go to sleep," said Gates.

"You cocksocket." I charged him like a tiger.

He produced another little pointy friend which jolted me to a stop. "Enough of this." He turned to his accomplice. "We need to get to the bank, quickly. Clean yourself up and gather the paperwork. Then we're gone."

"Are you sure the birth certificate is enough?"

"Gretchen, the ends of your stupidity are boundless. If that doesn't help, we have the hospital records."

"What about the other man listed on the document? At least, that would give us some extra insurance."

"This is already too messy." He shot me a glare. "Let's go."

I spat blood at him. And maybe a tooth. "No way, douchenozzle."

It was difficult to argue with whatever was in that needle, so a few minutes later, after I washed up according to orders, Gates shoved me into the driver's seat of a car.

"You do anything stupid and I won't just kill you," he growled. "I'll infect you with a disease that will make you wish you were dead."

I glanced at Gretchen in the rearview mirror. She had the nerve to look defeated. Or maybe it was her black eye, crazy hair, and torn blouse. She was clicking her jaw as if to check that it was still hinged together. I'm sure I didn't look much better. Everything hurt. I made a mental note to get back to combat training if I ever got out of this alive.

Gates instructed me to follow a long, winding road that stretched about six miles out of town. The car climbed up a steep embankment that led to a modern cottage with windows for walls, allowing for spectacular vistas.

What kind of a hideout had that many windows?

Dr. Dread walked around the driver's side, opened the door, and spat, "Get out."

He pushed me along a flagstone path that wound to a large, oak door.

"By the time they find out about this place, I will be long gone with your grandfather's money. This house is rented under Samantha's name."

I just stared at him.

"You didn't think her real name was Gretchen, did you?" Gates laughed. "I'm not even sure it's Samantha."

He moved me into a large bathroom and handcuffed me to the sink. Then he began flipping through the medicine cabinet, which was about the size of my Jeep. The needle drawer alone held more tools than Monique's makeup chest.

"Ah, here we go. Something to make you sleep."

"Look, can we discuss this?" I squirmed on the toilet. "You don't have to do this. You said yourself, no one would find me." I really didn't want to die on a toilet.

He rolled his eyes. Then he grabbed a vial. "Wouldn't want you to scream. Not that anyone could hear you out here."

He put the needle in his shirt pocket. Then he prepared a new syringe.

As Gates leaned in, the shiny point of the needle reflected in his glasses just long enough to make him squint.

I kicked it from his hand and it rolled near the tub. Close

enough for me to smash it with my foot. The liquid spilled out.

He stood up, hands on hips. Not a very masculine stance for a cold-blooded killer. "We could be here all day or you could just trust that I am not going to kill you. You will only be unconscious for a while."

Said the Big Bad Wolf to Goldilocks.

"What if I'm allergic?"

"You're not allergic."

"How do you know?"

"Do I have to gag you?"

"I wish you wouldn't."

"Are you going to cooperate?"

"Not likely."

"Fine. Then I will tie you to the bed so you can't move and then I will kill you."

If he tried to move me, I might have a fighting chance. "Excellent."

Gates raised his eyebrows. "You'd rather take that option?"

"I'm pretty sure you're going to kill me either way. I find it more dignified to die in bed than squatting on the porcelain throne."

"Fine."

Gates stepped out of the room for a minute, and I scanned my surroundings for a way out. It was the only space in the cottage without windows.

Soap, shampoo, toilet paper, towels. Not even a hair dryer. Or a towel bar. Linens were stacked in a wicker unit, which I gathered wouldn't knock anyone out. Unless I could loosen up the sink basin, there was no weapon except the needles. And I had no idea which drugs were inside of them. I heard the faint rumble of a freight train approaching as I tugged at the sink leg through the handcuffs.

Before I knew what was happening, Gates roared in seconds later, stabbed me with the needle in his pocket, and ran out.

The train got closer and I thought I heard glass breaking right before my eyes closed and the world slipped away.

39

*I*t wasn't a freight train. It was a hulking group of old men on motorcycles led by none other than Wildcat.

By the time I came to, there was a lot of broken glass, a kicked-in door, and a doctor who wish he'd never been born. Samantha managed to slip away, but I doubted she was going to get very far in the woods. Leo was looking for her now. Apparently, Gramps' friend had seen me driving the doctor's car and knew something was wrong. Wildcat made a few calls, rounded up his posse, and well, here we were.

Wildcat's crew didn't waste any time ringing the bell when they reached the place. Someone spotted Gates holding a needle through the huge glass windows and decided to park his bike in the living room. A few of them took turns playing dodge ball with the doctor before calling the police, and since these were not the most law-abiding citizens, it was either get on the back of a bike or wait at the scene where Samantha could have shown up at any moment. I chose option A.

I was at Muddy Waters Coffee Shop now with my cousin, sitting at an outdoor table littered with sandwich wrappers, gently applying ice and a bit of Birdie's remedy to my lip. A couple of hours had passed and the sedative that Gates drugged me with had worn off. Who knew he was telling the truth when he said he wasn't going to kill me?

Wildcat's Harley pulled up to the sidewalk then. With the engine still idling, he shouted, "Listen, girls, you need anything, ask for me at the Elk's Lodge. They'll find me."

"Are you leaving?" I asked.

His face met the sky. "I think it's time I moved on. The road is calling."

"What about War Games?" Cin asked.

His eyes sparked. "Just a pipe dream. My true passion is wanderlust. Keeps me young. Besides, I'm guessing the cops won't be too happy that I bent the law a little bit back there." He grinned.

Damn near broke it off, I'd say.

Cin and I watched him head down the road until he disappeared over the horizon. I wondered if I would ever see him again.

Tony walked up to the table carrying two coffees. He set one in front of Cinnamon, who smiled at him and he kissed her. A small piece of my heart leapt at that. Maybe things would get back to normal. At least normal for those two.

"Leo said you can come down to the station tomorrow to draw up the statement if you're not feeling well." Tony set the other coffee in front of me, and I thanked him.

"Good. I'm exhausted." I lifted the lid on the coffee and blew on it.

A loud grumble followed by an impressive snore erupted from beneath the table. I peeked under at Thor who was dreaming of something that made his lip curl and his tail thump. Tony thought it would be funny to dress him in a Batman costume for the parade, but if I were to be honest, I think the dog liked it. There was an extra perk in his step when he greeted me.

Cin sipped her coffee as Tony stared adoringly at her. "Are you're staying for Samhain?"

I met her eyes, but said nothing.

"Birdie would want you there," she said.

Birdie was home now, all charges dropped since she recanted her 'confession' and it was clear she had nothing to do with Gramps' illness. Pearl had not been so fortunate. Sweet, loving Pearl. She didn't deserve to die like that. We'll never know why Gates used a lethal dose on her and not myself. Maybe it was an accident. Maybe he hadn't meant to kill her. Perhaps she was on a medication that caused a bad reaction to whatever drug Gates injected into her. Or maybe he hadn't meant to spare me. It could be that Wildcat and company got him so flustered that he mixed up the needles. Either way, it meant that Gramps would now be alone again and it twisted my heart to think of the pain he would be in. Almost as much as when I first got the phone call that he was sick.

I wrinkled my brow, thinking about that, and something knocked on my brain. A missing puzzle piece.

Cin asked, "What is it? You okay?"

"There's something that still bothers me." I tapped my chin. "Neither of them mentioned anything about putting Gramps in the hospital in the first place. How did that happen? Why would Gates go to the trouble of poisoning Pearl and myself, but not admit to that? And what about the break-in at the cottage? The antifreeze?"

Cinnamon put her hand on mine. "You can't possibly still think Chance stalked you."

"No." It couldn't have been Chance. I just had to believe it couldn't be him.

"I'm sure they had something to do with it, Stacy." Tony scooted a chair close to Cinnamon.

Thor rose from the table, toppling my coffee, but I caught it before it spilled. He stretched and yawned, and I scratched him behind his big pointy ear. "You're probably right."

Cin was watching me. "You know, Thor isn't *just* the God of Thunder." She and Tony exchanged glances.

I eyed her. "Yeah? What else?"

Cin nudged Tony.

"Well, he represents lots of things." Tony looked at the huge canine. "Let's see, there's health." He counted on one finger.

"Agriculture." Cinnamon stuck out two fingers.

Tony added, "Protection."

I didn't like where this was heading.

"But most importantly, he's the god of moral right and wrong." Cin sat back and crossed her legs.

Tony leaned forward. "You might say *justice.*"

I shook my head, looked from one to the other of them. "Oh hell no. I know you are not asking me to take this beast."

Thor grouched at me.

I bent down to look at him. "No offense, buddy."

"Tony and I were thinking of renting an apartment close to the shop and they don't accept pets." Cin gave me a pouty look. "Besides, I worry about you in the city. There's a lot of nuts out there."

"There's a lot of nuts right here." I watched Shea Parker approach our table.

He came over and pulled up a chair, interrupting this

awkward exchange. For once, I was grateful to see him. He swung the chair around and sat on it backward.

"Hey, Lois," he greeted me. Parker was in a Clark Kent costume and munching an apple.

"Where's your cape?" Cinnamon asked, and sipped her coffee.

"Wouldn't you like to know?" Parker winked.

Tony pulled his fake gun on him. He was dressed as a cowboy.

"Just kidding." He turned to me. "You going to write the whole story?"

I took a swig of my coffee, the last few days' events swirling in my mind. I hadn't realized how much I missed Amethyst until just then. I missed my family. I missed this crazy ass town. "You gonna make me an offer I can't refuse?"

Cin spit out her coffee, and Tony swung his head to me.

"Are you serious?" Parker asked.

I smiled. "I don't think I could handle the slow pace of the city anymore."

Jumping out of his chair, Parker kissed me on the cheek.

"Agh." I wiped his slobber away. "Boundaries, dude, boundaries."

"See you Monday." He hurried off before I could change my mind.

Monique passed him on the street, waving her knockers at him, and teetered over to us. She was wearing a Charlie's Angels costume, complete with fuzzy handcuffs slung over her hips and a squirt gun tucked in her cleavage. I think she was going for Farrah, but the tight, white jumpsuit, platform heels, and dog collar around her neck made her look more like Farrah's slutty sister from the trailer park.

Tony jumped up and mumbled something about the bathroom.

Monique watched him leave. "Well, aren't you all cozy?"

"Nice shiner." I grinned at her.

She had attempted to cover the bruise with a thick coat of foundation, but the purple splotch pushed its way through.

She smirked. "Compliments of your cousin."

"I aim to please." Cin bowed her head.

"Look, I just wanted to say that I'd like to call a truce." Monique glanced from me to Cin. "With both of you."

I raised my eyebrows and watched my cousin.

She flicked her eyes to Monique. "Bite me."

"Get bent," Monique sniped, and tottered away.

"I think you two may have reached a plateau in your relationship." I sipped my coffee.

"A good ass kicking will do that."

And with that, everything was as it should be.

40

October's full moon is often referred to as the "Blood Moon" because hunters would track enough prey to last through the winter under her illumination. Tonight the blood moon stamped the sky, tinted by an orange hue. There was a thick ring around it that gave my stomach a turn as I snaked through crowds of tourists dressed as ninjas, witches, nurses, and knights. The parade had ended and I was heading to the cottage to change and rest before the Samhain celebration. My entire body hurt and I was exhausted, but after everything that happened, I needed the ritual. I needed my family.

I was about to walk up the steps off Main Street when I caught a glimpse of flaming red hair. Not light like mine, or auburn like Birdie's, but deep, rich red. Only one person on Earth had that color hair.

She turned then, a black cape shielding her as she wafted through the crowd. She lifted the hood and I followed, stepping on toes and weaving through kids still collecting candy.

She was a block ahead, the cape billowing behind her

like a shadowy warning, but I was gaining momentum, sailing past storefronts and groups of trick-or-treaters.

"Mom!"

She darted down an alley then, and I ran to the spot where she had just turned seconds before, but there was no one. Just a dumpster stuffed with cardboard boxes and a broken old chair.

"You really are losing it, Stacy," I muttered.

I hiked up the hill to the cottage where Moonlight greeted me with a yawn and a demand for dinner so I obliged him. I was utterly spent, but decided to put the blue cape on first because Birdie would have wanted me to wear that for the festival and I didn't feel like arguing about it. Then I went to rest my eyes for a few minutes.

I MUST HAVE FALLEN asleep because when I woke up my head was pounding and Zorro was standing over me with a whip.

I blinked for several seconds, trying to decide if I was dreaming and then Zorro said softly, "Hi."

Chance.

Sitting up, I rubbed my eyes. "Hi. Didn't expect to see you here." I was still half asleep and I'm pretty sure I had drooled all over my cape.

He walked over to the dresser and leaned against it. "Thought I'd give you a sneak preview of my costume." His voice sounded strange. Hoarse. He fingered the whip.

"Do you have a cold?" I swung my legs over the side of the bed and yawned.

He shook his head.

I stood up. "Well, just let me splash some cold water on

my face and we can head to the festival." I looked out the window and didn't see his truck.

"Did you walk here?" Chance always drove.

He nodded.

"Are you okay?" I stepped forward and my stomach roiled then, so much so that I thought I might puke. *Uh-oh. How did he get in anyway? Didn't I lock the door?* This was not good. Not. Good. And Thor wasn't here either.

He stepped closer to me, bent his head to kiss me, and ice shot down my spine.

I backed away. "What are you doing?" Nothing about this felt right. This wasn't the Chance I knew. Not *my* Chance.

That's when I saw his eyes. Not blue. These were light brown, nearly amber. And angry. So angry.

Birdie's voice shot through my head. *Harmful intent.*

I pretended to play along until I could get to the door or a weapon, making a mental note to always keep a knife in my boot. "Let's just go to the festival, Chance."

"Well, I thought it would be nicer if we kept the party here." That voice. It was disguised, yet familiar. But I couldn't place it.

"Sure. I think I have some beer in the fridge." I walked toward the bedroom door. Who was he?

He grabbed my wrist and threw me on the bed. Hard. His voice was gruff, like his hands. "No, I mean *here*." He kicked the door shut behind him and locked it.

He pounced on me before I could lift my aching body off the bed.

"You know, Chance, it isn't a good time. I've got PMS, I haven't showered—"

"Shut up!"

For once in my life, I did. I mentally crawled around my

mind and my sore body for a sign, any indication of who this mad man was on top of me. I inched a knee up, but his grip on my arms was strong and he was positioned in a way that blocked his groin.

"You've always brushed me off. Like I didn't even exist. Treated me like a leper."

"Now that's just silly, I don't even know any lepers."

What was he talking about? He sounded like a stalker. I didn't have any stalkers. Not even a disgruntled ex.

"Everything is a joke to you, isn't it? *I* was a joke to you."

"You're wearing a Zorro costume, so ..."

He cast his eyes away. That's when I saw the rope dangling from a back pocket. What the hell was he planning to do with that?

"Yes, the costume. You'd be surprised how easy it is to masquerade in this town. No one locks their doors. So easy to just break in, borrow some keys, some clothing."

Clothing? Was he talking about the shirt? The damn red and black plaid shirt fabric stuck in my doorframe? I must have had an expression of clarity on my face because, he said, "Now you're catching on." He smiled. Wait a minute. I knew that smile. That crooked smile. The smile of a crocodile.

I can take this sonofabitch. I did it once before when we were kids.

"Nothing ever impressed you. Not my sense of humor, or my clothes, or how hard I worked. The sacrifices I made for you, for your family." He was practically spitting. "And you wouldn't even have one lousy dinner with me."

Because you're a disgusting creep. And apparently, a psychopath.

I had written about men like this. Men who thought that just because they want a woman, she should return the favor. Men who became obsessed with controlling the object of their desire. And when they can't—bad things happened. Things like shooting up shopping centers. Or burning witches.

He kept talking. "So I decided if I couldn't be the *kind* of man you wanted, I would just be the man you've had."

He really was crazy. Did he honestly think a Halloween costume would change everything?

There was a clink in my brain and the sound of a hundred pennies falling to the floor filled it. It made sense now. There were two pennies from the year I was born. One for me, one for Chance. And another one from the previous year. I couldn't place the significance at first, but I could now. It was the year this man was born. The year he was given up for adoption.

The face of Gladys popped in my head. *"He say he owe him."*

I knew what that meant now. Pain pierced my skull as I tried to halt the spinning. Then I saw it. Pearl in a hospital, crying, holding an infant. This was the baby she put up for adoption.

"You're Pearl's son." *Pearl's son. Pearl's son.* It played over and over in my head.

"I was," he shouted. "But you destroyed that, too. She's dead and it's all *your* fault."

"I called Eddie," Pearl had told me.

Ed Entwhistle dug into my biceps and I took my one shot. I slammed my head so hard into his, he bounced off the bed.

The impact dazed me, probably gave me a concussion to go along with the 678 other injuries. Ed was groaning on the floor between the bed and the door so I dragged myself over to the window. The lock was giving me a hard time for precious seconds before I realized the window was painted shut. I swung my legs up to break the glass.

That's when a cloth clamped over my mouth, smelling of ether.

"Now I'm sorry to have to do this, but you've misbe-haved," Ed growled.

For the second time that day, the world blackened.

41

I woke up in a dark, damp room, hands tied behind my back, still wearing the blue cape the Geraghty Girls had given me. Blinking a few times, I tried to acclimate myself to the darkness. Felt stone walls. My head throbbed as I wondered where I was. Something sparkled in a far corner. Not a light. Something glittery.

It came back to me in bits. Ed Entwhistle. Pretending he was Chance. Probably the person who spiked Gramps' drink with antifreeze too at the Elk's Lodge. How could I have missed it? Birdie was right. I didn't pay attention. I should have seen this coming. And now what? He blamed *me* for Pearl's death?

Oh, he is so out of the will when I tell Gramps about this.

Standing up, I noticed there was damp dirt beneath my feet. My eyes began to adjust to the darkness. I pivoted around and caught a familiar scent. Vanilla and lavender and sage all whipped into one.

Wait a minute. I know this space. That was an amethyst cluster sparkling in the corner. Amethyst for protection, spiritual enhancement, and to guard against psychic attack.

Although right now I was more concerned with a physical attack.

But I knew where I was. The old fruit cellar under the Geraghty House. This was where they used to store much of their herbs and where they cleansed some of their magic tools, at least the ones that benefited from re-charging within the earth. When I was a kid, I would play hide and seek down here. It had the best nooks and alcoves. But the Geraghty Girls hadn't come down here in ages. Not with their trick knees and arthritis.

But why would he bring me *here?*

Then I recalled the festival. It would be going on for hours if this were still the night of Samhain. Until dawn even. And no one would find me down here. Not for a long time. Not until the smell got to them and they searched for a dead raccoon.

Seeker of Justice. A lot of freaking good that did me. I just get pennies flung at me. Bet the Warrior got a set of throwing stars.

I studied the corner where the amethyst sat. It was something, at least. I shuffled back toward the wall, squatted, and tried to pick up the crystal. It was heavy, larger than I anticipated. I couldn't lift it with both hands tied behind my back, so I tried another approach. The gemstone had a few sharp edges, but since I had been bound with that stupid costume whip, I only made my wrists bleed trying to sever the ties.

Think, Stacy. What did they use in their spellcasting? Candles, crystals, paper, cords, herbs, a chalice, an athame.

Right. Now, was any of that stuff down here still?

A soft shadow of light from the moon crept through the window well. It didn't offer much, but I could make out some shapes. There were shelves built into the stones at varying heights, and I trailed around them. I found some mason jars filled with herbs, spent matches, dusty crystals, and a dead mouse.

It was even darker near the stairwell. The knots in my stomach twisted, and I knew he would be back soon.

I swept the ground with my hands, covering as much of it as I could until I hit something. It felt like a box. I flipped my hands up, trying to open the lid. No luck there. I circled back and faced the container, tipping the lid up with my right foot. I had to kick it three times, but it finally flipped open. Inside sat a few white candles and a dirty, long-forgotten athame.

Pivoting again, I sat down, my back to the box. The knife was in reach. I felt for the handle, picked it up, and poked the tip lightly through the ties, then shoved the blade away from my body, slicing through the bindings, freeing my hands. I tucked the knife in the back of my pants and tore through the box. I couldn't find any matches for the candles. However, I found a bloodstone, a quartz wand, and a sprig of dried out rosemary.

So I decided to do what I hadn't done in a long time.

Cast a spell.

I rubbed the rosemary all over my head and ate the sprig for strength, swallowing a cobweb in the process. I took the wand, walked toward the center of the space, and drew a circle all around me in the dirt. The bloodstone, a stone that banishes evil, was secure in my pocket. Then I sat down in the circle, cross-legged and chanted: "Spirits come forth from every direction. Cast around me a web of protection." Over and over.

The cellar door creaked open after a while and footsteps fell on the stairs.

I shoved my hands behind my back, pretending to still be tied, and felt for the athame.

"What's this, Stacy? Is the little witch doing a spell?" He was holding a stool as he descended the stairs. He set it down and put his foot on it.

I didn't say anything.

"Well, chant all you want, it won't do any good. That only works if you believe. And I don't." He lit a kerosene lamp and placed it on the ground. "In fact, I am so offended by your beliefs that I've decided to give you a proper witch's send-off."

He looked up. I looked up.

There was a noose wrapped around one of the beams directly above my head.

"Well, Ed, that's why it never would have worked between us. We come from two different worlds. I'm pagan and you're crazy."

He reached over and backhanded me across the face. I tasted blood where my lip split open again. I swallowed it, swallowed all the fear and pain, and vowed that no man would ever get the best of me again.

"When are you going to learn to shut your mouth?" He dragged me to my feet and tugged on the rope.

He was bigger and stronger than I was, but I had two advantages. He didn't know my hands were untied, and he didn't know I had a knife in my pants. Plus, I had a cooler cape.

"Well, that should hold you." He laughed. "I wish I could see the expression on Birdie's face when she finds you dangling from the rafters, your body burned."

Was he going to hang me or burn me? Or both? I hadn't thought through a plan, but I was pretty sure I wanted to make my move before he put the noose around my neck.

I made a face at the rope. "My head will never fit in that hole."

Ed sized me up. "What are you talking about? It's big enough."

I shrugged. "Hey, you're the boss, but I'm telling you the hole is too small."

Ed reached for the noose, and I pulled out the knife and lunged for him.

He tried to grab my arm but he fell backward over the stool and we both crashed into the dirt. The blade slipped from my fingers.

I scrambled for it, but he got to it first and swung his arm, slicing through my left shoulder.

Perfect. Now the bad guy had a weapon and all *I* had was a damn cape.

Hot, searing pain gripped my flesh. I rolled away and he came at me again, so I darted to the right. The knife smashed into the stone wall, breaking the tip.

The amethyst cluster was near me. I scrambled for it as Ed found his footing. I picked it up, hoisted it above my head, and smashed it over Ed's skull.

He fell back, blood seeping from his wound. I ran to the steps and shoved at the cellar door, but it was heavy and my shoulder throbbed.

Ed moaned, and I heaved with every bit of strength I had. The door lifted, my legs scrambling to pull me out. Just as I reached the opening, he grabbed my ankle, pulled me down, and the door slammed shut on my fingers.

I screamed and kicked his head with my other foot. He yelped but held on, dragging me back to the dirt floor. I sprang up then, and jumped for the noose. Then I swung like Tarzan, barely connecting with his chest.

He staggered, the wind knocked from him.

My legs carried me back up the stairs, where I flipped

the door open again and crawled out, running to the back screen door, Ed close behind.

A chair was tucked under the doorknob, and I hurled it at him and slid the lock open.

Before I could twist the knob, he grabbed me by the waist and tossed me across the center island. Then he jumped on top of me, clawing at me, slapping my face.

The pot rack dangled above us, holding cast iron and copper pans, but I couldn't reach anything. Ed's hands were everywhere. Scratching, pinching, slapping, tugging. He pinned me, and I felt his breath on my face, hot and demanding. I clamped my teeth onto his lip and pulled hard. Blood spurted across my cheek. His blood.

He screamed and wrenched back, giving me just enough reach to grab a cast iron skillet and yank. The pot rack crashed on top of us.

I rolled and landed on the floor in a heap, scrambling until I gained purchase near the stove. Grabbing a knob, I hauled my body up, then turned, keeping an eye on the monster in the room. I felt around behind me for a frying pan, but wasn't fast enough.

Ed got to it first. He pulled back and raised it over his head.

I leaned back, over the stove, my hands flailing behind me ... searching for a knife, a wooden spoon, anything.

There was nothing.

*T*he burner must have twisted into place because I heard the whoosh and felt the heat.

"Say goodnight, Stacy."

I closed my eyes, shielded my head.

The crash sounded like thunder raining down on me. Only it didn't hurt. I felt nothing, but I heard it, loud as a tornado.

When I opened my eyes, Thor was sailing through the backdoor, snapping his jaws and roaring like a lion. I scrambled out of the way just as he leapt onto Ed, slamming his mighty paws into the man. Ed screamed as Thor attacked, his canines flashing in the dark kitchen like lightning bolts.

It was the most terrifying and awesome thing I had ever seen.

"Get him off!" Ed screeched.

His shout fueled Thor's rage and the giant dog intensified his attack.

Ed tried to escape by climbing on top of the stove.

You know how they warn that Halloween costumes are flammable? They aren't kidding.

*C*innamon saw me first as I made my way to the woods. Thor was at my side, and I knew somehow that he always would be.

"Oh my God!" she screamed and ran over to us.

There was a good chance one of my lungs had collapsed because all I could do was point toward the house.

Tony ran in that direction before I could say a word.

LATER THAT NIGHT, with every muscle in my body aching and ice on my head, I watched the orange and red flames of the bonfire shoot twenty feet in the air. It was much prettier than the blue and red cherries of the ambulance that had carted Ed off with what were likely third degree burns.

I took my place around the ritual circle and tossed the pennies that had found me these last few days into the fire. "For you, Dad, I hope you'll visit me."

Cinnamon stepped up and sailed a paper badge into the flames. "Miss you, Pop."

The clearing in this part of the woods made room for

crowds of people eating, drinking, singing, and dancing. Birdie floated forward and made an offering to her mother. Lolly and Fiona did the same.

My arm was still stinging from the gash, but Fiona had patched me up and Lolly applied a poultice of lady's mantle, comfrey, and calendula to stop the bleeding and heal the wound. There was nothing broken, just bruises and flesh wounds, and I refused to go to the hospital tonight. At least, until the festival was over.

Tonight was for my family and for myself. I didn't want another year to go by that I didn't spend this important night with them.

Birdie came up and put her arm around my shoulder just before the sun rose. "I'm proud of you."

I touched her hand. "You're just happy I finally listened to you."

"Don't get cocky. You have more to learn. But I think you have graduated to another level."

"Good, because I need a new cape." I twirled in the bloody, torn, blue one Lolly had made.

Birdie smiled. "And what have you learned?"

"Stay away from needles."

"And?"

"Never trust a guy with a whip."

"And?"

I shook my head and shrugged. "I got nothing."

She whispered in my ear, "Follow your instincts." Then she strolled away.

Chance came up from behind me and put his arms around me. "I'm glad you're okay."

Smiling, I turned into him. "Guess you can't always save me."

"No, you do a pretty good job of that yourself, Stacy." Chance kissed my cheek and walked away.

I watched him go, feeling a tiny bit sad.

From across the woods, Leo smiled at me and started in my direction.

Behind him, I caught a glimpse of a woman in a black cape, fading into the shadows.

THANK YOU FOR READING! If you enjoyed the book, please consider leaving a review at your favorite site. Reviews help me to bring you more books that you love.

Read on for a sneak peak of the next book in the series, OPAL FIRE.

For even more Stacy Justice, tap here.

For important news on upcoming publications, sales and free stories, sign up at www.authorbarbraannino.com. You can also follow me on social media at Facebook, Instagram BookBub, and Amazon. You'll always get notified of new releases and great deals if you follow me on BookBub and Amazon.

* There's also a PRIVATE reader group filled with amazing, supportive people and a whole lot of fun. Feel free to stop by and say hello. Or shoot me an email at author@ authorbarbraannino.com. I'd love to hear from you!

SNEAK PEEK OF OPAL FIRE
CHAPTER 1

You might say everything was fine until the fire.

I was back in my hometown and living in my grandmother's guest cottage. I had a steady boyfriend, a steady job, and a sturdy dog.

Right now, my main concern was the dog.

"Stacy!" Cinnamon yelled through the haze of hot smoke. "Are you still in here?" The panic in her voice matched the fear pumping through my veins.

"I can't find Thor!" I coughed back.

"He'll be fine. Just get out!" Cinnamon was about to step forward when a beam whistled, then cracked and plunged into the floorboards. A wave of sparks shot into the air, barricading her in the back room of the bar.

I sure hoped that exit wasn't locked and if it was, I prayed Cinnamon had the keys with her.

"Cin," I choked. I couldn't see my cousin anymore through the thick fog and debris, so I stepped forward.

A wave of fire licked the air—too close to my eyebrows for comfort. It forced me to lunge backwards into a beer barrel. I lost my footing, scrambling for anything to sustain a landing. My arm caught the edge of the brass foot rail as I went down—the searing pain instant and vicious.

Then I saw him.

My recently adopted Great Dane was wedged between the keg that toppled me and another, set close to the bar. We hadn't had a chance to hook them up before the fire erupted.

"Thor! Come!" The desperation in my voice shook me to the core.

His rear end was wiggling while the kegs blocked him like linebackers. I couldn't figure out what was holding him there. My eyes flashed to the front entrance of the bar. The flames hadn't reached it yet, but I was certain we had minutes, maybe only seconds to escape.

Sirens screamed not far off.

I flopped on my belly and skidded quickly to Thor, ignoring the burn. I managed to get my head around the first keg. The dog's eyes met mine, pleading with me not to leave him there. Not to let him die as waves of heat threatened his long, tan tail.

The ornamental footrest that trailed the bar was intricately carved, and Thor's tag had locked onto one of the decorative loops.

"Hang on, buddy." I heard another whistling sound and looked up. A second beam had caught a spark.

Thor whimpered.

My fingers crawled around the keg to grab the tag, but my arm wasn't long enough.

Thor yanked his head back, the muscles in his huge neck bulging as if they would burst right through his fur. The tag bent beneath his force, but he didn't have enough leverage to move his head, or I was sure that collar would have broken apart. It wouldn't have been the first one that couldn't contain Thor.

I sure hoped it wouldn't be the last.

With one good arm, I shoved at the first keg, hoping for enough room to free him.

It wouldn't budge.

The sirens screeched closer.

Or was that Thor wailing?

The bottle opener! It was in my back pocket and it might get me just enough length to lift that stupid tag over the brass.

Just as an ugly orange flame crept closer to Thor, I heard a familiar voice.

"Stacy!" Leo yelled, and a bottle burst.

Then another.

I kicked my foot. "Down here! Help me get Thor!"

Leo covered me with a tarp and yanked me back by my ankles as Thor howled like a wolf beneath a full moon.

"Get out!" Leo yelled and grabbed his utility knife. To cut the nylon collar, I guessed. There was no time for that.

I grabbed the gun from his holster and fired three shots into the far keg. Beer shot up, then showered down on the bar, my dog, and the floor. It was enough liquid to set the flames at bay.

Leo shoved the first keg out of the way and cut the collar off Thor. The three of us sprinted from the Black Opal, spilling onto the street where a crowd had already gathered.

Leo grabbed his gun from my hand and guided me through the red, white, and blue lights—a rare sight in the tiny tourist town where we lived. Firefighters zigzagged across Main Street, hosing down the nineteenth-century building as volunteers ran around asking how they could help.

It was late afternoon in February, but I wasn't cold. We headed to Leo's police cruiser, and I leaned against it, coughing out a sigh as he handed me a towel to wipe my face.

We stood there for a moment in silence and I felt a lecture coming.

"Are you crazy?" he finally asked.

I looked at him, pointedly. "Don't call me crazy. You know that drives me nuts."

Leo set his incredibly sexy, always-stubbly jawline.

"You could have been killed," he said in a low voice.

"But I wasn't, so let it go." I was too pumped with adrenaline to let my guard down. Had I stopped and thought about what might have happened...I shivered at the possibilities.

Leo ran his fingers through his thick black hair and sighed. He pulled me into him and rubbed my shoulders. I flinched as my arm met his leather jacket, and he stood back to examine it. He snapped his fingers and an EMT promptly said, "Sure, Chief," and shoved an oxygen mask in my face.

Leo was my boyfriend and chief of police of Amethyst, Illinois, where the pie is homemade, the pump is full-service, and quirky is a compliment. He has a Mediterranean look about him and a slight temper to match. Mostly when I put myself in life-threatening situations. Which was hardly ever.

"Look at that burn too," Leo said to the EMT.

"Nah, it's fine," I said. "The aunts and Birdie will take care of it." No co-pay when you lived with witches.

Thor was leaning against me, licking the beer off his backside. I began to towel him off with my tarp.

Leo said, "You two get in the car and stay warm. Give me

a minute to straighten out this mess and then you can tell me what happened."

I looked over at the crowd. It had developed its own heartbeat.

"I need to find Cinnamon, Leo."

Leo pulled out his radio and called to Gus, his right-hand man. He opened the door to the backseat, and Thor and I slid in.

A few minutes later, he knocked on the window.

"She's fine. Not a scratch. Now, sit tight so I can ask you some questions before the mayor has a coronary and I have to explain why my girlfriend is always caught up in the chaos that surrounds this town like the *Twilight Zone* on steroids."

He shut the door again, and a firefighter approached him.

I drank in the scene around me. Some people were directing traffic, some were throwing buckets full of water on the flames (the whole bucket too, not just the contents), some were snapping photos, and one guy, who I recognized as a regular of the Black Opal, Scully, was clutching a stool and crying.

It was like the bleacher seats at a Cubs game when the beer gets cut off, but how was that my fault?

Before Leo turned back toward the car, a small group of men, all dressed in purple polo shirts with plastic badges, approached him.

"Chief, where did ya want me?" a man asked.

"I can close off the streets," another offered.

"Hey, I called that," said a third.

I rolled down the window. "Leo, what's this?" I asked as the three men neared the squad car.

Leo turned back and said in a low voice. "Remember I told you we were hosting a citizens' academy class?"

I nodded.

"Today was graduation."

I winced. In a matter of seconds, the rent-a-cops swarmed Leo like a group of bees in a bed of sunflowers. Actually, they weren't even rent-a-cops. They were rent-a-cop wannabes. It was disturbing.

While Leo fought them off, I seized the opportunity to slip away. Thor and I snuck out the other side of the car and headed down the street.

I needed to find my cousin. See her. Touch her.

We made it about a block when I noticed, displaced from the crowd, a pimply faced teenager with hair like a Brillo pad staring at me, an oddly satisfied look on his face.

I stopped and stared back. He smiled wildly. Then he bolted like a cat attached to a firecracker.

And a chill rumbled through my veins.

ALSO BY BARBRA ANNINO

The Stacy Justice World

A spellbinding series that dazzles with magic, mystery, and mayhem.

Amethyst Witch

Opal Fire

Bloodstone

Tiger's Eye

Emerald Isle

Obsidian Curse

Phantom Quartz (Tisiphone cameo)

Jaded Witch – Coming Soon

A Tale of Three Witches – Novella

Deadly Diamonds – Novella

Witches Be Crazy – Novella

Thor and Peace – Spin-off

Thor Games – Spin-off

Geraghty Girls Recipes – Recipe Companion

The Everafter World

A laugh out loud fairy tale featuring modern-day princesses with attitude.

The Bitches of Everafter

The Bitches of Enchantment

The Bitches of Oz – Coming soon

Fury Rising (Stacy Justice cameo)

If you like your heroines fierce and your heroes tough and no nonsense then you'll love Tisi and Archer!

ABOUT THE AUTHOR

Barbra Annino lives in North Carolina with her husband and their goofy Great Danes. When she's not writing, she can be found somewhere in nature plotting her next story.

Made in the USA
Monee, IL
27 October 2021